Gavin

A Reverse Harem Romance

- Book 3 in the Nadia's Boys Series -

By Alyssa Clark

Published by
Scarlet Lantern Publishing

SCARLET LANTERN
Publishing

1

Nadia

"Are you sure you want to give up this place?" Gavin asked. He had a box in his arms. "I know it was my idea for you to move in with us," he shifted from foot to foot. "But having to deal with that first night where Landon has to warm up to us all over again is pretty fucking tiring."

"Deidre assured me that the older he gets the more used to us he will be," I said as I packed plates into a box. "It shouldn't be that way every time Austin brings Landon home." I paused to think of the last time I'd see the infant. Was he still considered an infant? He was closer to six months. I didn't know how those definitions worked and I was really going to have to look that up because I didn't want to be stupid and ask. "He's not fussy for tummy time anymore. He sleeps at night. What's the problem?"

"There's not a problem. I just figured I'd ask," he shrugged as he went to the door. The living room was empty. All that was left was the few things that I had in my kitchen. "Trying to make sure everything isn't going to go to shit once you actually move in. For real."

"You are really just looking for a place to crash if Landon got too fussy for you to handle, aren't you?" I asked.

"I mean, I didn't think I was being that obvious," he huffed as he walked out the door.

"I think you forget Vaughn still has his apartment," I shouted after him.

He didn't respond, but I knew he heard me. The neighbors heard me, too. But it didn't matter. They weren't my neighbors anymore. I still had a week left for the notice I'd given Mr. Coleman. It left me plenty of time to clean the apartment so I got the measly deposit back. That little bit that I would get back could go towards putting new windows in the house.

It was summer now, but if we were going to have a baby in the house we would need to get that taken care of before it started getting cool. That was five hundred out of four grand. Yeah. That barely made a dent.

I rubbed my fingers into my brow. I needed to do more. I needed to find a way to make this easier on him. I needed to pull my weight.

"First," Gavin said as he traipsed back into my apartment, "I forgot about Vaughn. I was used to the idea of this being the three of us. You, me, and Austin." He came into the kitchen and looked down at me, his hands on his hips. "He's involved, but it doesn't feel like it's at the same level. But I think it's because the bar's almost done and he's trying to help my parents get a house here." One of his hands went to the back of his neck, he went from looking irritated with me to embarrassed. "He's got a lot on his plate."

"Your other house sold?" I asked, trying to steer the conversation onto something that, hopefully, he wouldn't be bothered by. I went back to wrapping and packing plates.

"Yeah," he sounded surprised when he said it. "It went pretty fast, too. Someone else on the team picked it up. I'm not even out as much as I thought I would be." He released a breath and leaned against the counter as he watched me. He was the pack mule that hauled everything downstairs to his truck, I just packed the boxes.

He fell silent, watching me as I put a t-shirt between each breakable dish. I hated buying boxes for this, I wasn't willing to splurge even further on the packing paper. When I closed the box up and picked it to hand to him, I was confronted with that same expression.

"What is it?" I asked, finally.

"It wasn't an issue with Austin, when you met Kirstin," he began warily. "What do we do about meeting parents? Does this stay between us or do we get to go to family events and shit?" He bit his lip as he looked down at me, "I've not brought a girl home since high school and I wasn't serious with any of them. When my mom comes back home, she's gonna want to know why I stayed here. I want to tell her the truth."

I damn near dropped the box. "What?"

"I want you to meet my parents," he said carefully. "We're tight knit and used to have a lot of gatherings when I was a kid. With them coming back home I'm kind of expecting that to happen again."

I just blinked at him. It went against everything he suggested from the beginning. How was I supposed to react to this?

"I don't know how that would work." I admitted. "Especially considering your parents know Vaughn and Austin. Are you going to tell them what we're doing? Or am I going to be introduced as just your girlfriend?"

Gavin opened his mouth to speak then stalled out. "I don't think mom would freak out about it," he finally shrugged at me. "I think she probably wouldn't want to know the details. She'd probably just be happy that I was in a committed relationship with someone that I'm serious about," he looked at me then. His jaw was tight and it looked like he was waiting for me to shoot down the idea.

I swallowed hard as I tried to imagine how my mom would react to me being in a relationship with more than one man. "This means you're gonna need to meet my parents, too, doesn't it?" I asked.

A grin started to work its way across his lips only to suddenly falter. "I wanna say sure, unless you think your dad might end up shooting me," he suddenly looked uncomfortable. "Especially when he finds out I'm the one that started all of this."

2

Nadia

The day had been a long one. Moving up and down stairs had been a work out that I hadn't been able to avoid. Then unpacking the three boxes that represented my kitchen and the two that were my bedroom, while having the existential crisis about the fact that my life was just five boxes full. That was all that I had amassed in the last twenty eight years.

"You're being weird," Gavin said as he shoved my pots into the cabinet by the stove. He had insisted on helping me pack up and now he was helping me unpack. I think it was to help me digest the idea of meeting his family.

I could understand. If I didn't think my parents would freak out I would have said something to them about the relationship I was in now. They weren't overly judging, I was sure Mama knew I wasn't the blushing virgin waiting for my husband. Dad probably just elected to ignore all of it and was just waiting for me to bring a man in front of him that had proposed.

How would they react to me bringing home three men? I couldn't even begin to guess. Gavin thought the biggest problem would be Dad shooting him. I was pretty sure that Mama was more dangerous. She was fierce and protective, I was sure she would take one look at Vaughn and flay him alive.

That was assuming she wouldn't remember their names from high school. "Maybe it was a good thing I called you by your last names," I thought out loud. "She's more likely to remember Stockton, Price, and Fowler than she would know your first names."

"You are overthinking it," Gavin said, he had a stack of my plates in hand now. "I want you to meet my mom," he said as he put the plates into another cabinet. "Have you ever felt that you disappointed your parents?" he asked without looking at me.

"I never played professional football," I pointed out. "I'm a waitress in a non-chain diner. What do you think?"

He made an irritated noise. "I think if I introduced her to a girl that I liked," he finally turned to me. "I think there would be less of a reason for her to be disappointed. If you don't want to, I get it. But just say so."

I stopped washing the dishes that I thought we might actually use. I looked at him and I saw that he was upset with the way I was handling this. I guess I was being more than a little callous. "I think you're selling yourself short to assume that you're a disappointment," I began carefully. "You went to college. You have a degree, right? You're not in crippling debt and you're actively working to get yourself into a good position financially. You're not a failure. There's no reason for you to feel like you've disappointed your family."

"As much as I appreciate the reassurance you're trying to give me, I'd like it if you would answer me," he said, pinning me with his expression. He was waiting for rejection. He was waiting to hear the fact that I didn't want to meet his family.

"My only question is," I began slowly. "am I just your girlfriend? Or am I Vaughn and Austin's, too?"

"Kirstin doesn't know about it," he said evenly as he leaned back against the counter. "Is it something that we're going to need to air out right now? How would you suggest I do this?" He stepped away from the counter and closer to me, "Is it something you want to do? Because I won't argue with it. I can't lie for shit to my mom." He wasn't angry, his voice wasn't raised and he didn't look perturbed. "We could just keep things simple and play it by ear."

Gavin was afraid.

"Out of everyone involved, who is the most likely to come out of this looking like the bad guy?" I asked. "If your mom finds out you're sharing a girl with your friends, who is she going to blame for this?" I took a deep breath and tried my best to get him to see the logic behind what I was saying, "Even if this was your idea, I can't expect anyone not involved to see me favorably. If you hide this from your parents and then they come to visit the house, there would be no hiding the fact that it's not just me and you in this."

"I guess that means the next time Kirstin comes to town we will be telling Austin's sister the truth?" He didn't give me the chance to answer the question. He just shook his head, his hand moving into his hair, "I didn't think about how you would be perceived."

"I'm more than willing to meet your parents," I told him. "But if I'm going to be a slut or a whore for giving into your idea when Austin or Vaughn get friendly with me in front of them it's going to create a bigger problem." I shrugged uneasily as I considered the comment about Austin's sister. "I was willing to let him take the lead in that situation because of everything he was dealing with. I understand why he didn't tell her the truth." I tilted my head a little as I took in Gavin's frustrated features. "Is there a reason why you wouldn't tell your mom about what you started here? Do you think maybe we should talk about this with Vaughn and Austin?"

He took a breath and straightened, the anxiety melting away to reveal his usual flirtation. "I'm more than willing to tell my mom about what we have going on," he leaned closer to me, invading my space in a way he tended to do when he was trying to talk me into something. "As long as you're willing to tell your parents and I get to meet them."

It threw me off like it did when he first mentioned the prospect in my apartment. "Why?" It came out of me without a thought. The answer should have been obvious, but for some reason it just didn't connect. "If it goes bad with your mom and dad, how do you think it'll go with mine?"

He shrugged after a beat, "If both our parents disown us for poor choices then we'll still have each other, right?" He gave me a big grin, "Plus Austin and Vaughn."

"I guess that's one way to go. But if I get any derogatory names hurled in my direction I'm blaming you," I told him.

"My mother works in disapproving looks and guilt trips," he assured me as he drew closer. He pressed a kiss against my brow, his hand coming to rest on the small of my back. "It seems like everything is coming together. All I want is for this to come together, too."

"You're a mama's boy?" I asked, trying to take the edge off the conversation.

"Without a doubt," he admitted before he got back into helping me unpack.

3

Nadia

By the time Vaughn walked in the door I was satisfied by the work Gavin and I had put in. It looked like I lived here and wasn't just taking part in an extended sleepover. I put the afghan that usually stayed on my couch across the back of the sofa in the living room. It was a dark brown and I felt like the blue of my blanket went with it nicely. I went as far as tossing the matching pillow on it, too.

There was just enough room to accommodate my coffee table and my little television and its stand sat in the corner. I couldn't put into words the feeling it gave me to see some of my things meld into the house. It was like another piece fitting into place.

That was until Vaughn came in, flopped onto the couch and kicked a foot up onto my coffee table. The bright red of the sole to his leather shoes caught my eye. I wanted to get frustrated with the fact that he seemed to brush off what I brought into the house. But it didn't seem fair, especially since I had given him as much of a chance as I'd give Gavin and Austin.

He seemed to realize what he was doing when he noticed the pillow that he had pressed against the armrest of the couch. Vaughn looked around the living room to take in the little pieces I'd added. "She's moved in?" he asked.

"Yep," Gavin came from down the hall. "The only thing we didn't get done was putting her bed together. I drug my feet with that for obvious reasons," he said as he sat down and stretched out in Austin's armchair. "Aside from probably needing a tetanus shot after going up and down her stairs, they were rusty as fuck, it was pretty easy. She didn't do any kicking or screaming."

I rolled my eyes, "I considered it after you mentioned meeting your parents."

"What?" The tired look Vaughn had been sporting immediately vanished. His attention was on Gavin. "What did she just say?"

"I thought since they're coming home it would be a good time for her to meet them," Gavin answered with only a moment of hesitation.

"Why do you think that would be a good idea?" Vaughn's foot dropped off the coffee table and he leaned forward, resting his elbows on his knees. "Do you have any idea how Kelli will react? This isn't like any of the girls you used to take over there. The situation between now and then has changed a lot."

"How do I keep them from meeting her?" Gavin shot back. "They're going to stay here. Nadia lives here, too. There's no way we can hide the fact that we're all sleeping in one bed. Even if we were to keep things PG while they're in the house. There'd be no hiding it. Why try?" He shrugged as he relaxed back in the chair, rocking it lightly.

"They can stay at my place and there's no reason for them to know what goes on here," Vaughn argued. "Kelli is going to be shocked and pissed that we're sharing her. This isn't going to be a big happy family reunion if you come right out the gate exposing what we're doing."

"And how would she react later down the road?" I asked, not pleased with having to have this conversation again.

"Why does anyone even need to know?" Vaughn shot back.

That seemed to be the wrong thing to say. Gavin sat back up and threw a hand back into my direction,

"You can't tell me that you don't want to show her off. That you don't want to take her out and shit." He was speaking with a little heat that surprised me. He actually wanted to take me on dates? We'd gone out as a group before but I never thought there was anything telling about it. I'd hoped outside observers would assume we were just friends. "I think Mom would love her," he said, sounding as if he didn't doubt his own words.

Vaughn turned his attention to me, eyeing me where I stood just in the living room. I folded my arms over my chest and tried to not let all of it bother me. I didn't want to guess what he was thinking, or looking for.

"This wasn't my idea," I offered stubbornly.

"I know it's coming from him," Vaughn said as he nodded towards Gavin. "Guy is full of bad ideas and worse decisions. The only thing I'm going to ask you is why would you agree to it?" He raised an eyebrow, "It's been what? Three months? Not even that. You said Austin was worried about things moving fast, you were complaining about it when we first started talking about you moving in. Why make the leap to meeting parents?" He leaned forward, his eyes narrowed at Gavin. "You aren't going fucking ring shopping, are you?"

"I'm pretty positive all my disposable funds are tied up here in the house, the bar, and helping Austin with attorney fees. I've not got enough money to even consider something like that," Gavin said with heat. It seemed like he was triggered by his friend's words. "The only thing I pressured and pushed forward was sex. And maybe her moving in. One of those you can't really complain about. Her meeting Mom just seemed like the natural step when they come into town. I haven't even made plans, ring shopping is at least another two steps from here."

"Calm down," I objected a little too sharply. "That kind of leap isn't necessary."

Vaughn just gave me a blank expression, "After everything you're going to make that conclusion?"

"After everything you're going to assume that's the next step after such a short period of time? Marriage? Really?" I asked, trying to not be bothered by what he was suggesting.

Vaughn stood up and closed the space that was between us. "I think you're missing something here," he said to me. "You're just looking at the recent past," he leaned down a little, getting into my personal space as he spoke. "You're just taking into account when you started having sex."

"When you started using first names instead of last names," Gavin supplied quietly.

"You're forgetting the history goes back a little further back than that," Vaughn continued like he hadn't heard Gav. "I think it's been proven already that some of the emotions involved aren't something that just developed."

I swallowed hard, focusing on the line of Vaughn's jaw and trying to not get sucked in by his words. He was suggesting that they cared back in high school. While I could believe that Austin did, that the crush he had for me left him with an inability to express himself to me, I didn't think it was the same for the man in front of me. Gavin's feelings developed because I wasn't charmed by his open and flamboyant personality, I resisted giving him the attention he wanted. I didn't want to reflect on why I had gotten Vaughn's attention.

Not with him standing so close. Thinking about the notes he left in my locker always produced unwanted feelings of vulnerability. I still didn't want him to have that power over me.

"Crushes," I started finally, "aren't something that should be a cause for a fast moving relationship. Just because you felt a certain way back then doesn't mean that I should take them into account now. Time changes feelings just like it changes everything else." I took a breath and I forced myself to meet Vaughn's gaze. His eyes were hooded and it felt like he didn't believe me. "It might lead you to being more than willing to rush into bed with me. It's not going to lead you into wanting a committed long term thing."

"I thought I was pretty clear," Gavin said from the chair. His hands dug into the cushioned fabric of the armrests and he didn't look at me. "That's what I want. I said I just wanted this to be a fling in the beginning but," he paused, shaking his head and giving me his full attention, "I don't want it to be over. It's like I'm still riding on the high I got from the first time I had you between me and Austin. Even after all the bullshit. I don't want to let go of it."

They were putting me on the spot. Austin wasn't here as a buffer and, usually, he was quick to come to my defense. He was taking Landon home and there was no one here to help me, I was stuck. I didn't know what to say and I fought to not look at Vaughn.

"I agreed to meet his parents," I closed my eyes as I struggled through it. "I just don't want anyone to think I'm a bad person for agreeing to this," I waved my hand aimlessly hoping I didn't need to clarify. "I caved, I gave in to all three of you," I looked up at Vaughn then. "But that doesn't make me easy and that definitely doesn't make me a slut or a whore."

I thought I'd been stuck before. The way Vaughn's eyes narrowed and his eyebrows drew down made me think I might've said the wrong thing. He stepped closer, leaving just a breath between us. "If someone calls you that," he said lowly, "say something." Intimidation kept me silent. It was like he suddenly held a power over me. "I will handle it," his tone offered no argument.

I looked down, afraid of the tightness in my chest. I nodded, my arms dropping from where they'd been crossed over my breasts. I hooked my fingers together and took extra interest in the hangnail on my index finger.

He gave me a break, surprisingly. He didn't step back but he pulled his phone from his pocket. "We've got about an hour before we have to go pick up Austin. Why don't you go get dressed so we can get dinner afterwards?"

"I had planned on cooking," I protested, looking up at him. "I figured after the flight and leaving Landon he'd be too tired to do anything."

"No," he said with authority. "We are going to dinner after we get Austin." He turned away from me then said gentler, "Let's make believe it's a date between the four of us. God knows it's something that we need to do."

4

Austin

Flying with Landon was slowly becoming easier, he'd cry after the initial ear popping take off but it didn't take him long to be lulled to sleep. That was the comfort. But after the jolt of landing and the waiting in a diaper that probably needed to be changed, I knew the short nap on the flight hadn't done either of us any good. He cried until I got him changed and I'd made a point to carry him on my arm while we waited for Lauren outside of security.

I had about an hour before I had to go back through security to get on my flight back home. I didn't have any luggage to worry about so her being late wasn't something that was bothering me. Landon wasn't fussing. His head jerked a little as he watched the people passing, his little hand fisted in my shirt. I didn't know if he was looking for *her* or if it was just the crowd of unfamiliar people that had his attention.

I didn't know a lot when it came to babies and their development, but Landon was definitely teaching me. He cooed, sounding elated. I tried to spot what he saw, raising up on my toes to see if he'd managed to see Lauren before I did. She had a way of standing out.

"Where is she?" I asked him, hoping I could get a hint.

Landon turned to me, giving me a gummy grin. His two front teeth had begun to peak out and it made any smile he gave me extra adorable. But it had definitely made the nights harder to manage. I knew he'd been cranky the last time I had him but seeing those two teeth now made me realize why. I couldn't imagine how Lauren handled it.

She never said a word about teething. All I ever got when we communicated was whether she'd run into traffic. I pulled my phone from my pocket with my freehand, turning it on to see if she was just running late. There were no texts or emails.

My stomach tightened into a knot and I let her know I had Landon in the waiting area just outside of baggage claim and the car rental kiosk. I didn't wait for a response, I just found some seating on what might pass for carpeting and pulled a baby blanket out from the diaper bag I had stuffed into the car seat. I thought my lifting routine had me prepared for anything. Standing around holding fifteen pounds on one arm and twenty pounds of plastic on another was proving me wrong.

I carefully spread the blanket onto the dingy looking carpet and placed him onto his stomach. He started hiccupping a protest cry before he got his hands under him and pushed himself up. His attention went back to people watching. I was counting that as a small victory.

Now if only Lauren would show up.

I tried to keep my focus on the infant in front of me, watching and cheering quietly as he managed to roll himself over. He gave me another gummy grin at the praise. It was damn impossible not to keep looking at my phone. Especially when the battery percentage got lower and lower.

It was when I had a half an hour to get through security to the boarding gate that I began to panic. After changing Landon and seeing that I didn't have enough diapers for an overnight stay. After some quick digging I found an extra onesie and I had enough formula for at least two more bottles.

What was I supposed to do? Could I just go home and take Landon with me if she decided to not show up? Would I get in trouble for that?

Afraid and more than a little lost, I went to the check in desk of the airline I'd been booking flights through for the last few weeks. I carefully balanced Landon on my arm and put the loaded down car seat between my feet. I shoved it along the tiles until it was my turn and the clerk immediately cooed at Landon, earning a happy face from him.

"What can I do to help?" she asked, giving him more attention than she gave me.

"I've got half an hour to board my flight," I started. "But mom hasn't shown up to pick him up," I bounced Landon a little. "I've no idea what to do," I admitted, hoping she could give me some direction.

The girl blinked at me and the man beside her gave me a once over. He gave her a nod, "Can I get your ID?"

I carefully balanced Landon on the counter, keeping a hand on his back. I went for my wallet and with some maneuvering I managed to get it out one handed. After some speed typing she hummed and the man beside her looked at her screen. "I thought he looked familiar. Go ahead."

"What we can do is we can put you on standby for the next available flight," the girl in front of me said. "In the meantime you can try to get a hold of mom or maybe your case worker. That way you can find out what you need to do to cover yourself and keep the baby safe," as she said it, she gave Landon another big grin that he mirrored. "If you can keep us up to date when mom gets here we can see how quick we can get you home. Aside from the flight that you were on, I have another at ten and another at two."

The prospect of being stuck in the airport until two am suddenly made Landon feel heavier. "I'll keep you posted," I said before picking up everything so I could leave the line.

That was some direction, a plan as to what to do if Lauren suddenly showed up. But what do I do until then? I had my phone in hand and I called Mr. Lange, my attorney through all of this. It was after five and I was sure this would probably be another expensive call, but I couldn't just sit here and wait.

"You are very lucky you caught me just as I was leaving the office, Mr. Fowler. What can I do for you?" He said as a greeting. He didn't sound annoyed which was something of a relief.

"I'm stuck at the airport with Landon. Lauren hasn't shown up, yet. They put me on standby in case she's just running late. But at this point," I paused to breathe, heaving out that breath, "she's over an hour late and she's not made any attempt to get into contact with me. I don't know what I'm supposed to do from here."

The other line was quiet for a beat. "This could be a case of abandonment," he began slowly. "But let us cover all the important bases before we make that leap. I'll get into contact with her local law enforcement office so they can do a wellness check on her. Stay at the airport and save your receipts for anything you have to buy. Whether it is diapers or baby food. We shall get this handled as quickly as possible." He paused to speak to his secretary, "Vanessa get Mr. Fowler's file for me." He directed his attention back to me, "Find yourself a comfortable place to sit for now and I will get back to you as soon as I know something."

That made me feel better. Someone was doing something and would find out if she was okay, at least. I would get direction and right now. That's what I needed.

Giving the battery life on my phone a glance I decided the next best course of action was to call Vaughn, he'd agreed to pick me up from the airport. I needed to let him know I was going to be late. Maybe arrange it so Gavin or Nadia picked me up. Squeezing into Nadia's little sedan wasn't ideal, but if she was willing to come get me I wouldn't be looking a gift horse in the mouth. The call went to voicemail, I didn't think to do the smart thing and leave a message. I let it go in favor of watching the time and looking for Lauren.

After an hour and a missed flight, whatever relief I'd gotten from talking to Mr. Lange was gone. I hadn't gotten a single call from him or from Lauren. The fact that I'd been checking my phone every ten minutes had me switching on battery saving mode and only ten percent left. What would happen if my phone died?

Finally, it started buzzing in my hand, distracting me. I didn't even look at the caller I just answered. "What's happening?"

"Well, your flight wasn't delayed. We're here at the airport. Where the hell are you?" Vaughn asked.

Had my flight already landed? Shit I forgot to call him and let him know I wouldn't be on it. I sent a worried glance at the television that displayed the departing and arriving flights. What had my flight number been? At some point the number had slipped my mind.

Landon started fuss from the floor. He had rolled a few times and mushed up the blanket I had him on. From the sound of it, he was tired. That was something I felt, I stooped down to pick him up. Wedging the phone between my ear and shoulder, I tried to calm him down. Would he nap for me here? Was it too noisy for that?

"Why do you still have Landon?" Vaughn asked, sounding annoyed.

"She didn't show up at the airport." I snapped. The infant on me twitched, feeling my irritation. His mouth pulled down in an exaggerated frown and I could see him getting wound up. I patted his back gently, shushing him in an effort to fight off the melt down. "I missed my flight because I didn't think I could just leave and bring Landon home with me," I gritted out while trying to maintain a non-hostile tone.

"The fuck?" Vaughn took the tone I was refraining from expressing.

"I called Mr. Lange, but he hasn't gotten back to me," I explained carefully, pressing Landon down so he rested his head just under my chin. "My phone is going to die before he's going to give me an idea as to what to do."

The line was quiet. Landon became heavier as he gave into the exhaustion. I slouched further in the metal seat so he would be more comfortable on me. My arm went under his bottom and I felt a slight firmness to the diaper, this nap was going to be short lived because I would need to change him.

"What do I do?" I asked, whispering into the phone.

"You didn't bring your charger? You can't tell me that the airport doesn't have an overpriced store you can buy shit from. Get you another one," he barked into the phone. "Get your phone charged and start blowing hers up like you know she would yours. And while you're at it, go to the airline desk and get them to give you a receipt showing you had to be moved to standby. Get fucking receipts for everything and then get on the next plane. Come home. If she's going to do this shit to you the bitch can come get him from you."

It was like he pulled the anger and resentment right out of me. The direction, a plan, was just what I needed. "I'll get right on it."

5

Nadia

I was driving Gavin's truck. The wheels rolled smoothly over the pavement, the engine purred just low enough for me to know it was there over the music that he had playing. As far as I could tell he favored alternative music, though the band was unfamiliar. The sound of the drums and the low pitch of the singer's voice seemed to make for a good enough lullaby as the two men in the truck with me were out cold.

Gavin's head was tilted back against the headrest, the angle seemed to encourage snoring because he made more noise than usual. It wasn't obnoxious, it blended well enough with the music that it wasn't distracting. Except for that first exaggerated snort that startled me. The car ride had gotten quiet for just a minute and suddenly he belted that out made me swerve just a little.

Vaughn was in the back seat, quiet and the last time I glanced back there he had his eyes closed. It was nearing four in the morning. Austin had called as he was boarding the plane, letting us know about the arrival time. I could hear Landon's fussing in the background of the call.

It had been a long day for the both of them and it was going to be a longer day tomorrow. Or today, I should say. If I was lucky I might get four hours of sleep. But that depended on how long we had to wait for them to get off the plane and the ride back to the house.

I pulled into the parking lot and I was relieved to see that it wasn't packed. As nice as it was to drive a vehicle that wasn't on the verge of falling apart, Gavin's truck was a lot larger than the beater. I didn't feel bad when I didn't get the truck parked perfectly between the lines. I was just happy that I didn't have to worry about hitting another car.

I sat back and picked up my phone, looking for a text to let us know he had landed. The two men that were asleep in the truck were the only thing that kept me from going in. "They should've stayed home," I thought out loud.

"No," came from the back seat. I guess Vaughn wasn't asleep after all. "You are going to need help hauling the baby out to the truck. Driving in the middle of the night alone doesn't sound safe either. You should call in sick tomorrow."

"No," I said it without looking back at him. "He's helping me out by not charging me too much in rent. I'm not going to take advantage just because something like this happens. I'm going to do what I can to help him out." I looked out at the nearly empty lot, "you've affected my income enough. I don't need you to jeopardize my other job."

"I said I would replace the job you had at the bookstore," he said evenly. "I can replace it with something that will pay more." He took a breath and the truck shook slightly as he stretched, "but you haven't taken me up on the offer."

"I don't think it would be a good idea for me to work for you," I tried to offer him gently.

"Funny that you think I would want you to," he didn't sound amused. "I'm a realtor, I don't work for myself, I work for my father," he admitted. "Unless you wanted to be a receptionist or a secretary, you wouldn't work with me. Much less directly for me." He paused, smothering a yawn behind a hand. "I know contractors. I know building managers. It's called connections. It wouldn't be hard for me to pull strings with someone I know to get you a better job."

I had assumed a lot with him. I looked at the steering wheel in front of me and felt guilt and shame twist up my insides. *Idiot,* that didn't seem to be an adequate enough insult to encompass just what I was. *Asshole is better. He's trying to help.*

"I can't just quit and leave my boss in a bad spot having to replace me," I muttered to my lap. I felt bad and while there was some truth to my words, it still felt like an excuse. I was making a stretch, assuming things that weren't true. Was asshole a good enough descriptive word for me? It didn't seem to be at this moment.

"Are you as loyal to people as you are to your job?" he asked quietly.

I looked at him in the rearview mirror, his eyes were closed and his brow was pressed against the window. It looked as if he were asleep. "I've not proven that?" I struggled to keep the offense out of my voice, but I felt like I'd done nothing in the past month but prove that I'm more than willing to see where this goes. I turned in my seat, the mirror not good enough anymore. I glared at Vaughn, hoping to gather something from his expression.

It was blank and when his eyes opened to meet my gaze he only raised an eyebrow at me. "There's a pretty good chance that this went from being every other weekend to full time. Are you going to still be loyal?"

I ground my teeth together. I looked away from him and settled back into the seat. "I'm not so much of an asshole that I would leave him because of Landon. Regardless as to whether or not he has him full time."

"And that's not an issue coupled with meeting Gavin's parents? The further along we go with this, the more you're willing to do, the more attached the two of them are going to become," he said after a length. "Is there a line that you've got drawn for them? Where do I come into this?"

"I thought we've already got you settled," I huffed out.

"Maybe," he murmured.

My phone chimed, notifying me of a text I just received. I looked to see a message from Austin, 'We just landed. We're waiting for them to let us off the plane.'

It was a distraction but I knew it wouldn't solve anything. "Let's go help him with the baby," I said as I got out of the truck. "We can leave Gavin in the car."

"It's not like he's got work," Vaughn argued as he got out of the truck. He fell into step with me, all without looking like he was making an effort. "This isn't just about me being involved," he said easily. He wasn't going to let go of the conversation and I was stuck until he got the answer he wanted. "This is about everyone else getting comfortable with your position in the house. Gavin wants things to move forward, probably faster than they should. Austin's situation is going to make or break things. I've just been trying to figure out where I stand in all of this."

I sighed, "Because you've gotten attached, too."

He didn't answer me.

"Are you doubting my position in this relationship because I've done something?" I asked as we stepped into the building at baggage claim. "Or is this an insecurity from hearing me express feelings for Austin?" I went into the direction of security, figuring that the exit for the gate would be close by. I saw a long hallway that was blocked off with a tired looking security officer standing to one side of it. "I would like to think that just me being here would prove my loyalty."

"To him," Vaughn said at last. "But if Gavin or I were in a similar situation, would you?"

I opened my mouth to answer him, because it was a hypothetical question. How often were they based in truth? I looked at Vaughn. He was a well put together man, even at four o'clock in the morning. He had a pair of slacks and a button down on, not the basketball shorts that Austin and Gavin favored. He was slightly wrinkled, but at this hour that was to be expected, right?

I knew for a fact that he went through damn near every girl in high school. That wouldn't have been any different in college, would it? He wouldn't be any different now, would he?

"Do you have a kid?" I asked him.

He rolled his eyes and looked down at me. "No," he said with a surety that I knew Gavin wouldn't have. "But that's answer enough for me."

"That question doesn't really give you an answer," I held up a hand, trying to keep him from assuming anything. "I've got an idea about your history. Gavin is the same way." I shook my head, "I can accept that people have changes of heart and decide to settle down. We're at that age," I dug my hand through my hair and looked up at him. "But when it comes to you, I'm never not going to come back to the fact that you are way out of my league. You are so much more attractive than I am, I shouldn't have been on your radar in high school." I tilted my head a little when his expression didn't show me anything. "You're trying to solidify something between us and I can't begin to guess why. Instead of casting doubt on my position here, maybe you should explain what you're getting out of it."

Vaughn's eyes narrowed at me and I felt a little triumph in knowing that I had managed to throw him off just like he had been doing with me. It was almost like we were on equal ground now. "Have you ever thought that there might have been some validity to the notes I put in your locker?"

I eyed him, I didn't want to believe that. The men I was with shouldn't be with me. I looked away, down the concourse hoping that Austin would appear and save me.

People were slowly starting to trickle down the hallway, but there wasn't any sight of the broad shouldered man I was looking for.

"You can't accept that, can you?" he asked, ignoring my discomfort. "That I could have had a crush on you?"

"I just find it hard to believe that someone like you would want me," I admitted, trying to keep my focus on the hallway as a person that fit Austin's build and looked like he was struggling with an infant seat. "You could do better. All of you could." I shook my head. "Back then I thought that the notes were an elaborate joke. Especially considering the reactions from your various girlfriends."

"They were more social climbers than girlfriends," Vaughn said after a beat. "You still have that skewed view of yourself, don't you?"

I didn't want to answer him, so I nodded to the person approaching that was still beyond the security barrier. "There's Austin," I said as I rubbed my hands on my jeans. "Let's shelve your analysis of me and my inability to move on from the past."

"You can blame me if you want," he said evenly. He had been standing close, but as his friend got within view of us he stepped aside. "You never bothered to find out back then if you were wrong. I just don't want this to end badly because you're being stubborn."

I wanted to argue with him. I wasn't stubborn. Stubborn and cautious were two different things. There was nothing wrong with being cautious.

I heaved a sigh instead, "Rain check on the date you wanted. My next day off we'll do it, even if we have to bring the baby with us." I smiled a little unwillingly, "it would probably do us all a lot of good to just go out together."

"Look at that, I didn't even have to twist your arm for it," he sounded amused. Unfortunately, he said it loud enough for Austin to hear.

"What?" Austin asked. Fatigue was evident around his eyes, his hair was twisted up in different angles and he was slightly paler than usual. The stress he was dealing with was way too obvious that it was an effort to wait until he made it to us. "You two should be in bed. Gavin could've picked me up."

Vaughn took the carrier that held Landon, he looked down at the infant speculatively. The baby just looked back, a pacifier in his mouth and a blanket between his little fists. Austin wasn't the only one exhausted. "He take the trip okay?" he asked before addressing what the other man said. "We were all concerned so we all came up here."

"I think the fact that it's been a really long fucking day is what's kept him from having a meltdown," Austin said as he let me take the diaper bag from him. "I changed him before the seatbelt light came on so he should be good for the ride home. I'm out of formula so he'll probably want a bottle before we crash for the night. Where's Gavin?"

"Sleeping in the truck," I supplied as I started us out towards the parking lot.

"Out of the three of you he should be in here while you two slept," Austin grumbled.

"Already sent an email letting the old man know that I had a cough. Something that was probably contagious so I didn't need to see clients. Went ahead and rescheduled what I had going on tomorrow," Vaughn told him. He paused and coughed pointedly into his fist, as if he had to prove to the two of us he was sick. "In the off chance he calls you, I might need you to develop a cough, too. I imagine that Naddy has to be close to death to miss work."

"Bills," Austin said before I could. "After all the money I spent within the last month I'm not gonna say shit about how often she works," he lagged between Vaughn and I. "As long as I get to see her and she's overlooking all my extra baggage I'm definitely not going to complain." He paused and stretched, his arms going up to the air and his back arching until it popped audibly. When he fell into step with us again he had a hand in his hair, "She's moving in. What more do you want?"

"Gavin wants me to meet his parents," I informed him as we got to the truck. I unlocked it with the fob and as far as I could tell the man in question was still asleep.

Vaughn didn't say a word, he just opened the back door. He put Landon and his seat ahead of him. The truck shook slightly as he wrestled with getting the infant seat secured. He didn't make any effort to share his thoughts on what I had told Austin.

"It's fair," the man beside me said after a length. He gave me a sleepy look, I couldn't tell if he had really digested it. "If this is going to be long term, family has to be met at some point. Isn't it better to meet them without any sort of crisis behind it?"

Or maybe he had. The fact that he made a good point didn't help. It wasn't the time to get elbow deep on Austin's lack of concern when it came to meeting Gavin's parents. We needed to get home.

Austin went to the other side of the truck, slapping a heavy hand against the passenger side front window before he got in. The truck shook again and Gavin barked out a curse. I got in the truck just as Landon started to fuss.

"That's my fault. He's tired," Austin croaked. "Just get rolling and he should settle down."

"We're all tired," Gavin complained, but didn't protest when I started in the direction of home. It only took ten minutes of listening to a baby cry and a grown man grumble before both nodded off.

"Next time Gavin gets cranky we'll remember to just take him for a car ride," Vaughn said quietly, in a tone that suggested that he might not have been talking to me. A quick glance into the rear view mirror showed him leaning over the infant seat. He wasn't speaking to me, or to even Austin who had already fallen asleep. "Don't worry, Landon," he whispered. "We will get him handled."

He was talking to the baby. Fatigue was still obvious on his face, but his features had softened around the edges. There wasn't any sign of arrogance or even the cool demeanor I usually saw. Vaughn looked sweet and I wasn't prepared for how it struck me.

I swerved, just a little. The tires had moved onto the shoulder just enough to startle me. It was a reminder that I needed to focus on the road and not what was going on in the backseat.

I didn't need to dwell on the unexpected view of the man behind me. While the sun hadn't started to peak over the horizon the sky was lightening. More cars were getting on the road, early commuters getting up to start their daily grind.

"You okay?" Vaughn asked in the same gentle tone he used for Landon. "Do I need to drive?"

"I'm good," I said, trying to sound reassuring.

"I'd like to make it home in one piece," he said without changing his tone. It hinted at the idea that the baby hadn't fallen asleep like Austin had assumed he would.

I was chalking up the distraction to fatigue. Vaughn only softened up for the baby. The tone didn't reflect the words. I pursed my lips… he probably wouldn't soften up for me.

6

Nadia

I thought I'd been dead on my feet before. Coasting through my day would've made it easier. There was more than one occasion where I stood there to take an order and for some reason nothing connected. I had to have a few tables to repeat their orders for me.

"You're not sick, are you?" Jodie asked, she cocked her hip out to one side. "Because you said you would work my Friday for me. If you're going to get sick on me, I need some kind of notice."

"I like how that works seeing how she's doing *you* a favor," Deidre snorted as she passed.

"I just had a really long night," I rubbed an eye as I spoke, smudging the mascara I had on. "I'm gonna have to go out to my car for a nap when it comes time for lunch otherwise I'm just gonna start grunting at people."

"We could probably turn it into a theme," Jodie looked entertained by the idea. She clapped her receipt pad between her hands, "We could do our makeup like we were zombified waitresses for Halloween!"

"Girl, you know you're gonna be trying to wiggle your way out of work," Dee said as she began to fix a drink. "Don't get all pumped up for us doing a dress up thing when you know you're not going to be here for it. Even with us having months away, you're gonna start planning for things you ain't gonna participate in," She nudged me, "You do look like you're about to fall asleep. What were *you* doing last night that kept you up?"

"Not what you think," I said without looking at her. I was filling cups up with ice and I needed to get drinks for my own table. I had the receipt pad in my hand to keep track of what I needed. I was arranging cups to fill with soft drinks when a thought occurred to me. "I've got something serious to ask you. When you get the chance," I tried to give her a meaningful look.

"Little girl over there is closing with you, not me," Dee pointed out as she left the waiting station.

Jodie looked between us, confused. "This isn't about me, is it?"

"No," I said as I started to load up my tray with cups. "She's just really good about encouraging my bad ideas."

"I can do that, too," she said just loud enough for me to hear.

I didn't have anything to say to that. I took the drinks to their appropriate table and passed them out. I should feel bad but I didn't have it in me to be peppy or friendly with Jodie. I was just barely making it through my shift as it was.

By the time Deidre went on her lunch, I damn near forgot that I wanted to talk to her. But she was quick to remind me after I brought her sandwich. "Was there something important you wanted to talk to me about?"

"Huh?" I blinked at her before it connected. I eyed the diner's tables, Jodie was two tables down flirting with the people seated in her section. My tables looked like they were okay, no one needing my attention. I sat down across from Dee and tried to assess her mood. She looked tired, but patient. I bet this was an expression she showed her children. "I wanted to admit something to you and gage your reaction."

She looked curious, but began eating. When I didn't immediately speak, she cocked her head to one side. "You are poaching my lunch break, Nadia," she said as she chewed. "What were you going to say?"

"You know Gavin?" I struggled with a way to begin. I was on borrowed time for the both of us and I gave an uneasy glance to the dining room around us.

"Your curly haired thing?" She asked with a knowing look.

"Yeah," I shrugged a little. "One of them."

Dee didn't miss my choice of words. She sat the sandwich down and leaned back in her seat. She eyed me hard, "One of them?" Her eyes narrowed and I got the distinct feeling she was giving me the judging mom face. "Don't tell me you've got that boy plus a side piece."

"One or two," I cringed as I said it. I raised both my hands up when her mouth opened, "They know about each other. They aren't what I would call 'side pieces.'"

She looked confused, the judging disappointment left her face. "What would you call them?"

"My boyfriends," I offered simply.

"And they know about one another?"

"We live together for the most part," I told her.

Deidre gawked at me for a beat then leaned over the table, "you and how many?"

"Three," I supplied. "Four including me." I felt nervous watching her digest the information, I saw shock but there wasn't disgust or judgment.

"I guess that explains all those days you were in here walking funny," she said as she put a hand to her chest. She eyed me again, "I just thought Curly was skilled. That was part of the reason why I liked him. A good looking man that gives it to you so good that you have a hard time walking. That's something every girl wants. But if it's not just him…"

"I mean, just because there's two other men involved doesn't mean Gavin isn't skilled," I added hastily without thinking. I shouldn't need to defend his abilities. Even if we hadn't had the chance to repeat the moment we had in Vaughn's bathroom, it was still something that was hot and fresh in my mind.

Dee just looked at me. "So, that doesn't mean you let all three of them at you at the same time?"

"Well," I winced a little at her question. The way she worded it made it sound worse than I thought it would. I guess it was because someone else was saying it out loud.

"All three of them?" her eyes widened, "At the same time, girl?"

"All three of what?" Jodie appeared at the table beside us.

It took both of us by surprise and I'd almost forgotten I was at work. "It's nothing," I said to Jodie.

"We're gossiping," Deidre said at the same time. "Don't worry about it, it's not something you need to worry about."

Jodie looked a little ruffled at that and she turned her attention down to me. She frowned, probably upset at being excluded, "Are you going to take your break now, too? I just want to know if I need to be looking after your tables, too." She was being snide about it and I was willing to bet that she'd have a complaint to Freddy when she got the opportunity.

"Sorry," I stood up as I spoke. "I got distracted." I felt sheepish considering all the flack I'd given her about her phone.

"What were you talking about?" Jodie asked, moving in step with me. "Has this got anything to do with the diner? I had a friend of mine fill out an application. I figured if we had another person working I could get days off without having to worry about anyone getting over time."

I released a breath, "Freddy hiring another person isn't a bad idea. But I'm a little worried about losing hours just so it would be worth their while to work here."

"You say that," she said, lingering close to my side. "But how often does one of Deidre's kids get sick? Having Megan come in to work, even part time, would keep us from having to be stressed when it's really busy."

"Sorry you guys," I said to the couple that was in my section. "You need some refills?" I picked up an empty plate.

"We're good," the man said, waving me off. He looked like he was half my age and he was vaguely familiar. Almost like he had been here earlier in the day. I couldn't call him on it but I was willing to bet he was playing the same game Gavin used to. "Just give me the check," he said with a wink.

"Alright," I said a little too brightly as I pulled my pad from my apron pocket. I set the bill on the table top. "Take your time."

He put a twenty on top of the bill without looking at it. The total was fifteen forty seven. "Keep the change," he said with a grin.

Okay. I guess I could be paid off by a player. I gave him my biggest smile then looked at the girl, she looked to be the same age as him. She was pretty while probably not being so attractive she would be high in the popularity scale. With the boy's letterman jacket it was easy to see what was happening.

Would this have been the way things went if I'd given in during high school? Would Gavin played me then? I couldn't begin to guess.

I picked up the bill and my cheeriness was more forced, "You guys have a good night." As soon as I went to the next table I bit the inside of my cheek to keep from letting the shift in my mood get to me. Too bad it didn't keep me from reflecting on the past.

Maybe things were working like they were intended to. I wasn't being played, that much was obvious now. I couldn't delude myself anymore despite how cold Vaughn acted. Maybe it was time I stopped holding people at arm's length.

After I settled the tables I had in my section, Dee flagged me down. When I got close enough she leaned out of the booth so I didn't sit back down. "You are going to have to tell me how this works," she said earnestly. "I want details."

"Like dirty details?" I asked, unable to hide my chagrin.

"Girl, I've got an imagination. I don't need you to tell me how you have sex with all three of them," she deadpanned. "Tell me how you manage to balance them all."

"Balance them?" I echoed in confusion.

"Every time you get into a relationship with a man, you give him a piece of you," she began seriously. Her hand closed around my wrist and when I looked closer at her I didn't see judgment, I saw worry. "You've given pieces of you to three different men. How do you keep you?"

I opened my mouth to answer and drew a blank. "I got pieces of them in return?" It seemed like an easy enough answer, it came right out of me before I could even put thought to it.

It seemed like the truth. For everything that I did for them there was something given in return. I didn't feel like they were using me, I wasn't getting played. I had come to realize that this wasn't a joke.

Dee let go of me, eyeing me carefully. "You and I are gonna talk about this off the clock," she decided aloud. The worry was still evident. "I just want to make sure you're okay."

"Okay," I agreed. "As long as I don't have to hear you calling me anything derogatory."

"Baby girl," she said evenly. "You are my friend. I'm just worried that you've gotten yourself into a bad situation because some pretty men are using you. I know damn well that I have no room to be judging you."

That was reassuring. While Dee and my mother were two different people, they were both level headed. Mom always looked at the whole picture and if all Dee did was worry, I was sure Mom would have a similar reaction. There'd be no reason for me to find her an alibi or anything rash. "I appreciate it," I said to her.

This would be okay. I could introduce the guys to Mom and everything would be alright. All I had to do was meet Gavin's parents.

7

Nadia

Somehow I ended up face down in bed. I couldn't quite recall how I'd gotten there, but the best assumption was that autopilot took over and guided me home. Funny how it brought me to the house instead of the apartment. I guess after spending the majority of my time here, before I even moved in, that my subconscious just decided this was home now.

Or I was overthinking it because I was way too tired.

There were two bodies already in bed. I didn't have it in me to pay attention to who was who, all that mattered that I was in my spot, between two of them at least. The bed shifted and a set of hands pulled my shoes off. I groaned appreciatively, my feet ached. They reached under me and unbuttons and zipped my khakis before tugging them down my hips.

I didn't fight as one of my guys decided to undress me. I lifted my butt up into the air and wiggled so it would be easier to get them off my hips. Then the collared shirt was pulled up and over my head, it was only a little difficult with my laying on my belly. The helpful hands even went as far as to unhook my bra, the fingers slid down my back almost making me wish I could purr.

"You want a shirt to sleep in?" Vaughn asked, voice low.

I tensed a little, surprised he was going through the motions of taking care of me. I don't know why it wouldn't occur to me that he'd be eager to do it. This aspect of our relationship still felt new, the fact that he hadn't really changed in demeanor just added to the weariness.

"Nadia," his low voice growling my name twisted something up in me. "Do you want to sleep like this or not?"

"This is fine," I mumbled. Was I talking about the way I was undressed? I usually wore a t-shirt and panties to bed. Now I was just in my panties. In comparison, the three of them usually wore about the same. Would it be so bad?

His hands came up under my armpits, he wasn't going to leave me with my legs hanging off the bed. He hefted me up to the top of the bed so my face was pressed into my pillow. "That good?" He sounded tired as he settled in beside me.

"Where's Austin?" I asked, because as far as I could tell there were only two of them in the bed.

"He's got Landon in the crib," Vaughn began as he shifted the blanket around me. "Separation anxiety has him in your bed in the spare room." He paused to yawn, "Probably going to end up getting a new mattress for you."

"He doesn't need to be spending any more money," I protested.

"Worry about in the morning," he huffed back at me. "Go to sleep. You're exhausted."

"You can't just say something like that to me and expect me to be able to go right to sleep," I grumbled as I rolled onto my side so that I faced what could only be Gavin. He was peacefully unaware, snoozing as if I hadn't joined the two of them in bed. And, despite how tired I was, I was finding it hard to close my eyes now.

"I can get you a shirt," Vaughn grumbled beside me.

"This is fine," I insisted.

"Then why are you still awake?"

"You're trying to tell me that you've never had moments where you're so tired that you're not able to sleep?" I asked him.

"Come here," he said with a sigh.

There was this temptation to resist but it didn't take me long to realize I didn't have it in me to start a fight. He was probably in the same boat as I was. I rolled back over so I was facing him. He ushered me to his side, his hand coming to rest against my bare back. My cheek pressed against his pec and I couldn't make myself relax.

He didn't seem to have that problem, he wasn't tense. He usually wasn't much for cuddling before now so the fact that he was unaffected was surprising. Like his readiness to help with the baby, his insistence on making sure Austin was okay, and him bothering to undress me so I could go to bed comfortably. He hadn't copped a feel, yet. If this was Gavin, he'd have both hands full of my breasts.

"Quit overthinking," he murmured and the hand on my back began to run up and down the length of me. "Worry about it in the morning."

With my ear pressed against his chest I could feel the rumble of his voice. "Are you going to be like this in the morning?" I asked.

The hand on my back didn't falter. His fingers steadily traced my spine. Gooseflesh broke out and I shivered. I closed my eyes and leaned further against him, his nails were trimmed short but he was still teasing me.

"I'm like this all the time," he started softly. "You just don't pay attention."

"Is that why you're such an ass?"

The hand on my back stopped. He sighed lightly, "Maybe I'm an ass because I'm still the third wheel. I don't know how to change it." His hand went to his face and he scrubbed at it, "But instead of going through those motions again we can agree to disagree, or whatever gets you to go to sleep."

His hand landed solidly against my back and I jumped a little. He didn't go back to stroking my skin, it just rested there heavily. I didn't try to prod further into the problem between us, both of us being sleep deprived meant that it would probably be harder to slog our way through a solution. It would only lead to more frustration.

His breathing deepened, giving me a clue that he'd fallen asleep. It was such a man thing to do to be able to fall asleep after opening up a can of worms like this. I sighed and closed my eyes, letting the rise and fall of his chest lull me. I wrapped an arm around his middle. I guess I would just have to start paying more attention to him.

If there was a difference in him that I just wasn't seeing, maybe it was because I hadn't been looking for it.

***

I rolled onto my side, shifting closer to the warm body on my right. The body shifted closer and an arm slung around me. I snuggled into the warm body, prepared to fall back into the deeper sleep. Gavin hummed, his hand curling down from my back to skim along my side. It seemed like he was taking in my state of undress.

His hand cupped my breast, the thumb skirting around the curve until he found my nipple. He tweaked the numb, like he was confirming what he was fondling was what he thought it had been. "This is new," he murmured. "But I like it."

I kept my eyes closed, hoping he'd assume I was asleep and would just let me stay that way. I never really cared when he got handsy, but I wasn't ready to let go of the illusion that I could roll over and go right back to sleep.

A door opened accompanied with the loud rumble of pipes as the toilet flushed. "Let her sleep," Vaughn barked. That's probably what ruined any chances of me going to sleep. "It's too early for that."

"You're only saying that because you took the day off," Gavin whispered. "It's not like the sun isn't up."

"What time is it?" I asked, not opening my eyes in the hopes that I at least had another thirty minutes before my alarm went off.

"Just after eight," Vaughn supplied. "What time is your alarm set to?"

I sighed, trying to ignore Gavin's hand as his fingers shifted to toy with my nipple more. "Nine," I said as I started to stretch. It did nothing but give the man next to me more access to my chest. I should swat his hand away, I should stop him because all he was going to do is get things going and it wasn't going to be long before I needed to get ready for work.

I shifted onto my back, not breaking the hold Gavin had on my breast. He readily pressed against my side and the hand on me became a little more insistent. "That an okay to go?" He asked, sat up and leaned over me as he waited for my answer. His hair was in disarray, swept upward in tangled curls that made him look wild. He looked down at me with half lidded eyes, hunger simmering in his eyes.

I glanced at Vaughn, he stood at the edge of the bed looking curious. He sat my phone down and didn't immediately join us in the bed. I reached a hand towards him. "I just woke up," I said. "So, I probably have some serious morning breath. If that's not going to kill the mood for you I'm not going to protest."

"There are workarounds for that," Gavin said before he stretched back out beside me. He didn't hesitate to illustrate his meaning. He cupped both of my breasts now, pressing them together so he could rub his face between them. The stubble on his face raked against my skin, making me inhale sharply before he even began to press open mouth kisses against me.

Vaughn just seemed content to watch, ignoring my hand. I dropped it. I didn't know how to feel about it, his expression was placid and he wasn't really looking at me. His attention seemed to be focused on what Gavin was doing. Did that mean he was just going to watch?

"Touch me," I said without thinking. But clearly it was something I wanted.

Vaughn's gaze connected with mine, somehow he still managed to look cool even with the growing tent in his boxers. He sat on the bed and reached for me. He moved Gavin's hand out of the way and began to lightly tease breast he claimed.

"Is this what you want?" he asked, his thumb circled the areola pointedly avoiding the nipple. "Or did you want this?" His hand left my chest and drifted down my side to slip into my panties. He spread the outer lips of my pussy with his fingers so he could trace my slit.

I spread my legs, arching in response. I closed my eyes and rolled my hips against Vaughn's hand. I hoped it would be answer enough for him, but he didn't make any attempt to enter me with his fingers. Combined with Gavin's mouth traveling to my other breast, I felt a twinge of impatience go through me.

"Quit playing with me," I huffed out.

"Tell me what you want," Vaughn said evenly, without any frustration. "I don't want there to be any sort of miscommunication. I want to make sure *I'm* paying attention to give you what you want."

Gavin let go of me to look at his friend, "is everything okay?"

"Just trying to be clear," Vaughn said without looking at the other man.

Gavin looked between the two of us, his brows drawn together. He pushed himself up, "Is this going to be a problem? Like," he paused to purse his lips and tilted his head, "the kind of problem that's going to blow things up unnecessarily?"

Vaughn pulled his hand out of my panties. I couldn't contain the whine that erupted from me at the loss, even if it had been more teasing than anything. "I'm a third wheel," he said after a length. "The only time I've not been is when it was just me and her. Every effort I make is ignored."

Gavin deflated onto me and groaned, "We're not going to be able to fuck now."

"What?" I asked, trying to push him off of me so I could sit up. The fact that he jumped to that conclusion confused me.

"Sex doesn't fix the situation," he said as he moved to sit up with me. "That much is obvious. Even if it were just you and him or if all of us were involved, it's only a matter of time before it implodes. I don't want that to happen," he said to the other man on the bed. "As far as I could tell since I walked in on the two of you, I thought we were fine. Now we're not?"

Vaughn's brows twitched and he turned away from me and Gavin. He rubbed his face with both hands, "I'm the asshole, the prick."

"Well, yeah," Gavin said, not waiting for his friend to get to the point. "That's the way it's always been."

"Fuck off," Vaughn shot him a glare over his shoulder. "I don't give a shit about how other people view me. That's never bothered me," he continued evenly. "But when you're trying to appeal to someone that you want to be in a relationship with and that's all they see you as …"

"It's like Austin said in the beginning," Gavin offered gently. "Shit's gotta be earned."

"What the hell?" Austin called out from the other end of the house. It was loud enough to startle the three of us in bed. He had Landon balanced on one arm with his hand shielding the infant's eyes like he might see something. I was topless and up to that point there hadn't been anyone that cared. I tugged the sheet up to cover myself trying not to feel chastised. "I realize that asking you guys to keep it PG while my son is in the house is a lot, especially with him being here off schedule. Do you think you could close the door if you're going to do that?"

"We were trying to do shit," Gavin said, "but we hit a roadblock."

Austin came closer to the bedroom, his hand still covering Landon's eyes. "Didn't we already do this?" He eyed the three of us, "Why go through this again? What's the point?"

"I think the point might not be obvious to you," Vaughn snapped at him, "because you're safe. You're in a good spot. There's nothing to soil your situation."

"Are you sure?" Austin asked, dropping his hand from Landon's eyes to rest on the small of the child's back. "Because I'm pretty sure my situation just got shittier. Especially considering the fact that I just changed the situation's diaper and I can feel him pooping now." He grimaced as the baby grunted, Landon's blue eyes flicking from each of us before he closed them for another pointed strained noise. "Maybe you should reconsider your wording."

"I think maybe we should stop dwelling on the possible conclusion of this," I interrupted. "I realize there has been and is some strain between us," I said to Vaughn. "I have a preconceived opinion of you from a period in my life that wasn't so great." I ran my fingers through my hair, pausing when I ran into a tangle, "You have to admit when you have a view of someone. It takes time for that to change. I get talking about it might help, but demanding that I suddenly see you as a doting boyfriend instead of a jackass is a little much."

He didn't look at me, but I could see his jaw working and his shoulders stiffening. I scooted closer, hesitating before I touched his back. "Patience," I started. "I'm paying attention."

"Shit doesn't happen overnight," Gavin said from behind me.

"It just happens," Austin said in agreement. Then he looked at the infant he was holding, still making a face. "Are you done?" he asked his son.

Landon just gave him a grin. His little hand slapped against Austin's chest and he turned the same grin to the three of us. "It feels damp," Austin said as he turned to go back down the hall. "I hope you didn't have a blowout."

"If you can find a way to have him be distracted for twenty minutes or so we still might be able to salvage this," Gavin called after him. "Have it be all four of us. Have some great morning sex." He prodded, his voice raising, "Get some much needed release after a long ass week."

"Not today," Austin called back down. "But if you make me a bottle I'll get some breakfast ready."

"We're gonna have to find something to do with the kid for us to be able to have that kind of fun, aren't we?" Gavin asked.

"Probably," Vaughn said, seeming to give in. "Kelli should be in town to do that."

Gavin groaned as he pushed himself out of bed. He went into the kitchen, preparing a bottle like Austin asked. "I don't know that I can wait that long."

8

Nadia

At least for today work was less exhausting because I'd got something that resembled a decent night's sleep. I had the next day off to play catch up and I might even get the house to myself. Well, considering that Austin would be there with the baby and Gavin didn't really work, probably not.

That was the disadvantage of commitment. I guess if I ever needed time to myself or if I ever got legitimately angry at the three of them I could always go stay with my parents. That was a painful thought.

There was a chance that I could use mom as a babysitter. After this morning I was wishing that we would've been able to celebrate a child-free house like usual. But we didn't get that opportunity. Maybe mom would be willing to accept Landon as a grandchild by proxy. I guess to find out I had to introduce all of them to my parents.

Hopefully mom would be on a similar page as Deidre. I passed my coworker as I headed towards a table with a tray full of drinks. I was grateful for the older woman I worked with, even more so that kids apparently affected her memory that she had forgotten about the talk we were supposed to have.

"You seen that?" Dee asked as she nodded towards the hooks in the kitchen window. Each hook on the little spinning wheel was full. "We that busy?"

I paused, it felt like I had just given someone their plates. I looked at my tables, there were two that were still waiting on their meals. But that wasn't entirely out of the ordinary. "I don't think so," I said as I glanced into the window I didn't see Freddy. There was food sizzling on the cooktop and the fryer was going. The back door was propped open. "He might be out smoking a cigarette," I suggested.

Dee hummed, but didn't argue. She went back into her section and looked apologetic as she spoke to the people at her table. Had they been waiting longer than usual? It took Freddy some time to put complicated meals together but he usually had a method that put out meals at a fairly decent pace.

I delivered the drinks to my table and decided when a plate didn't appear in the window I'd go check on him. Jodie was at the waiting station with her phone in hand, her tables look handled. No one was pointedly looking at her.

"When was your last pick up?" I asked her at the door to the kitchen. I knew if I went in there and Fred was busy he'd get crabby if I asked about food.

"It's been forever," she said without looking up from her phone. "I haven't had anyone complain, every time I pass by my tables I just let them know it'll be done soon." She shrugged unconcerned with it, "I figured I would just take the time to text my friend. She applied here and I hadn't got the chance to talk to the boss about whether or not he had looked at her application." She gave me her full attention, "But you could do that for me… tell him we need another person to work at least part time."

"You need to understand if he even decides to hire a new person, and it's your friend, that it's unlikely you guys will work the same shifts," I said as I leaned on the kitchen door. I made the decision then to check on Freddy, just to flee the conversation. "He's not gonna pay you two to hang out."

"But you and Dee are friends," Jodie protested.

I pushed the door open, "She was working here before I was. We became friends when we started working together. There's a difference." I stepped into the kitchen and let the door swing closed behind me, "Plus we still do our jobs."

Then I smelled it. Something burning. I saw burger patties on the cooktop, smoking and blackening at the edges. I reached over to begin to turn each of the knobs off. I'd address the food later and the likelihood that Freddy would be mad at me for touching his grill. The fryer was in a similar state and I carefully picked the basket up out of the bubbling oil. I curled my lip, it was very unlikely the fries in it were edible.

I looked at the open door, afraid now for an inexplicable reason. "Freddy?" I called out. "If you're smoking you're screwing up orders."

He didn't answer.

"Fred?" I called again, drifting to the open door. My heart was in my throat.

There was a groan and as soon as I took in the back lot behind the diner I saw the dumpster. Freddy was hunched over on his knees, one hand gripping the front of his shirt and the other pressed against the metal exterior of the trash can. He looked like he was breathing laboriously and he was staring ahead, he didn't even look up at me when I approached.

"Dee!" I yelled back into the kitchen before I fell on my knees next to Freddy. I put my hands under his arm and tried to pull him up. "Are you okay?" I shifted so I was kneeling, but I wanted him to stand. I couldn't deal with him looking like this. His shirt was damp, he was sweating so profusely that I felt it through the fabric as I tried to heave him up. "Come on, get up."

"Nadia," he wheezed but didn't make any move to get up like I wanted him to.

"Dee," I hollered again. "Come on, Freddy," I gritted out to him. "We need you to get up."

"It hurts," he said through his teeth.

"Why do I hear you hollering at me?" Deidre finally appeared in the door frame of the kitchen. Then she gasped, "Lemme get my phone."

"I don't know what to do," I shouted after her when she disappeared.

"I'm calling nine one one, girl," she said as she reappeared. "Jodie, watch the tables if anyone asks we're having an emergency. If there's anyone that's a doctor or a nurse send them back here." She came to kneel by Freddy and I, thrusting her phone between us.

"Nine one one, what is your emergency?"

"We found our boss doubled over in the back lot," Dee supplied readily. "He's breathing hard and looks like he's in pain."

"He's also really sweaty," I offered, feeling more than a little hysterical. "He's said he hurts."

"Are we on speaker phone?"

"Yes," Dee confirmed.

"Sir?" The operator began to direct the question to Fred. "Are you experiencing chest pain?"

Fred nodded shakily, his eyes clenching closed. Dee reported that in a matter of fact tone. I resisted the urge to pull him up again, but I couldn't make myself let go of his arm. I felt shaky and I was so grateful that the woman next to me had some idea as to what to do.

"Can I get your name and age, sir?"

When Fred didn't answer immediately Dee took the wheel, "Fred Dobbs. He's the owner of Fred's diner. He's fifty three. Maybe two eighty."

"Dee," he gritted out, glaring at her.

"You're what? Five eleven? Don't be mad at me, Boss. I'm trying to get you help," she pursed her lips at him. She perked up a little bit and I could hear sirens in the distance, but they were growing louder. It suggested that the ambulance was moving fast and getting closer.

"I've got an ambulance on the way, but I want you to stay on the line with me," the operator said seriously. It made the dread in me grow.

"Our diner is full of customers," Dee said evenly, looking between me and Fred. It was the first instance where she looked less like she was in control. "Do I need to clear them out?"

"Are they obstructing access for EMTs to get to Mr. Dobbs?"

"There's a back drive where the dumpster is at," I managed to speak up. "There's no cars blocking it and he's right here. Or should we try to move him inside?" I didn't know but I knew my knees were hurting from the gravel on the broken up concrete that made up the back lot.

"If it's convenient for EMTs to get to Mr. Dobbs where he's at then you should stay right where you're at. That way they can easily get to you and help."

"Okay, we hear them coming," Dee offered her phone to me. "I'm going to wave them down to make sure they get back here. You take this because they're going to want to monitor him."

"That's not necessary, ma'am," the operator spoke up even though Dee had already shoved the phone into my hand. "I've kept them up to date on what's going on throughout our entire conversation."

"Sure it isn't," Dee said as she got up and started to follow the little driveway down to the curb.

I winced as she left us, I doubted I was strong enough to handle this. My stomach was in a knot and I felt nauseous. "What am I supposed to do?"

"Is he still breathing?" the operator asked.

I turned to look at Freddy, his face was a worrying shade of red and his eyes were clenched closed. But his mouth was open and he panted for breath. He leaned slightly against me, but it felt like he was still balancing the majority of his weight against the dumpster.

"He is," I confirmed.

"Have you had a heart attack before, Mr. Dobbs?"

He shook his head and I reported that, "He is a smoker though. That's something that could cause heart problems, right?"

"It can."

"Snitch," Fred managed to wheeze out.

"Yeah, well," I laughed and there seemed like there was an edge to it. "I told you to quit a long time ago and where are we now." My eyes started to burn, even when the sound of the sirens became unbearably loud. "You can't die," I said it low and I doubted he would've been able to hear me over the noise.

"Do you see the ambulance?" the operator asked, politely ignoring what I said.

"Yeah, they're coming down the drive now." The large truck backed down the drive, giving me a view of the big truck. The light reflected off the yellow and white stripes on the back of it and I should've been relieved. It still felt like I was on the edge of panicking.

"Do you need me to stay on the line with you?"

Could they tell I was about to fall apart? I cleared my throat as the back doors opened and a man in a dark blue uniform came out of it. Another came from around the front of the vehicle and helped pull out the gurney. This meant everything was going to be alright, right?

"I need to get out of the way," I said to myself, shaking my head.

"Mr. Dobbs?" one of the men squatted next to me as the other arranged the gurney close to us. "The ladies called us and said you're having chest pains?" he asked, sparing me only a glance. "Do you think you can sit on the gurney for me so we can get you checked out?"

A set of hands gently touched my shoulders, "Come on, ma'am. Let us do the work now."

I let him help me to my feet and take my place as him and his partner carefully maneuvered Freddy to the gurney, first to sit and, with a pained noise, to lay down. I could feel my chin wobbling beyond my control, my throat burned and tears were just at the surface.

"You got my phone?" Deidre appeared at my side. I held the device tightly between my hands, but when she tugged it from me I didn't make any effort to keep it from her. "Baby girl," she made a noise as they began to load Fred up into the ambulance. "It's gonna be okay."

I couldn't contain it anymore. I turned to her and she pulled me into a tight hug. I broke down then, trembling and sobbing onto her shoulder. It seemed way too out of hand but despite every effort I couldn't reel myself in. Even when she hushed me and assured me that everything was going to be alright, I couldn't stop.

"Are either of you going to go with him?"

"No, we need to clean up and close up shop. We're not related to him, just employees," Dee told him while she held me. "What hospital are you taking him to?"

"Mercy."

"We'll be there later," she said as she pulled away from me. "You gotta dry it up now, baby. We got to take care of the diner before we can go make sure the old man is alright. So, let's go. Jodie isn't gonna know what to do so you need to pull it together, okay?"

I nodded shakily and rubbed my cheeks, "Yeah, sorry." I turned to watch the ambulance pull out of the drive. The sirens started again, blaring so loudly I could feel it in my skull.

"No reason to be sorry, but let's hurry this up so we can go check on him," she directed me back into the kitchen. Her hand was gently rubbing my back and it left me wishing I had the same strength she did.

9

Vaughn

I should've just fucked her when I had the chance this morning. As it was now, I had my back to Gavin in bed, unwillingly listening to the video he was watching on the phone. There was a Naddy sized gap between us that was annoyingly empty.

"Turn it down," I demanded, it was probably the third time.

"I'm trying to stay awake," Gavin complained as the volume went down just a notch. "If I doze off and end up cuddling with you, you're gonna punch me. Then I'll have to punch you back, we'll fight. I'll win, more than just your ego will be bruised. Do you really want that to happen?"

I rolled my eyes and regretted this arrangement I had fitted myself into. If I was at home I wouldn't have to deal with this. It would leave me in my own bed. Alone. I had enjoyed sleeping next to Nadia, she could be just as bad as Gavin when it came to sleeping in bed with her but it was much more pleasant to have her pressed against me. I wouldn't complain about that. But with her working late it often left me going to bed without her. And either laying between Austin and Gavin or beside one.

It felt like I hadn't quite found where I fit into this. If I even fit at all. Sometimes I wondered if I was just fooling myself into believing that I did.

"What time is it?" I asked when the video he was watching broke into an ad.

"Quarter after one."

"She isn't normally this late, is she?" I asked, shifting onto my back. He didn't appear concerned. Since

I started staying here she was usually home around midnight. It was now an hour past that. "Why aren't you worried?"

"What are you worried about?" he gave me a look, "What do you think she's doing? Cheating on us?"

"You're an idiot," I sat up and reached for my phone. "That's not what I was getting at." I found her number in my contacts and called her, if the jackass beside me wasn't going to make any effort to soothe my nerves then I would just call Naddy myself.

She picked up on the second ring and before she even said anything I put my feet onto the floor, sitting forward and ready to get out of bed. "Hey," her voice was a whisper, filled with emotions like she was on the verge of tears. "Sorry I'm not home, yet. It's just been a long day. I was trying to calm myself down before I headed that way."

"What happened?" I demanded as several different scenarios crossed my mind. Had she been attacked while trying to get into her car? Was she in a car accident? She was a fairly decent driver, but that didn't take other drivers into account. I stood and went to the dresser, pulling out a shirt. "Where are you?"

"I'm at Mercy hospital," she supplied with a sniffle. That didn't help me at all, "In the parking lot. It's just taken me a little bit to calm down. I'm sorry," she sounded so small.

"If you don't think you can drive, give me a minute. I'll be out there to get you," I instructed as I tugged my shirt on, taking just a beat to hold the phone away from my ear. "Don't try to drive."

"You have to work tomorrow," she sniffled again. "I don't want to be the reason you're exhausted at work."

"It's not up for debate," I turned to Gavin. "Get your ass up and get dressed so we can go get her." I directed my attention back to her, "Did something happen to you? Is that why you're crying?"

That got Gavin up and out of the bed and he was pointedly listening to the conversation even though he was hearing just my side of it. He had shorts and a shirt on, then sat back down on the bed and was shoving his feet into his shoes. "We're taking my truck," he announced without waiting to get the answers to my questions.

"I'm fine," she told me weakly. "Nothing happened to me, I'm crying because it's been a rough day." She sighed heavily over the line. "I didn't want you to know I was crying. I wish you hadn't called."

That hurt. More than it should have. "My opinion of you isn't going to change just because I see you cry," I tried to say it gently because she sounded emotional. Was it because of me? Was that why she was crying? This couldn't be because of what I said this morning.

She sniffled noisily over the line. "I don't like to feel weak," she admitted finally. "And that's how I feel right now. I didn't even have the common sense to do anything other than call for Dee for help," her voice cracked and it sounded like she was falling into a new wave of tears. "And they didn't let us see him because we're not family and I don't even know if he has family or who to contact."

I nodded towards the door at Gavin as I slipped my feet into my own shoes. I looked ridiculous with the loafers on, paired with a wrinkled shirt and bright red shorts, but my appearance wasn't important. "Who? Maybe I can help?" I offered.

"Fred," she supplied. "H-he had a heart attack. I found him outside and I have no idea how long he was out there," she broke then. "I didn't think it was a big deal that plates were a little behind. I thought he'd gotten distracted, but no."

"But he's okay?" I asked.

"I don't know," she hiccupped. "They wouldn't tell us. All they told us was that he was in surgery."

"We're on our way," I told her. "Just sit in your car and we'll be there. Okay? Did you go directly to the hospital with him?"

"No," she took a deep breath and let it out slowly. "We had to take care of the customers that were still in the diner. Most of them were understanding and left big tips even though they didn't get their food. There was only one person being an asshole but Jodie was pretty good on making them feel guilty so they left. I'm kind of surprised, I didn't know she had that in her." She made a frustrated noise, "Everyone managed to have their shit together and know what to do, but I fucking crumbled under pressure."

"You found him?" I asked as I led Gavin out of the house. I waited for him by the truck, when the headlights flashed I got in. "It's a stressful situation to come across someone that's collapsed, it's scary. The reaction you're having is completely normal. There is nothing wrong with you crying." I didn't have any clue behind my words, all I had was the drive to make her feel better.

Gavin got in the truck beside me, his eyes were wide when he looked at me. "She's crying?" He asked. "Where are we going?"

"Mercy Hospital," I said to him.

"You didn't wake Gavin and Austin up did you?" There was something accusatory in her voice.

"They don't have jobs and we can't just leave your car at the hospital, can we?" I shot back at her. "Austin is still in bed. I'm not such an asshole that I'd keep him up late when I know Landon is going to wake him up early."

That quieted her. But the fact that she fired up for me had me worrying a little less. "Okay," she relented. "I'll keep an eye out for you."

"Do you want to stay on the phone with me?" I asked, hoping she would. Even if it just left me listening to her breathe.

She hesitated, "I don't know. I look like a mess. I should try to clean myself up before I frighten you off."

"I've woken up next to you while you were still asleep a few times now," I began. "I've heard you snore loud enough to shake the windows in my car. I don't really care what you look like."

"Okay," and I thought for a minute she was going to hang up on me. "I feel so stupid," her breathing stuttered over the phone. "I should've just come home as soon as we closed up the diner, but I couldn't imagine just leaving him up here by himself. And then they wouldn't tell me anything, they just told me everything else was restricted to immediate family members and I would have to wait until visiting hours to find anything out. But even then," she huffed out a gasp, "I'd probably just see him hooked up to a bunch of tubes and wires."

"You don't owe him anything," I said as she grew silent again. I had said the wrong thing. "But I understand," I began in an attempt to back track. "He was important and I bet he will appreciate you looking in on him."

She didn't argue, but she didn't hang up either. When we got to the hospital she directed us to where she was parked. We found her standing outside her car, her phone held to her ear until she spotted us. Then she ended the call, shoved her phone in her pocket. As soon as I got out of Gavin's truck she was on me.

Nadia's arms wound tightly around my waist and I was caught off guard. Not just by the feel of her holding onto me so desperately, but from the feeling that went through me. I carefully wrapped my arms around her shoulders, at a loss for words. I held onto her even as I felt a quiver go through her.

Did she hold onto people that hard? Is that why she was reacting like this? Would she ever feel like this about me?

Her face was buried against my chest and while she shuddered a little, she didn't make the same amount of noise she did while we had been on the phone. Was I a bastard for enjoying this? The way she held onto me almost felt like she needed me. I wanted her to need me.

"Is everything okay?" Gavin asked, I looked up at him.

Was he jealous? He didn't give any signs that he was. Then Naddy reached out a hand for him. Gavin came to her readily, he didn't pay me any mind as she hooked her arm around his waist and she tugged him closer. His shoulder bumped into mine and I had a moment of discomfort. The forced closeness bothered me while I was caught up in the emotions she was making me feel.

"Can we just go home?" she asked.

"Your keys in your car?" I asked her. When she nodded I broke the hold she had on me, stepping away. "Ride with him and I'll be just behind you. We can go home and go to bed."

She only resisted a little before she let Gavin guide her to the passenger side door. I got into her car and immediately regretted the offer I made. I banged my head against the frame, I guess that was from cracking her jaw the last time her and I had been together solo. I had to slide her seat back all the way to have any hope of being able to drive it.

Naddy left her key in the ignition, which was helpful. When I started up the tiny car it made me question how she got anywhere. The engine rumbled in a way that suggested that it was only a matter of time before it decided to quit. I followed Gavin closely, just in case it suddenly failed. I wasn't looking forward to having to walk the rest of the way to Austin's.

We came up to a gas station and on a whim, I pulled into it. I could only hope that Gavin kept Naddy distracted and neither were paying attention to what I was doing. If I filled her gas tank up maybe that would improve the ride. The fuel gage wasn't empty, but it was close. My hope was she wouldn't notice, that after the day she had that she would question whether she had gotten the gas herself.

At most, I would expect her to get angry at me. I was used to her glares, it was something I was willing to face again. It didn't take much to fill up her tank, anyway. Twenty five bucks shouldn't earn me grief for long.

While I was wrong about the fact that filling her car up would make it run better, it got me home. I put her keys on the coffee table and went to the bedroom door. They hadn't waited for me but the lamp on the bedside table was left on.

Naddy was already wrapped up in Gavin's arms. But they left plenty of room for me in bed. I kicked my shoes off and tugged the shirt over my head. I dropped it on the floor and I noticed I had an audience.

I stalled out when I met her gaze. I felt pinned watching the swirl of greens and browns of her eyes. "You should be asleep," I pointed out, not recognizing the sound of my own voice.

She didn't say anything, didn't give me any snark. She pulled the sheet and blanket back from the bed, offering me room. Then she reached out to me.

It didn't occur to me before now where I stood with her. But as I climbed into the bed beside her. As I let her tug me closer so I was pressed to her side and by proxy Gavin. As her hand rested against my chest, my heart beating heavily under her fingers.

I was too far gone to do anything but what she wanted, I cared in a way I wasn't familiar with. I knew now how Austin felt and had felt since high school. What I thought was infatuation in the beginning was more than that.

I swallowed hard, resting my hand on top of hers. I looked up at the ceiling and I tried to figure out what I was supposed to do next. What could I do to make sure nothing bad happened to this?

10

Nadia

There was a familiar buzzing that cut through the fog of sleep. My head hurt and I had the blurred worry that I was hung over before I realized that wasn't it. I hadn't had any alcohol last night. But I cried yesterday, I put a hand to my face and I felt heat in my cheeks but if there had been puffiness it wasn't there anymore. But there was pressure behind my eyes and in my forehead that made me ache.

There was a body next to me that was firmly plastered to my side. When I sat up I found the other side of the bed empty. It looks like Vaughn went to work after all.

The buzzing started again and I managed to untangle myself from Gavin without disturbing him too much. I found my phone in the pocket of the khaki's I wore yesterday. I hadn't bothered to plug it up and the battery life was glaring at me. Hopefully it could wait to die until after my phone call.

"Girl," Deidre started as a greeting. "If you're gonna ignore my call because you're surrounded by men, me and you are gonna fight."

"I'm sorry, I was asleep," I huffed into the phone. "Yesterday was kind of a trying day and I was really tired."

"You think yesterday was bad, try to be me this morning," she snapped into the line. "I rode by here to make sure the diner was alright. There were cars in the parking lot, people were waiting on it to open. I had to tell all these people that Fred had a damn heart attack and we were going to be closed for a while." She made a noise, "I don't even know what this means when it comes to our paychecks and what we're supposed to do between now and the time he's back on his feet."

"That's if he gets back on his feet," I interrupted as I sat back on the edge of the bed. I put a hand to my brow and I could feel my throat starting to burn again. "What if he doesn't make it? What happens then?"

"Nadia," Dee snapped into my ear. "We are not having that conversation. We are not talking like Fred just died on us. Now you stop it. He didn't say much yesterday, but he was conscious and responsive when they picked him up." She sounded strong at first but there was a little waiver in her voice, giving me a hint that she wasn't as unaffected as I thought she had been. "He'll be okay. Boss man has to be okay."

Hearing her crumble, even if just a little, made me feel better for some reason. Dee wasn't cold or uncaring, she just didn't readily show that emotion. She had better control of it than I did. "Sorry," I took a breath and released it slowly. "What do we do now?"

"I called you because I thought you might know," she said evenly. "I was wondering if I need to start looking for another job or not. What's going to happen to our last paycheck?"

I shook my head, "I don't know. Even after you left the hospital to go home, they refused to tell me anything. I've never had this happen before."

"Me either," she sighed. "At least not with a job that was owned by one person," she made a noise. "I'm gonna try to call up at the hospital, see if they'll tell me anything over the phone."

"If you decide to go up there, let me know. I'll meet you there. Have you heard anything from Jodie?"

"Girl ain't stressin'," she said after a length. "She's treating it like it's a vacation. But I got her number so I can get on her butt if I need to. Find out if she's gonna quit right away or not." She paused, "Was she after you about talking up her friend to Fred, too?"

"Yeah," I rubbed my face as I answered her. "I haven't said anything to Freddy about her friend. I didn't think it would be a good idea to try to hire another person, even part time."

"Girl, if we get someone to cook we can keep on while he's in the hospital," she said evenly. "All we need is access to do payroll and be able to make orders for food. We could run that business while he recovers."

"We would have to get his permission to do this," I argued. "Can he even agree to something while he's in the hospital?"

"I called you to ask you this mess because I thought you might know," she sounded exacerbated. "How about this, you do some research on what we need to run the diner. I'll get in contact with the hospital. Let's see if they will tell someone who is a bigger bitch than you are what we want to know."

"Let me know what you find out?"

"I will. And don't think this gets you out of any sort of conversation on how I can get a few men to take care of me," she said before she hung up on me.

It was a plan, something to do. Otherwise I would be in the same boat Deidre was having to find a replacement job. Losing two jobs in such a short amount of time wasn't good, even if in both instances it wasn't my fault. It was harder to find a job when you didn't have one.

"What's going on?" Austin asked, peering in from the kitchen.

I hadn't heard him or noticed if he was even eavesdropping. I tangled my fingers in my bed head and looked up at him, he had a bottle in hand and while I didn't see Landon I could hear him in the kitchen. He was most likely in the second hand high chair that we bought off of Dee, I could hear his little hands patting against the heavy plastic top accompanied with a gurgle.

"My boss had a heart attack," I told him, twitching as everything in me wanted nothing more than to dissolve back into that sobbing mess that I'd been yesterday. I couldn't, I needed to pull myself together. I needed to make a plan. "So, I guess I'm out of a job. I know that's the last thing you need to hear after I just moved in."

He started to step into the room then Landon made a noise, not really a fussy sound but one that suggested he might just be on the verge of kicking one up. Austin's shoulders slumped a little and he stepped back out of the bedroom into the view of the infant. "Don't worry about it, Nadia. I know you're not a leech like some people," he nodded his head towards the bed, indicating Gavin that still laid stretched out behind me. "Besides, this isn't something that happens every day. It happened out of nowhere, it's not like you could have planned for it."

That was true. I guess that helped the gnawing feeling in my gut. "It doesn't mean I know what to do from here," I said lowly and looked at my phone, the battery symbol in the upper right hand corner of the screen was empty. The screen went black. I'd need to plug it up so Dee would be able to get in touch with me. But if I plugged it up and I was still empty handed, I'd feel useless.

"You were on the phone with someone," he prodded before disappearing. I heard Landon make an approving sound that Austin responded to before he came back into view. This time he was empty handed, his attention clearly on his son that I couldn't see. "It sounded like they were trying to work out a plan of action with you. If you're lost, maybe give Vaughn a call. I bet he can give you a little direction. He's good at that."

"Comes from being QB," Gavin said with a yawn, stretching. "Why are we up so early talking?"

I glanced over my shoulder at him then a loud crash echoed from the kitchen. Austin gave a mock gasp of surprise, despite the fact that I had jumped. "How are you supposed to eat breakfast if you throw it?" he demanded before he drifted back out of sight.

"It's not early," I shot back at Gavin. "It's eight." I put my phone on the bedside table and plugged it up, despite the fact that I would've liked nothing more than to avoid reality. Seeing him stretched out behind me seemed to pose an idea as to what I could do to distance myself from reality, at least for a little while.

Gavin just squinted at me, he was stretched up with the blanket and shoved down to his hips. It put his abs on full display and I didn't bother to look away. This felt like a mirror of yesterday, the only thing missing was Vaughn.

"If you give me a minute," Austin spoke from the kitchen. "I can get something to cook for breakfast." After he said it there was a loud smack suggesting that Landon had repeated the act of dumping his own liquid meal onto the floor. Austin sighed, "This is gonna happen a lot, isn't it?"

"I see you," Gavin said quietly to me. "You can get up and close the door. We could fuck real quick and have something to eat." He turned on his side and stretched an arm up and over his head, drawing my eyes back down to his stomach and how the muscles moved. To the defined v that made my mouth dry. "Or we can just go get some lunch."

"It wouldn't be fair," I whispered back.

I didn't look up at his face and he laughed a little and shoved the blankets down a little further, "The thirst is so obvious here, Naddy. Are you sure?"

I winced and I pushed up to my feet, "We're gonna have to figure out a way where we can be together while the baby is here anyway. I need the distraction and I want you." I went into the kitchen and saw the bottle on the floor, leaking a growing puddle on the floor.

Austin was in the fridge, he had a carton of eggs in one hand and seemed to be struggling to decide just what he wanted to do. He hadn't made an attempt to retrieve the bottle, likely because it had just been flung to the floor. Either that or he was losing patience with it.

I picked up the bottle and took it to the sink, I carefully rinsed off the nipple before sitting it back on the plastic tray in front of Landon. He looked up at me, his father's blue eyes huge framed with a fan of lashes that only babies found a way to have. He blinked owlishly at me before grinning broadly with that gummy smile and sending the bottle crashing back down to the floor.

Maybe kids just weren't my thing.

I studied his round cheeks and tilted my head. He put a little fist into his mouth without breaking the stare between us. He gnawed on it, still looking right through me. "Is his face usually this shade of pink?"

"What?" Austin perked up with an arm full from the fridge. He put the carton of eggs down with what looked like spinach and dill. Or maybe it was kale?

God, I hope he wasn't planning on trying kale in an omelet. I could take spinach, but the taste of kale wasn't something I enjoyed and I really didn't want to start my day with it.

"He's a little pink," I said and carefully reached out to touch one of the baby's round cheeks. "I guess he could've gotten some coloring from Lauren. But I didn't think the one good look I had of her was something I could base an opinion on." Lauren, Landon's mother, had been hysterical when I actually met her. The first time it was a snooty glimpse the second was more of a meltdown. "He's a little warm."

While Landon was fully capable of packing a meltdown of epic proportions, I wouldn't equate it to the same thing Lauren did. Baby meltdowns weren't on the same level as an angry ex-girlfriend. They were close but different. Just not by much.

Austin stood beside me, looking down at his son with a little concern. He cupped both of Landon's cheeks in his hand, his brows drawn together. Then he pressed his hand against the baby's forehead followed by pressing a kiss against it. "He does feel warm," he said after he pulled away from him. "He was fussing hard when he woke me up. I just thought it was because he was hungry." He looked down at the bottle that was on the floor, "Is that why he's not touching his bottle? He's sick?"

"I don't know," I shrugged helplessly at him. "Has he thrown up at all? Or had diarrhea? I don't have kids so I have no idea."

Austin carefully pulled Landon up from the highchair. The baby whimpered but didn't resist when his father pulled him close, "I don't have a doctor for him. I don't even know what to do?" He looked at me, "What if he caught something on the airplane?"

"It might not be that serious," I tried to calm him down. "Do you have a thermometer?"

"I think there's one in the first aid kit I bought when he first came home," he said as he swayed with his son. "I've been so used to him being a little fussy in the mornings that I didn't think anything of it. God I hope he isn't getting sick on me."

I went back to the room that Austin had converted into the nursery. It took a little searching before I found it in one of the drawers of the changing table. When I pulled out the digital thermometer and frowned. "How are you going to be able to get him to hold this under his tongue?" I asked as I came down the hall. "That's not something an infant is going to know how to do."

"I should take him to the urgent care," Austin said and it sounded like he was talking to himself.

"That's an hour ride from here," Gavin said, standing in the door of the bedroom. "I bet you can call it in before riding all the way out there. Or," he gave me a look then turned his attention back to Austin and Landon. "Call a mom."

"Dee's busy," I said without thinking. "She's supposed to be checking on Freddy."

"And your mom?" He asked, his hands behind his back.

I blinked. It felt like it had been such a long time since we had a conversation about meeting each other's parents that I was caught off guard. "My mom?"

"Yeah, the lady that brought you into this world," he said like it should've been obvious. "She knew how to handle you and your siblings, right?"

"I'm an only child," I told him point blank. "You banking on the idea of my mom knowing how to handle an infant after twenty eight years is a little much."

It was pretty evident then that his plan hadn't been well thought out. He wasn't expecting that answer. He had been pretty open with his own family situation, the fact that he had younger brothers. Or the fact he was close enough to his parents that he bought them a house so they could be close to him. Gavin just never bothered to ask if my family was anything like that.

Here he was just now realizing that. His mouth opened and then closed before he looked down and away. I was taking that as an admission of defeat.

"Would you call her?" Austin asked, having ignored our exchange. "Maybe she has an idea?"

I swallowed, "Yeah. I don't have any guarantees that she can do anything. She's just a manager at a grocery store." I felt bad just as I said it and went to get my phone. I brushed past Gavin and sat on the bed as I powered the device back on. I checked to see if I had any messages from Dee first, but when one didn't pop up I figured she was still working on the hospital staff.

When Deidre was determined she got what she wanted. That meant as soon as she was free of distractions she would be grilling me about the things she wanted to know. While I didn't know exactly what that was, I could guess. I wasn't sure I could handle just what she was going to ask.

Just like I wasn't sure how mom would react when she met the three men I was involved with. I found her number in my contacts and debated for a brief minute as to whether or not I should try the house phone. If she was already at work then there was nothing I could do, really.

Then Landon began to cry.

I hit the phone icon and put it on speaker phone. It was a bad idea, because she would definitely hear the baby crying. But hopefully it would induce a sense of urgency and I wouldn't have to worry about any questions.

It only took a few rings before she answered, "Hey there stranger. It's been a while. Your dad said you might be calling me about coming to cashier at the store. I don't have a whole lot of free space on my schedule, but it looks like I got a girl that's ready to pop on me any day now. So you could probably fill in for her while she's on maternity for about a month or so."

"Hey mom," I said then paused as I tried to think of an answer. "I'll keep that in mind, I guess I could probably part time it for when you have people needing time off like I used to."

"That's not what you called her for," Gavin protested, not even bothering to lower his voice.

"That's fine," she said, acting as if she hadn't heard a male talk. But she did quiet, telling me it was likely she heard Landon crying. "Is that a baby?"

"Yeah," I cleared my throat. "I was hoping you could help me out about that."

"Help you with that? Little girl if you had a kid without saying anything to me, I don't care that I brought you into this world. I will take you out of it," she growled over the line. "You can't have babies and not tell me about it."

Gavin snorted, covering his mouth with his hand. When I glared at him I gathered he had heard that more than a few times. He edged out of the bedroom and waved Austin over, patting his hand on the other man's shoulder like that would appease the infant he held.

"The baby isn't mine, mom," I said after rolling my eyes. "He belongs to a friend and well," I tried to figure out the best way to handle the situation. "The dad is new to parenting."

"I don't know why you think I would be the person to go to," she said immediately. "Where's the baby's mama? Where's *his* mama? What do I get out of this?"

"We don't really know where the baby mama is," Austin spoke up. "My mother is, also, missing in action and has been since I was a kid. I just," he sounded helpless. "Because I don't have sole custody of him and we can't find her, I'm at a loss as to what to do." He bounced a little bit, trying to soothe Landon, "I guess I could take him to the ER."

"I have two hours before I have to get to work. I was going to go get some lunch," she said with a huff. "Is he running a fever? He sounds tired."

"He's warm," Austin told her. "He's been fussy on and off since yesterday."

"We can bring you lunch," Gavin spoke up finally. "You name it and it's on me."

Mom hesitated for a second, like she was aware that there was more than one man here. "Okay. You can bring me a Big Mac with fries. I'll take a strawberry shake since you're paying. You can bring the baby but I will be holding him," she said it with authority. "You don't get to bring a baby into my house without me getting to love on it."

"I wouldn't protest at all," Austin said before turning to go into the back bedrooms. "I'm getting his diaper bag and we're loading up."

"I will see you when you get here. If this baby gives me any sort of bug, I will be taking it out on your hide," she said to me. "I'm in the same boat as you are, I can't miss any days."

"I know, mom," I sighed and I got up. "I'll see you in a minute." I ended the call to glare at Gavin. "Get dressed. It's funny you were scared of my dad. The person you should be afraid of is my mom."

11

Gavin

Of course the drive through took forever. By the time I got to the address that Naddy texted me it felt like I was beyond late to the party. I carried the shake, burger, and fries to the front door of a tiny little brick house. It did give me time to scrutinize what was clearly her childhood home.

It wasn't in the middle class neighborhood I had grown up in. The yard was cared for but from the weeds and brown spots in the grass it was obvious that they didn't have the benefit of a sprinkler system. The fact that the guy living next to them had a yard that resembled a jungle told me that this probably wasn't the type of area where Naddy spent her days playing outside with friends.

It made me reflect on how I saw her in school. She always dressed plainly, like she does now. Jeans, shirts, nothing that looked like it had a brand name on it. I knew she got picked on quite a bit because of it. Because of me, Vaughn, and Austin.

The door opened and a woman that could only be Nadia's mother stood in front of me. She was short, just like her daughter, and a little rounder in the hips. Not that it was a bad thing. Her hair was a light brown with red streaks. Her facial structure was damn near a mirrored image, too. The only difference was the coloring, Mrs. Evans was a whole lot paler and more tired.

She looked up at me with brown eyes that looked like they could cut a man down. "Who are you?" She asked, even though she held Landon and the baby reacted to me. Naddy and Austin had to be inside, why wouldn't they tell her I was coming?

"Delivery boy," I cheesed as I held up the shake and bag of food. I hoped the joke and the food would be enough to keep her from looking so damn hard at me.

She eyed me speculatively and I fought to think if I'd ever seen her before. Aside from how I could see Naddy in her features but I wouldn't be able to say the same thing before that. Have I run into her while being a jackass as a kid? She turned to look back in the house, "Don't tell me you used one of those delivery services to order me McDonald's."

"No, mom," Nadia sounded irritated as she said it. "That's Gavin. He doesn't work for DoorDash or anything like that."

"This is your roommate?" she asked as she turned to let me into the house. She didn't leave me to stand in the tiny living room, something that I wanted to do especially when I caught the family photo over the couch.

Naddy looked like she couldn't have been more than six with a gap toothed grin. Her hair was in pigtails and there was a sprinkling of freckles across her nose. When I saw her in the kitchen I mirrored the grin that I'd seen pictured. I was willing to overlook the fact that she had labeled me as a roommate just because of the fact that I got to see that.

Even if it hurt a little.

"You got Landon good to go?" I asked her mother. "Cracked the baby code?"

She just gave me a look, the tired mom look. Something my own mom had given me a million times while I was a kid. I'm sure I'd probably get it from her when I introduced her to Naddy. "There's not a code, it's more along the lines of paying attention. If you helped your friend you might learn it," she said evenly to me as she sat down at the table, still holding Landon.

He had his head against her shoulder, one little hand stuffed into his mouth. His cheeks were still a solid shade of pink, but his eyes were closed like he was on the verge of sleep. I doubted it took her long to get him into this position either, the hand she rubbed against his back. "Cutting teeth is tough and doing several at once is big business."

"Nothing serious then?" I asked, shifting from foot to foot. I looked at Naddy, she was leaning back against the sink. Her full attention on her mother and how she was holding Austin's son.

"No," her mom said with a smile as Landon opened his eyes owlishly at her. "You're gonna be just fine bright eyes. It hurts now, but daddy knows what to do and he'll make it easier." She looked up at me and in the same pleasant tone she used for the baby she said, "But the question I have, with all the extra you brought with you. Are you going to help him? Hinder him? Or just watch?"

"What?" I asked.

Naddy's mother shot her a look, "Caring for a child is not easy. It is a handful, constantly. I know plenty of women are doing it all by themselves but if this is your *friend* you need to ask yourself." She gave Landon's brow a light kiss and the baby's eyes closed again, he gave a little whimper but settled against her. "Are you going to be there to help him with this?" She waved a hand at the baby. "Or are you going to be in the way?"

"Mama," Naddy protested.

"Nadia," she said evenly. "You came in here pretending that he's your roommate," she looked at Austin as she said it. "But then you say this guy is another roommate," she looked at me. "Now, I can pretend that it's a group effort to raise a child. But I know damn well you are keeping something from me." She picked up the milkshake and slurped at it. "I know this isn't your baby," she said after she set the cup down. "Why bring your *roommates* here?"

I feel like Naddy had tried to warn me. I guess this was why. I didn't try to lie to my mom often, she was pretty much aware of all the shit I got into as a kid. It looked like Naddy was in the same boat. She couldn't hide anything.

From the exaggerated frustration on her face, it was clear that she was giving up. "Fine, you really want to know?" She shrugged helplessly at me. "He's my boyfriend."

"This one?" she looked at Austin. Then she looked at me, because her daughter hadn't bothered to indicate which one of us she was talking about. I got an assessing look, like I was being sized up. "Which one?"

I waited to see if I was going to be claimed. It would be easy to just say I was a roommate, it would make sense that Nadia would bring her boyfriend's child to her mother for help. Wouldn't it? My position here didn't really make sense as anything more than a friend. I bit my lip, it wasn't my place to say.

"They both are," Nadia admitted in defeat. She tangled her hand into her hair. "And I have a third one that's at work right now."

For her credit, Naddy's mother didn't even blink. Her brows inched up her forehead, "Three?"

"Yeah."

She looked between Austin and me. "These are two of them?"

"Yeah."

"How are you going to introduce your boyfriends to me without actually introducing them to me?" her mother snapped finally, she stood with a huff but still managed to move without waking the baby that was resting on her shoulder. She offered me a hand, "Pamela Evans. I just thought you kids were friends. I figured she was dating one of you," she said, giving Austin a look. "I didn't think it would be more than that."

I took her hand and shook it, I couldn't put words to the feeling that was seated in my chest. I liked it. I liked that she was willing to be upfront about what was really going on. "Gavin Stockton," I said to her mother. I grinned at her then looked at her daughter. If there wasn't a kitchen table between us I probably would've pounced.

How soon could I get her out of here so we could go home? Would her mom be mad if I left her here with the baby? Would Austin protest?

Austin, for his credit, didn't look like he was affected like I was. He shook Pamela's hand and gave her his full name. He looked slightly nervous, before he had just been a roommate. Now he was boyfriend level and this wasn't with just his sister. Kirsten would bitch, but she wouldn't really endanger our relationship. Naddy's mom had a whole lot more power than Austin's sister.

"Why are their names familiar?" Pamela asked after she let go of Austin's hand. She looked at Naddy as she settled back down. "Help me with this," she motioned to the bag.

I stepped forward before Naddy could and began to unpack the bag. Setting down napkins in front of Pam and putting the fries on top of it. She smiled but nodded towards the baby that was resting on his chest. "Take over," she said to me and before I could protest, she was hefting Landon up and onto me.

He made a noise, something close to a fuss before she turned him over and pressed him to my chest. She gently eased his head against my shoulder, shushing lowly and rubbing a hand against his little back. She adjusted the arm that I awkwardly put under his butt so that he wasn't likely to slide off of me. Then she put my free hand against his back.

I stalled out, patting lightly on Landon's back. Whatever conversation was going to come with the familiarity of our names to Pamela Evans were lost. Landon didn't weigh as much as he looked like he did. I swallowed, the slight erection that I had at being labeled boyfriend deflated pretty damn quickly with a baby forced on me.

I guess any prospects of me reproducing were shot now. He got bigger since he first came home and I knew he was only gonna keep growing. I resisted the urge to ask Austin for help, this was a test. I could see the dubious expression on her face before she directed her attention to Nadia.

"I went to school with them," Nadia supplied.

"The only friend I remember you having from high school is Mara," her mother said evenly as she leveled a glare at me then she turned it to Austin. He faltered beneath the weight of the mama bear's gaze. "Fowler sounds pretty damn familiar."

"I'm stupid," he started. "I didn't know how to speak to her without sounding like a complete dumbass."

"And you know better now?" Her mother snapped before she looked at me. "Let me guess, you harassed your way into her good graces, didn't you?"

How did she read the truth so quickly? My mouth dropped open and I was grateful that I held Landon. I'm also willing to admit that I'm a shit for using a baby as a shield. "I wouldn't say harassed," I cringed. This wasn't going the way I thought it would at all.

I figured we'd come in here, meet her parents and put a seal on the three of us maintaining this for the long run. That was the code to make things work, right? Being there, great sex, and a solid approval from the parents. That had been the method even before I cared, because as far as I was concerned my parents were cool with just about everything.

I guess, everyone wasn't on the same page as mine.

"What would you call it then?" Pamela Evans asked with an arched brow.

"Call it a man knowing how to get his way," Nadia saved me. "Mom," she made a face as she drew out the word. "I know it's not conventional and this isn't the way I would've liked to broach the fact that I'm not in a normal relationship. But," she shrugged helplessly. "This is it. Well," she paused like she remembered that we weren't all here and accounted for. "Vaughn Price is the only party not present."

"I remember that name," her mother shoved back from the table to look at her daughter. "I remember the girl that wrote profanity across your locker and how much hell I had to raise to get them to paint over it when it wouldn't come off," she pointed a finger at me and I felt more than a little attacked as she spoke. "How is this something that's happening now? I am all for forgiving people for their trespasses, but Nadia. Are you serious?"

She didn't buckle under her mother's questioning. She was way stronger than I'd ever given her credit for. It made me reflect on all the issues that had come up from me worming my way into bed with her and Austin to the infant resting on my shoulder. And now, explaining how she had given up the earned animosity she felt towards us.

Did I have enough money in my bank account to shower this woman with jewelry? Was there any way I could make up for my shit? I looked at Austin to see if he was going to be able to help me out. He wasn't, he looked between the two women like he saw this all coming to an end right before his eyes.

I thought he knew Naddy better than that.

Her hand fell into her hair and she looked at her mother, irritation evident in her expression, "I don't have a good answer that you really want to hear, mom. I could but I'm going to have to look you in the face again sometime after this." She released a sharp breath and shrugged, "I didn't expect this to be something that happened. It wasn't something that I wanted to be neck deep into but here I am."

"Baby all you've got to do is give me an alibi. Go to work for me and I'll take care of both of them before your father gets home," she said without missing a beat.

I almost didn't catch onto the fact that she was threatening to kill us. Austin's eyes widened and he looked at me, whatever feeling he had before about being found out where we started in Naddy's life was gone. He looked like he was on the same page as me, though. Do we run? Would she come at me while I was holding a baby? Was Naddy going to take this opportunity to get rid of the both of us?

"I don't think that's necessary, mom," she said after a beat. "The more time I spend with them the more I see that things have changed," she folded her arms over her chest and looked at me. "The assholes from high school aren't there anymore." Her gaze met mine, "I think they've either learned their lessons or karma took care of it."

"I'd rather take care of it," her mother huffed out.

"Let's not leap to that," I stepped in carefully. My voice raised at the end and the child I was holding shifted a little. He whimpered before settling back down. "Instead of putting us six feet under, isn't it easier to just let us make amends, especially when that's what we want to do?"

"Are you the reason why she lost her second job?" Pamela asked.

"It wasn't my idea," I tried to explain. "I was more of a bystander. I didn't know she worked there. I always thought she would've left this place to go off and do better things," I kept on. "When we made the plans to open the bar she wasn't even considered because we didn't know where she worked. We didn't expect to see her outside of the reunion."

I never expected to be in the position I was in now. I never expected for her to give in. I never expected to want more than just sex from her. I cleared my throat and eyed her mother, "It was unexpected and probably not what she wanted in the beginning. But I don't want to let it go."

I had the attention of everyone now. Austin didn't look surprised or even bothered by the revelation. Nadia's expression was blank, but she didn't seem to be unhappy with it.

"If you change your mind," Pamela began as she redirected the conversation to her daughter. It was almost like she hadn't even heard me. "All I need is an alibi."

12

Nadia

The ride home had been quiet. Mostly because mom's magic had been enough for Landon to be passed out. There was something exhausting about what had gone on. I hadn't even had the time to digest the fact that mom wasn't bothered that I was in a relationship with three men. She was bothered because the three men happened to have bullied me in the past.

It was a relief. Something that felt so good to get off my chest.

"She said we need to help you," I said to the man beside me. "I don't know how to help."

"You've helped enough by moving in and helping me financially improve the house. I didn't expect to have Landon full time," he said evenly. "I don't know if I'm still going to have him full time. Mr. Lange is working on that and so far they haven't found Lauren." His shoulders hunched and I expected to see the stress of the situation, what we just walked out of, evident in how he sat beside me. He didn't grip the steering wheel like a vice as I expected, he balanced his palm against the top of the wheel and leaned heavily back in the seat. "These are the consequences of my actions on many different levels."

I sat beside him, letting his words sink in. "I feel like part of being in a relationship is that I should help you shoulder your burdens. I know that you have helped me carry mine," I took a breath and let it out slowly. "It doesn't seem fair to expect you to just carry me and not do the same for you."

"I think expecting you to do more after finding out I have a kid is too much," he pointed out. "I can't ask you to help parent a child that you have no ties to."

"You are what ties me to Landon," I said gently. But I wasn't going to argue with him. "I don't know what to do or how to help. Any contact I've ever had with children has been in passing, waiting tables or keeping an eye on Deidre's kids while they waited for their grandmother to pick them up. But even then, they weren't as young as your son."

"I've been trying to figure it out since I brought him home," Austin admitted after a beat. "One of the books said something about keeping him on a schedule of feeding and napping with tummy time in between. A blog suggested that I use a process of elimination to figure out what he was fussy about and so far that had been working for me. I just didn't take teething into consideration."

"Most people have help with their children," I pointed out.

"Most people aren't parenting part time."

"Are you still going to be part time after this?" I asked. "Even if that's the case it doesn't seem right to be a part of his life without helping."

He grew silent. I hoped that meant that he didn't have an argument and that he was accepting it. When we got home and out of the truck Landon was awake enough for a bottle. He and Austin ended up snoozing in the arm chair. Gavin sat on the couch, watching a movie with the volume set on low. He looked like he was on the verge of falling asleep, too.

We had about an hour before Vaughn came home so I decided to raid the fridge, see if there wasn't something that I could put together. I pulled out chicken breasts and spinach, there was milk and cheese that gave me hope. With a quick search I found pasta, surprising me to no end. It was vegetable based, but I hoped with enough cheese it wouldn't matter.

It didn't take me long to prepare and season it. Before long I had it sizzling in a pan. I went back and forth on making alfredo before I decided that I needed to keep it simple. Lessen the chances of me screwing it up. While I babysat the chicken, I pulled my phone out to check if I had any messages from Dee. I hadn't even bothered to do what she asked me to. I'd been so caught up at mom's that I hadn't paid any attention to the device, there was too much going on from Landon to 'coming out' to my mom. Was it considered coming out?

I needed to focus on what was important, *now*. Like finding out how Freddy was doing. I took a breath and found Dee in my contacts, turning my attention to the two men and a baby in the living room. Gavin had given in and nodded off, his head tilted back and a low snort I could hear from here.

"Girl," Dee answered on the second ring. "I would've called you back as soon as I got off the phone with the nurse, but my kids are acting like fools. They think just because I'm home for a change they can lose their minds," she sounded tired as she said it. But it was clear that it was directed at someone else. "Things aren't serious," she said as she seemed to get her point across to her children. "He's stable, but he's not conscious. She said the best thing we can do is wait until he comes to. So we're probably looking at two or three days without work." She made a pained noise, "I'm considering filing for unemployment, but we make most of our money in tips. So it's not gonna be much."

"It's an option," I said. "And if it's something you can do, let me know so I can do it, too. I don't want to go find another job and leave Freddy high and dry without any waitresses." The pan sizzled beside me and I flipped the chicken, trying to get an even browning on both sides. "Don't take that as you should wait around, though. You've got more important issues than I do."

"Your men gonna take care of you while your boss is in the hospital?"

"I haven't asked," I answered seriously. "I don't want to."

"That was a joke. But do you think they would?"

I looked at the two men in the living room. "Maybe? I don't want to be a freeloader." Then I remembered Vaughn's offer and I found myself wondering if he would be willing to help the two women I worked with out. "I might be able to ask if he could help you out."

"Help me out?" she asked, sounding confused. "I don't want to join your circle of fun. No offense," she cleared her throat. "Is it just you and them? Or are there other girls involved? I'm asking for a friend."

"That friend you?"

"Girl, don't judge me, I ain't judging you."

I snorted, "It's just me and them."

"That doesn't hurt?" she asked in a whisper.

"They are gentle and make sure it doesn't," I admitted.

Deidre made a noise and I flushed. I couldn't begin to guess what she was thinking now. I heard what sounded like a door closing, "How many Os you get between three men?"

I covered my mouth so she wouldn't hear me gasping. That's when I noticed that the pan sizzling beside me was accompanied with a billowing cloud of steam. "Shit," I barked and picked the pan up off the burner and cranked it off. What do I do, what do I do, what do I do? I put the pan on a different burner and reached for a plate from the cabinet. I plopped the chicken breast onto the plate to gage whether or not I'd ruined them.

"You were cooking?" she sounded surprised.

"I think I burned them," I sighed. "I wasn't expecting that question."

"Is it meat? What did you burn?"

"Chicken breast."

"Is it black?"

"No," I said, flipping one piece. "A dark brown, but not burnt to a crisp black."

"You can cut off the parts that don't look edible and cut the rest of it up instead of doing full breasts. If you do that, mix it with pasta or rice. They won't know unless they get an extra crispy piece." She advised without missing a beat, "mix in some chicken with buttered noodles and vegetables. Kids don't even bat an eye at it."

"These are grown men," I pointed out to her.

"Same thing."

I looked at what I had pulled out of the fridge and decided I could still make this work. "I guess I'll field complaints if they come," I said as I eyed the pan to see if I needed to clean it before cooking spinach in it. I shrugged before forging ahead. "Most of the time I can't keep track," I told her as I put a little oil into the pan. I knew I wouldn't be able to take my eyes off of this otherwise I would end up burning the spinach, too.

"What?"

"I answered your question."

"Girl," Dee barked. "You cannot say that all nonchalant like that. You are gonna give me expectations that no other man is gonna be able to meet."

"I'm pretty positive it ruined me," I told her. "It's had its moments that have been stressful and overwhelming," I took a breath as I stirred the wilting leaves in the pan. "It's new territory on a few different levels. Not just sex," I glanced back at the living room to make sure I didn't have anyone listening. "I never really bothered to get this far with just one person."

"Are they demanding more of you than you are prepared to give?" She asked. "Don't feel like you have to do something if it's not something you want to do."

"That's not it," I protested as I pulled out a pot to fill with water. "I just worry about doing something wrong, about being the asshole in the situation. You know?"

"I hate to tell you that no matter what kind of dance you try to do you are going to end up being an asshole at some points. I doubt there's a way to dodge that," Dee said quietly. "Just be careful."

I assured her as best I could, but I found that it was a soothing balm compared to mom's willingness to commit murder. Not that I didn't appreciate my mother. I felt like I walked away from both encounters unscathed. There wasn't judgment, just concern because the two people I opened up to about my nontraditional relationship loved me.

It made me realize just how lucky I was.

Vaughn came in just as I was cutting up the extra crispy chicken. He gave Gavin and Austin one look before he went into the bedroom, I assume to get into something more comfortable. As soon as I finished cutting up the chicken I went to the bedroom door. He had his suit jacket thrown over the end of the bed and he was rolling his tie up from where he sat on edge. He still had his dark blue slacks on and a soft gray button down. He looked tired, we had been having a string of late nights. Too many of them too frequently.

"Why are they passed out?" he asked.

"Landon's cutting teeth and apparently keeping Austin up," I told him as I leaned against the door frame. "I took them to meet my mother," I said after a beat. "Gavin thought a mom would know how to fix it."

Vaughn didn't look fazed. He nodded like it made sense, though I couldn't begin to guess which part of it did. "Did you tell your mother that they were your friends?" He asked, eyeing me as he did. "Or did you claim one?"

"I claimed both of them," I said without letting it bother me. "I claimed you, too."

He blinked at me before setting the rolled up tie on the bed so he could lean back. "How'd that go?"

"She threatened to kill the three of you," I said with a little bit of a laugh. "Though not why you think."

I had his attention, he didn't look disturbed in the same way Gavin and Austin did when mom insisted I be her alibi. Instead, he just looked intrigued. "I'm sure there's a few dozen reasons why she would want to kill the three of us. What's the reason for it?"

I guess he had a point. "I might've complained about you while I was growing up. I guess she remembered your names."

"A solid reason," he nodded. "Is that why you decided to cook dinner?"

I shook my head, this was going a whole lot easier than I expected it to. He wasn't angry or even worried. He just sat there and listened with a tired acceptance. "I cooked dinner because Austin was exhausted and I feel like," I shrugged as I struggled to think of a good reason, "I needed something to do."

"You hear anything about your boss?" he asked.

"He's stable, but I don't know how long the diner will be closed but I'm guessing people take a while to recover from a heart attack," I swallowed and I rubbed at the back of my neck. "Which brings me to ask you for a favor," I began with a grimace.

If I didn't have his attention before I had it now. His eyebrows rose and he straightened a little. He didn't say anything and it kind of didn't help my growing anxiety. Because I had no idea if he would give me grief for it.

"The ladies I work with are probably going to need new jobs," I said uneasily. "I know you offered to find me a replacement and I was hoping you would extend that offer to a friend or two of mine."

Vaughn stood up and closed the distance between us. "You said a friend? Is that just one of the women or both?" He eyed me, "Does this include you, too?"

"Deidre, specifically," I said without backing down. "I don't know about Jodie. I mean, she's young and pretty and she shouldn't have a hard time finding another job."

"You could send her to the bar," he suggested. "We've probably got another couple of weeks before I can start hiring staff." When I pulled a face he smirked a little, "We haven't decided that the cheerleading uniforms are definite. I was toying with the idea of making them dress like referees. That way it's not limiting the people I can choose to hire." He leaned down a little, "Though if you decided to fill out an application I would have to decline for the obvious reason."

I made a noise, deciding to ignore the last thing he said. "She's pretty and she's good with people. If she decides to go that route it would probably be good for her." I sighed, thinking about Dee and whether or not a bar would be somewhere she would even want to work. "But Deidre has kids. I don't think late nights waiting tables at a bar is a good idea. Maybe something that opens up her nights so she can be at home?"

He hummed, "The older woman? Give me her number and I'll see what I can do." He had his phone in his hand and his willingness to help Dee out had me pulling mine out as well. After I sent him a text containing her information he gave me a look I couldn't decipher. "What about you?"

I shook my head at first, "I can find my own job." Then I frowned and decided to admit the truth, "I'm afraid that he'll make a quick recovery and he'll come back to the diner with no employees so he'll have to start all over again."

"How long does it take to recover from a heart attack?" he asked with a dubious expression. "Who is going to pay your bills?"

"I'm gonna pay my bills," I snapped with a little misplaced heat. It wilted quickly when I realized I didn't have any idea how long Freddy would be in the hospital or when he could go back to work. "I don't know," I admitted after a beat. "I don't even know if he'll be able to go back to work. We don't know anything because we've not been able to talk to him."

I felt helpless then, "It could be months."

"I'll start with Deidre," he said without missing a beat. "I'll keep an ear out for anything I think might suit you," he paused with a frown as he looked at the screen of my phone. "But this is me doing you a favor, isn't it?"

I stiffened, "I thought this was you making up for me losing my second job."

"Finding you a job would be me making up for that," he began with a calculating smile. "But finding your friends a job is, as you said before, a favor."

"What do you want?" I asked. "You want me to suck your dick? You want that now or after dinner?" I was ready to get that done and over with.

"Normally, I wouldn't say no to that but I'm thinking something else," he started his gaze focused downward. I could only assume he was looking at my chest.

I didn't wait for him to delve into his idea, the memory of what Gavin and I had done in his bathroom not too long ago came screaming to my mind. Was Vaughn into stuff like that, too? "Are you wanting to do something weird?" I asked. "Maybe give me a breakdown as to what you want to do before I make my choice?"

A confused expression clouded his face, "I want to get you a new phone."

"You mean you don't want to do anything weird?" I asked, surprised. Why was I disappointed? I could see him looming over me while I was restrained to the bed. It did some things to me that I wasn't ready to admit to. I frowned at him. "I don't need a new phone, this one still works."

Vaughn took my phone from me and showed me the cracked screen. Then he flipped it to show where I had tape securing the case to the device. "Why is there tape?"

"I'm a little clumsy," I huffed. "Which is all the more reason why you shouldn't get me a new phone. I'll just drop it and break it."

He handed my phone back to me, "Do you have a preference for a brand and who is your carrier?"

13

Nadia

No one complained about dinner. I figured the women that cooked in their lives had taught them better. Gavin cleaned up dinner and Vaughn took Landon to the nursery and left Austin relaxing back into his chair. I had the option of doing some vegetating, too. But I couldn't sit still.

I went to help, though all Gavin ended up letting me do was dry. He washed and put away everything, though I still got his shoulder bumped into mine more than a few times. He was flirting with me without saying a word. I didn't resist the urge to give him kisses when the opportunity popped up.

"Do you think we could …" he trailed off but wiggled his eyebrows at me. "The kid seems to be out. What did your mom do before I got there?"

"She had an amber necklace from when I was a kid," I told him. "I don't know if that's what it is because Austin stopped to get some Tylenol for him. Mom swears by it, but," I shrugged. "I don't know that there is anything to prove the necklace has anything to do with it. It might just be exhaustion."

"That was what was around his little ankle?" Gavin asked, he looked curious. "I think Vaughn is putting him down without Austin in the room." His attention was down the hallway, "I didn't think that would be a thing."

"He helps more than we do," I pointed out and I leaned against the counter. My focus was on where Austin was kicked back in the chair. It looked like he might've been asleep. "I think mom was bothered by the fact that we weren't."

"Yeah I know my mom would have my ass, too," he sighed. "It seems like we were getting into a good routine and shit had to hit the fan again. Do you think this chick would just do this," he motioned down the hallway, "because she knew he was happy and she wanted to ruin it?"

"I don't think this is going to ruin Austin's happiness, Gav," I rolled my eyes and decided to check on Vaughn and the baby. I went towards the hall, "Anything could've happened to her and it could be that she just realized she couldn't hack it as a single parent. Honestly, I can't blame her." I didn't look to see if he was listening to me, the rest of the thought came out of me as I got to Landon's bedroom door. "I know I wouldn't be able to make it."

He didn't say a word, he just pressed his finger to his lips taking whatever question I was about to direct to him away from me. He was seated in the rocker that Austin had placed in there. Landon was curled against his chest and as far as I could see the infant was sleeping just as his father was in the living room.

"Bed?" I whispered, hoping he'd get my meaning.

He just nodded without upsetting the infant he held. I watched as he looked back down at Landon, rocking gently. It felt like I was intruding on something. It left me wondering how I would feel about him if I saw more of the man in front of me. Should I be concerned that seeing him hold a baby made me want to take him to bed?

It was because the arrogance that I usually had to face wasn't readily on the surface. It had nothing to do with Landon. I wasn't having any sort of maternal feelings because I saw an attractive man holding a baby. I'd seen Austin holding his son plenty of times and I didn't have moments like this that I could remember.

I turned to go back down the hall. This didn't mean I wanted kids. I was hard up and I was attracted to the softer appearance of Vaughn compared to how I usually saw him.

I meandered over to Austin, eyeing him where he laid back with the chair reclined as far as it could go. He had one arm behind his head and the other propped on his chest, he was just wearing a white shirt and with the position he was in it stretched the fabric across his pectorals. That was clue enough for me to realize what the real problem was.

I was hungry.

Austin stretched, inhaling sharply and his eyes fluttered open to look up at me. He hummed, rubbing an eye. "Didn't mean to fall asleep. I feel like that's all I've been doing," he stifled a yawn. "Getting up, taking care of Landon, then sleeping whenever I get the chance." He then went on to sit up a little, squinting up at me. "I forget how much it sucks to sleep by myself until I have to do it."

"You have a baby monitor," Gavin said from the kitchen, as he wiped down the table. "You just need to be able to cut the umbilical cord," he said with a snort. "Something that was never even attached to you."

"I read articles online about Sudden Infant Death Syndrome," Austin said as he put his face in his hands. "And I got so afraid that I would wake up one morning and he would be gone and there would be fuck all that I could do."

"The fuck is that?" Gavin asked as he tossed the sponge into the sink.

"When a baby dies for no explicable reason," Austin explained. "Sometimes it happens with little babies and," he shook his head. "I have this horrifying fear it'll happen to Landon."

"I think," Vaughn said as he came up the hallway, baby monitor in hand. "That you might be worrying over nothing. How old is he now? Six months?"

"Twenty two weeks," Austin said with a huff, dropping his hands so he could glare at his friend.

"Close enough," Vaughn said with a shrug. He held out the little speaker, "Any idea when SIDS becomes less of a worry?"

When Austin just shrugged I had my phone out. After a little bit of lagging I was able to find something, "Most cases occur before four months and the vast majority before six," I looked between the two men after reading off the first offering Google provided.

"Stay off the mommy blogs," Vaughn said as he turned to go into the bedroom. "Stressing yourself out over something that probably isn't going to happen on top of everything else you've got going on is just going to make you go nuts." He stood just where I could see him undoing the buttons of his shirt, "find some stress relief."

Austin looked up at me and in that moment I could kiss Vaughn for making the suggestion. "What if he wakes up?" Austin asked, "What am I supposed to do?"

"What?" Vaughn shot back, stepping out of the bedroom with his slacks open. "What are you talking about?"

"Well," Gavin grinned, having caught on quicker than the other man. "We can do a train and whoever ain't hitting it can go handle the baby while you finish up your turn," he offered reasonably. "Or we can all go at it like we usually do it and if he cries, you nut and go handle it."

"You're suggesting that we have sex?" Vaughn asked. He looked between the two of them before he gave me a narrow eyed look, "And you're okay with this plan?"

How was the best way to handle this? Would it be inappropriate to strip here in the living room? Would that be too forward?

The three men were looking at me like they were waiting for my answer. My mouth went dry and I grabbed Austin's wrist. With a little tug he was up off his chair and he followed me into the bedroom. I caught the open fly of Vaughn's slacks with my free hand. "Come on, Gav," I called as I directed Austin to the bed.

"So, train then?" Gavin asked. "Austin gets to ride it first?" He was at the bedside table, pulling out condoms and the bottle of lube.

"I want two of you in me," I said without thinking. Heat came rushing to my face and I tugged my shirt up over my head to cover it. It wasn't something that should bother me especially after this long. "If that means that someone switches out between the front or the back entrance, that's fine. I just," I released a breath. "I need this." I looked down at Austin then at Vaughn, lastly at Gavin. "I need you."

Vaughn stepped behind me and unhooked my bra. His fingers skimmed along my skin as he pushed the straps down my arms. Austin reached forward to tug the cups out of his way. He sat on the bed so he was level with my chest, he didn't hesitate to close his mouth around the tip of one breast while he palmed up the other breast. The pull of his mouth had me leaning back against Vaughn, my knees weak.

Hands traced the waist of my jeans, a mouth found my ear and my breath caught as teeth dug into the lobe. "What do you want me to do?" Vaughn rasped. One hand tugged at the button while the other inched down the zipper.

"Touch me," I breathed. I didn't know exactly what Vaughn wanted me to stay, but I hoped he wasn't going to pull away from me if I didn't say it.

One of the hands at my waist tugged my jeans the rest of the way open, the other delved beneath the denim and the panties I wore. I arched back into him as the hand in my panties cupped my mound and pressed fingers between my lower lips to trace the growing dampness there. Fortunately, he didn't ask further questions. He pressed against my back and his mouth went from my ear down to my neck, causing a trail of gooseflesh in his wake.

Austin had worked his way upward, his teeth scraping against my collar bone and I was drowning. This was what I had been hungering for. It was just missing one thing.

Gavin stood next to us, watching what his friends were doing to me with an expression that I was sure mirrored my own. "Are you just going to watch?" I asked when I found my voice.

"For a little bit," Gav said with a grin. He leaned forward and pressed his lips to mine, "I figured I would let them do all the work for me." He swept his tongue out to brush against mine, giving me a teasing taste of him.

"Push them together," Austin managed despite having his face pressed into my breasts. It made me realize that Gavin was doing more than watching. Especially when Austin rubbed his face between my boobs and released a sigh, "I've missed these."

"It's not been that long," Vaughn said. Though the erection that pressed against my ass suggested that he wasn't okay with waiting another week for us to have a moment like this.

I doubted I would be able to either.

I dug my fingers into Austin's hair, needing something to hold onto as my jeans were shoved off my hips. After Gavin got my jeans around my ankles my legs were nudged apart. It messed with my balance to the point that I was having to depend on the man behind me for balance. The hand in my panties pressed fingers into me, causing a moan to escape me.

"I guess there's only one thing for me to do," Gavin said with a sigh. "Is this how we're going in the first round," he nudged Vaughn with a shoulder. "You in the back and him in the front?"

"I want to be ball deep in her pussy," Vaughn said without missing a beat. "That okay with you?"

I didn't know whether or not the question was directed at me, but at Austin's nod it became apparent it wasn't. Neither man made any motions to move from their positions. Gavin grumbled, "I didn't want to touch your dick but you're not giving me much options here." He moved from my side for a beat to only return to it. "Greedy fuckers."

I reached for him in an attempt to make him feel better, fisting a handful of his shirt so I could pull him into a position where I could easily kiss him. Gavin hummed in appreciation even as he slipped his hand into the back of my panties and spread dampness along the crack of my ass. It lit me up with anticipation, even as his finger prodded my rear opening.

I wanted more. Even as he speared me with a finger, finding little to no resistance. He moved his finger into my rear entrance at the same pace that Vaughn was using on my pussy. It left my hips twitching but unaware of which direction I should go. Both seemed to be falling into a rhythm that mirrored the movements of the other's fingers.

"Hold up," Gavin said as his single finger pulled out of me. He was quick to replace it with two, "Okay."

I groaned when they began to move again, Gavin's fingers scissoring open to spread me further. He didn't come back in for a kiss, he seemed far too entertained with just watching. Then again it may have been because Austin had made his way up my neck, avoiding where Vaughn was still nibbling my shoulder.

"Just a few more minutes," Gavin said as he easily added another finger into me without breaking the rhythm.

"Shouldn't take long to make her come," Vaughn said as he stopped thrusting his fingers into me and began to search for that elusive bit of me that he enjoyed teasing way too much.

But even after the little search, I still buckled once he found it. The three of them were crowded around me, keeping me from falling even after I lost my footing. One leg ended up hitched up onto Austin's shoulder, giving wider access for Vaughn as he began to tease the button he found within me. It tore a cry from me and I was so grateful that I didn't have to rely on myself to stay vertical.

"That good?" Austin asked.

He must not have been able to see the liquid dripping down my leg. But I could feel it. It wasn't as distracting as the dampness that spread through my panties. I could feel the rush of heat through my face, *I hadn't peed. It wasn't urine. The only reason why there was so much was because it'd been a week since the last time we did this.*

Pep talks usually helped. But I was grateful when my panties were slipped off my legs and were added to my pile of clothing. Austin easily lifted me from the floor, pulling Gavin's fingers from me so that I could be laid onto my back. It gave me time to take in each man undressing.

Austin made quick work, oblivious to me watching as he shucked his shorts and boxers. His erection bobbed out in front of him, showing just how eager he was to give in. He didn't hesitate to roll a condom on. "I guess the best route would be to let me be on top," he said to the other two. "So, Vaughn lays down on his back and Nadia is on top of him."

"I don't protest that," I slurred a little as I propped myself up on my elbows, still drunk on endorphins. Vaughn had my full attention now, "Does he?'

His gaze connected with mine, having felt my scrutiny. He still wore his slacks, even though they were open and tented around his erection. He raised an eyebrow at me and I pointedly followed the line between his pectorals down to his open slacks, hoping he would get the hint. When the slacks slid down his thighs and I let my gaze linger on just how the front of his boxer briefs were tented forward.

I might've licked my lips, I was distracted.

"I've had you on top of me before," Vaughn said as he slowly pushed his underwear down his legs. He followed Austin's lead by rolling a condom onto his cock before he gave me another look. "Enjoying the show?"

I just hummed as he prowled on the bed beside me. He pressed into my side, catching my mouth with a hunger that ignited mine. I didn't resist him as shifted us so that I was sprawled across his chest. I was so eager for this that I moved to straddle his hips, I needed him in me. His teeth dug into my lip as my fingers closed around his cock, he didn't make any effort to help me position him at my entrance. He seemed more than content to let me press myself down onto him.

I didn't tug away from him as he slowly spread me apart. I didn't make any attempt to keep from groaning, either. Fortunately, he decided to meet me halfway thrusting forward so his cock was fully sheathed in me. Hands found my hips, stilling me as I tried to roll against him.

Patience at this moment wasn't a virtue I had.

"Let me get in here, too," Austin soothed from behind me. "You can ride the both of us."

Vaughn let go of my lip and I peered over a shoulder to watch as Austin pressed his thick fingers in me, testing the resistance of my anus. I hummed rocking as much as the man beneath me allowed. As good as it felt now, I knew how much better it could be once he slid into me.

I wanted it. I wanted the stretch that felt almost like it was too much. I wanted to be filled to the point where I couldn't recognize who was who, where they started and I began. I wanted the overwhelming feeling that made me drown in more than just the burning desire. I wanted all of it from all three of them.

I leaned down against Vaughn, my breasts pressed between us, and arched as Austin busied himself with judging whether or not I was ready for him. It had him thrusting his fingers into me instead of his cock a little longer than necessary. It left me whining out a plea, "Fuck me."

"I don't want to fucking hurt you," he grumbled before he pulled his fingers out of me. He pressed the head of his cock against my rear entrance, "There's no reason to not be careful even if Gav got you ready."

I released a breath, melting onto Vaughn as Austin finally started to ease into me. The stretch made me clench around the man beneath me, making a groan rumble through his chest. The noise he made doing just as much to me as the slight throb of his cock. I decided I wanted to hear the noise again and since he was keeping me still there was only one thing I could really do.

I dug my teeth into his collar and he made a surprised noise. "Not so hard," he rasped. My tongue soothed over the offended skin and I felt him shudder. An odd urge came over me and I closed my mouth over the path of skin at his collar. He inhaled sharply and his hips arched against mine, an expletive gritted out.

Then Austin surged forward until his hips were against my ass and he was fully seated in me. There was a chorus of noise from the three of us, he was a tight fit back there and I could feel the tremble in my lower extremities telling me it was almost too much.

I tried to push myself up on my hands, thinking that the change in angle would've made things feel better especially when they started moving. Only to have Austin begin to slowly ease out, the stretch making me keen and realize my arms weren't going to be able to hold me up. The shallow thrust back into me hand me melting down against Vaughn, accepting the fact that I couldn't do anything other than feel.

And maybe leave a few hickeys on the man under me.

However, I didn't get the opportunity to as both men began to move within me. Any thoughts I had outside of that was that someone was missing. I had enough thought still left to search for Gavin, he was the only one not in me.

He stood at the edge of the bed, shorts still on and his attention on where his friends moved against me. He didn't make any move to shed the rest of his clothing or take the opportunity to fill me, too. I reached out a hand for him, wavering only slightly as Vaughn's hips upward thrust began to carry a little force.

Gavin readily took my hand, climbing onto the bed with us. He pulled my hand to his lips, kissing my knuckles and teasingly sucking my index finger into his mouth. He swirled his tongue around it, mimicking what I should be doing to him.

I moaned his name, but didn't make any move to pull my hand from him. I let him nibble his way down to my wrist before I could say a word. "Gavin," my breath hitched and I clenched my eyes closed for a brief moment before I could try to speak again. "Fuck me," I demanded.

"Keeping an ear out," he said without even making an attempt to do as I asked him. "Someone has to play a distraction if his mini-me wakes up," he explained with a grin smothered by my hand. "As soon as one of them finishes I'll get mine, too. Don't worry."

Sound reasoning. I couldn't argue with him. I just clung to his hand as the other two continued to work into me. A hand fell on my shoulder and I could feel the strain begin from Austin. He was struggling to keep up with Vaughn.

"Let me help you," Gavin said. "So you don't embarrass yourself." He found a space between Vaughn and I, and his fingers combed through the curls above my sex teasingly. It was the only chance I got to prepare myself before I felt his fingers begin to circle my clit. He was using quick, solid strokes like he was following Austin's movements.

It had me clinging to the last bit of coherency that I could manage, it was a thread that I could barely hold onto. Then he pinched the little bundles of nerves that tore a wail from me. I buried my face in Vaughn's chest moving with him and Austin until the man thrusting into my ass began to stiffen. A long groan ripped from the man behind me, barely covering the string of curses coming from the man under me.

I felt the pulse of his release through my own. I felt his cock throb and I had the reckless thought of wanting to feel his come filling me. They wouldn't agree to it, not with the obvious consequences sleeping at the other end of the house. But it left a hungry burn in the pit of my stomach that only magnified when Austin slipped out of me.

I wanted this without barriers. I wanted to feel each of them as they erupted in me. I shifted upward, finding a last bit of strength so I could look down at Vaughn. I curled my hips against him, riding the wave of euphoria and extending it with each downward thrust I made on him.

Vaughn's eyes narrowed, the green looking bright as if he were on the same high as I was. He moved with me, changing his pace so it met mine and we moved together. My head dropped back and I basked in the feeling of control. The fact that I was on top of Vaughn, rocking as he pounded up into me, was an added bonus. Having power over a man that often left me on edge, or at a disadvantage was something I enjoyed more than I should admit.

His fingers dug into my hips and I thought for a moment he was going to stop, that he was going to slow us down. He bared his teeth and for a brief minute I thought he was going to fall in the same route Austin did. He arched upward and held me there, he was stiff.

"Take a breath," Gavin said from behind us. "Let him take a second so he doesn't bust when I slide in back here." He put his hands on my shoulders, "But lean forward so I can get in."

I didn't fight the gentle push that had my breasts pressed into Vaughn's chest again. I resisted the urge to rock my hips, but clenched around the cock that was still in me. It earned me a rumbled noise that I felt all the way through me.

I wanted him to make more noises like that. To be honest, I enjoyed the moans and groans all three of them made. But Gavin and Austin usually had no issues making noise for me. Vaughn usually was quieter. Maybe he wasn't as unaffected as he liked to present.

Gavin pressed his fingers into me, carefully testing the resistance of my ass before he crooned into my ear, "Gets easier every time." He still took the time to slick more lubricant between my cheeks before I felt the press of his cock against me. He slowly released a breath, sighing as if he was getting into one of his favorite places. "Fucking finally."

"It's not been that long," Vaughn protested.

"Tell that to the cheetah print she's got going on your chest," Gavin said with a laugh. "You're lucky she kept it below the collar."

"You didn't," Vaughn said, trying to sit up a little.

Gavin's arms hooked under mine and he pulled me back. It seemed to wedge him deeper into me and I caught myself on his thighs. I quaked, suddenly distracted from the conversation we had been having in favor of how every nerve ending seemed to be hyper focused on just how Gavin's cock pierced me like this.

The hands at my hips left and I managed to get a view of Vaughn checking out the peppering of purple bruises I'd left on his pecs and collar. That thrill of power went through me again, especially when his eyes connected with mine. I didn't see any anger, maybe some confusion but he wasn't mad about it.

Though that could've been Gavin's fault. He held me close, thrusting shallowly while Vaughn just seemed content to lay there. He instead reached up to cup both of my breasts, pressing them together and watching with a glazed look in his eyes. He wasn't far off from an orgasm and it only became clearer with every thrust Gavin made into me.

"I want to feel it," I said as I looked down at the man beneath me.

"You don't feel it now?" Gavin asked, misunderstanding. His arm went around my waist and his hand tangled in my hair, pulling it until I had to arch back. "Is that what you wanted to feel?" He growled in my ear.

It wasn't, but the way he pulled my hair had things tingling and magnifying everything else. I wasn't going to protest as Vaughn began to arch up into me again. It pushed me closer to the edge, it felt sharper than the first one, likely due to Gavin pulling my hair. Then his teeth dug into neck.

I had nothing to smother the moan it tore from me and nothing that could stave off the overflow of endorphins. The moan turned into a whine and I melted against Gavin, boneless. The hips beneath me hitched upward sharply, drawing out the waves of pleasure I was already drowning in.

"Fuck," Vaughn barked out and he clenched his hands around my breasts a little too hard. His hands dropped to my hips and he managed two more hard thrusts up into me before stiffening. His cock twitched in me, throbbing with his release.

That was as much as I could feel of it. "I wanted it," I admit out loud, brain cells still blissed out to the point that there wasn't any thought to the consequences of my words.

"What did you want?" Gavin asked, voice low as it coiled through my ear. "Baby, all you gotta do is tell me what you want and I'll give it to you."

I licked my lips, common sense just in the back of my mind screaming for me to say something else. Anything else. But my mind and mouth suddenly decided not to cooperate with good sense. "I wanted you to come in me," I said without trying to sound sexy. I was breathless, for obvious reasons, but it still came out like someone else was suddenly behind the wheel.

Gavin stalled out. The hand in my hair was loosening so that my scalp didn't have the tinge of pain going through it that probably influenced the words to come tumbling out. It left him full seated in my ass, his cock throbbing. "That's a bad idea," he said, though it sounded like he didn't necessarily believe that.

"All three of us?" Vaughn asked. He sat up a little and, even though his cock had gotten soft in me, he rolled his hips up. It was almost like he was testing whether or not he could keep going. "You want all three of us filling you up?" He sounded hoarse as he asked the question, his hands cupping my face as he started to pepper kisses against my jaw. "You want it from all of us?"

I can't find it in me to answer him. It's not that I don't know the answer, it's like common sense finally won out over what I wanted. Vaughn's teeth scraped against my jaw and I shuddered, my eyes fluttered closed.

I nodded. So much for common sense. This wasn't even something I could blame Vaughn for.

The fact that he started to stiffen inside me again and his hips began to move as he pressed his chest against mine. It fed into something that he wanted to hear from me, I realized. I didn't push him off and I didn't make any attempt to dissuade what he had been hungry for when it came to me. The fact that it seemed to reinvigorate him wasn't something I was about to protest either.

"It is a bad idea," Austin broke in, unsurprisingly agreeing with Gavin. He had been laying beside us, watching with a sleepy satisfaction. "The main reason why it's a bad idea is why we haven't done this lately," he said, motioning towards the other end of the house. "Babies come from unprotected sex. I've already proven that my pull out game is shit," he sat up and picked up the baby monitor, shaking it pointedly at us. "Why play with fire?"

Vaughn made an inexplicable frustrated noise, but he didn't offer any sort of argument. He just buried his face against my shoulder, his hips moved against mine shallowly before he seemed to give up. "There are alternatives," he said without moving back to look at the other man, "she's on birth control." He did pull back a little so he could see me. "Keeping track of her menstrual cycles and not being stupid about it will reduce risks of her getting pregnant."

"If we give up condoms," Gavin said from behind me. There was a slight quiver in his voice, showing that Vaughn's movements hadn't just been affecting me. "Does that mean we're admitting this is for keeps?" He huffed in my ear, "I know we have this conversation way too often. But," he released a breath, "I want it to be for keeps."

This wasn't the first time he brought that up, the first time he was chastising Austin for it. I had thought the agreement of meeting parents made that clear. I thought all the conversations made it clear. I'm surprised he still had doubts. "If that's what you want," I said without missing a beat. "I thought moving in made it obvious that I wasn't going anywhere."

"Not tonight," Austin said, still not looking as if he wasn't sold on the idea. "I think it's something that you should reconsider when you're not in between two people in the middle of it."

"Why talk her out of it?" Vaughn asked. "If shit is meant to happen let it happen."

"Let's finish this," Gavin began uneasily. "I hate to agree with Austin, but it feels like there should be some level headedness that isn't influenced by the sex we're currently having." His hands were at my back and he began to push, shoving me and Vaughn back down onto the bed. He didn't make any attempts to pull my hair.

One hand gripped my shoulder and the other was on my hip, he began to pump himself into me. The pace he set was fast, like he was focused on his own release. After the few I already had it only seemed fair to lean into Vaughn and let Gavin have his fill.

It didn't take him long, his rhythm began to stutter. The hold he had on me tightened. He hissed low and I clenched, pushed right over the edge again while I hadn't been focusing on anything other than the noise he had been making. He released a curse and I could feel him coming with me, as much as the condom he wore allowed.

He pressed against my back, sandwiching me between him and Vaughn. I didn't protest, even with the additional weight making my ribs hurt and bringing sudden attention to my bladder. I could wait a little longer.

I could wait until they realized that they ruined me for anything that might be considered normal.

14

Nadia

I woke up alone, something that surprised me quite a bit after last night. I wasn't surprised that Austin wasn't in bed with me. He was an early riser before he found out about Landon. Vaughn went to work early, even with a long week we've had he was still getting up early. Gavin, on the other hand, wasn't a morning person and was more than happy to stay cuddled up in bed with me.

After using the bathroom and pulling on a shirt, I got up to investigate the house. Austin was in the living room with Landon. The baby seemed like he was in a better mood and the little string of beads was still around his ankle. His little cheeks didn't have the same pink tinge I noticed yesterday and as far as I could tell from where he lay on the play mat, he looked well rested.

So did Austin for that matter.

"Where's Gavin?" I asked.

"Vaughn got him up before he left," Austin supplied from the floor. He was stretched out beside his son, shaking the little arch of plush toys that hung over him. "His parents are flying in today."

"Oh," I don't know why that didn't occur to me. They mentioned it here and there, but I didn't recall the exact date that they would be arriving. Nerves twisted up my stomach. Both Deidre and my mother handled the knowledge of my relationship status fairly well. Maybe his parents would be the same?

I turned to go back into the bedroom, I needed a shower. Maybe I could see how Freddy was doing in the hospital. At the very least I could get a check up on him.

"Nadia," Austin called after me. "I think we should talk about last night."

I turned to look at him, confused. He had sat up but stayed within each reach of the baby. "What?"

"I don't know if what you said you wanted was in the heat of the moment or if it was something you legitimately want," he began. "But I want to make sure you're fully aware of what you're asking for." He reached down and hefted up Landon, pulling the little boy to rest against his chest. "The consequences of it. Are you ready for kids? Do you even want them?" Suddenly he looked a little afraid. "Is what you're wanting for this to grow into some sort of family dynamic?"

I opened my mouth, wanting to admit that I didn't really know what I wanted. But I thought better of it. "I thought maybe it would put some of the insecurities that they have to rest," I shook my head then. "That's not a good answer," I huffed out. "I've been going through life not knowing what I want from it. I'm still kinda there. This," I waved my hands towards the house and him. "This is the closest thing that I've had to stability with someone else in my life since high school."

What did that say about me? Why did I tell him that? I put my hand in my hair as I looked at him, ready to face his judgment.

"You think having a kid will add stability to what we have going on?" He asked.

"Having unprotected sex with people that I intend to have a long term relationship with doesn't necessarily mean a kid will come from it," I sighed and I could see just how unsure he was. "I'm not Lauren. I'm not going to come up with schemes to keep you here if you wanted out."

"I doubt that I'll ever want out," he said as he carefully got up, without upsetting the baby he held. "This," he jostled Landon a little, earning us both a grin, "this is something I want to last. A baby won't guarantee that and I know it. I don't know if Gav and Vaughn have the same kind of sense as I do. I don't know if they'll think past their dicks." He looked a little uneasy, "They want you to feel about them what you do for me."

"I care about Gavin," I said without hesitation. Then I made a face, "And Vaughn. I should say it more often," I paused and bit my lip. "I thought last night would make it clearer how I felt without me having to say the words."

"I guess if it ends up with him having a brother or sister that'll just have to be it?" He asked, nodding his head down towards the baby in his arms. "Would you be okay with that?"

I looked at Landon, unable to put to words the feelings that welled up in me. "If it happens it happens," I croaked. "There's so many things that can go wrong with what we're doing now, being careful. My birth control isn't one hundred percent affective. Condoms break all the time. Every time we have sex, especially when it's the three of us, we're taking a risk." I shook my head and looked back up at Austin. "But I know for damn sure it's not something I'm willing to give up just because I don't want to take the risk."

He swallowed visibly. "Me either," he admitted. He nodded and seemed to accept my answer. "If we're going to go without them we just need to be careful and either avoid weeks before or," he shrugged, "just wrap it up when you're ovulating or whatever. I guess that means we need to keep a better track of your monthly stuff."

"I guess that's one way to do it," I said as I closed the distance between us. "If you would rather be safe, I understand." I didn't hesitate to press a kiss to Landon's temple before I leaned up to kiss Austin. "We haven't really been helping you a lot on the baby front.

"Vaughn has been a big help," he said as if to wave it away. "You didn't sign up for this."

"But I signed up for you," I said easily. "So I need to help more, especially since you so readily helped me out. If you need a minute, a nap, to go to the bathroom, anything I need you to tell me."

A buzzing broke the moment. Someone's phone was ringing and from the sound of it, broke and like it was two seconds from falling apart, it had to be my phone. I pulled away and went into the bedroom to hunt up the device.

I missed a call from Deidre. Before I got the chance to call her back she sent me a message, 'Stop messin' with your men and get ready to meet me at the hospital. The nurse I talked to said he was conscious and stable.'

'I need a shower, but I'll meet you there.' I stepped out of the bedroom, "I'm gonna meet Dee at the hospital to check on Freddy. I shouldn't be long."

"Take your time," he said with a shrug. "Just me and the boy in the house most of the time anyway, we can watch ESPN without having to worry about anyone complaining." He turned to go back into the living room.

I rushed through a shower and getting dressed. I piled my wet hair into a messy bun and I was out the door. I felt bad about leaving him at home with the baby by himself. Usually he had Gavin there with him. If something happened while I was out then he would have to deal with it on his own and my mom would probably be pissed if she found out about it.

I'd just have to keep tabs on them.

****

I didn't wait for Dee. After finding a nurse nice enough to not give me grief for not being family, I found Freddy's room. He was still in the ICU and while I had the drive to come up to the hospital and find his room, I couldn't get the nerve to go into it.

"You know the least you coulda done, since you weren't gonna wait on me, was tell me where his room was," Deidre complained as she found me standing in the little pod that the rooms were arranged in around a giant nurse station. "The guy at the information desk gave me mess about being the second person to ask about him." She heaved a sigh, "You ain't gonna find nothing standing out here."

"I'm gonna be stupid and cry," I said, knowing after the last time I saw him that there'd be no way I would be able to control myself. I thought of all the grief I'd given him since I started working there, all the banter we had. It wouldn't be the same, especially seeing him hooked up to machines and monitors.

"That's a given," she said without waiting on me as she knocked on the door. "But you either gotta face the music or you gotta take the route Jodie's taking. Pretend it didn't happen and act a fool, like you're on vacation." She took my hand in hers, holding it tightly. "I got you, baby girl."

She pushed the door open, not waiting for any cue that it was safe to enter. Dee didn't say a word as she edged in, peering past the curtain at the man that was on the bed. She took an audible breath and in a low voice said, "Hey Boss."

Freddy looked pale and it took everything in me to hold back the sudden burn in my throat. I could feel the tears building. He had a tube under his nose and bags under his eyes. His hair was in greasy disarray. His chest was slightly exposed, covered in electrodes and a large bandage. The blankets were just under that and from as far as I could tell, it looked like a nurse had just been in there.

His eyes were watery and it looked as if he were barely conscious. “Dee?” he croaked.

“I brought Nadia with me,” she announced as she tugged me into the room. “We just had to make sure you were gonna make it.”

He grunted, his eyes closing again. We waited a beat to see if he had fallen asleep. Deidre stayed at the foot of the bed, eyeing him with what I could only call worry. “They got you on the good stuff?”

He grunted again with what I could only call an affirmative. Or it might’ve been pained. I covered my mouth with my free hand, struggling to keep myself under control. Dee’s fingers tightened around mine, I doubted she thought I’d make a run for it. Maybe it was because she wasn’t as unmoved as she appeared.

“We closed up the diner for you,” she reported easily. “The last time I rode by there you had a few people asking about you. I had to tell them we weren’t sure when we could open again.”

“Need to clean out old food,” he said after a deep breath.

“Nadia and I can do that,” Dee volunteered. “We're gonna be on the clock for it,” she said after a beat but she nudged my shoulder. “We can get everything that’s gonna go bad while you’re down and out for you.” She eyed him again, “You think we’ll be able to call in for extensions for you while you’re in here?”

He nodded and he lifted a hand, pointed it towards a pile of clothes that were left on a chair. “Have a laptop that I do business on at the house,” he said and then nodded. “You can get that handled?”

Dee nodded, “We’ll handle your business while you’re here so you don’t have to worry about stuff getting cut off.”

Hearing him talk helped a little. I took a breath and released it slowly. "Do you have any family we can get into contact with?"

Freddy just shook his head. "You get the payroll figured out. I'll sign your checks. Don't rob me."

"Give us more credit," Dee huffed. "We wouldn't do that."

"Would you even be able to sign them while you're under the influence?" I asked.

He shook his head, I don't know if it was to answer my question or if it meant he was disoriented. I held my breath like I was waiting for him to answer me. When the door opened behind me I bounced into Dee before I felt stupid for being frightened. A nurse stood there, just as startled as I was.

"Mr. Dobbs," she began, looking between the three of us. "Is this your family?" She was cute, her dark hair was pulled back in a no nonsense bun and her brown eyes were narrowed just slightly, like she was suspicious.

"We're his employees," I offered. "We called the ambulance when we found him in the back lot of the diner."

"We just wanted to make sure he was gonna be alright," Dee added.

"Are you the girl that's been calling up here for the last few days?" the nurse asked, a frown clouding up her features. Clearly Dee had been an annoyance.

"If you would've just answered my questions when I first called I wouldn't have had to call so much," she snapped back.

"We can't give out a patient's personal information," the nurse shot back.

"Tell 'em," Freddy croaked after a beat. "Otherwise she'll be in your ass until you release me."

"He's stable," the nurse said with a sigh. "And they will be moving him out of the ICU later tonight into a private room. He's likely going to be stuck in the hospital for further observation while the cardiologist decides whether or not surgery is necessary."

"For how long?" Dee asked.

"Anywhere from a week to two weeks, depending on what the doctor says," the nurse crossed her arms over her chest. "I hate to tell you though it'll probably be longer before he's cleared to go back to work."

"We'll get things figured out," Deidre said with a bit of sass. She looked back at Freddy, taking him in where he rested in bed. "You get better," she said before moving to the pile of clothes he pointed at earlier. She tugged me with her because she hadn't let go of my hand. She found his keys and she shook them at him, "We will get things handled while you're stuck in here. Come on, Nadia."

Dee didn't wait for me to do or say anything. She tugged me past the nurse and into the hallway. She kept a death grip on my hand as we walked out of the ICU together. I thought for a minute she was going to drag me all the way down to the parking lot. But as soon as we came across a waiting room she whipped me around, let go of my hand so she could wrap me up with both arms. She held onto me tightly and at first I thought she was trying to comfort me. Then her shoulders began to quake.

Deidre was crying. I could feel it as she began to crumble. Me, like the big baby that I was, crumbled right along with her.

"It's okay," I sniffled. "He's gonna be okay. It's okay." I said it like a prayer and a mantra. Not just to comfort her, to comfort myself.

15

Gavin

"Fucking wake up," Vaughn said as he belted me with a pillow. "We've got shit to do and you don't get to sleep in today." He gave me a solid shake. "Don't make me wake up Naddy, too."

How he managed to not do that with me laying so close to her was surprising, but then again when the girl sawed logs there was no getting her up. Chalking that up to fucking her good. I sat up and rubbed a hand over my face, feeling the beginnings of a beard and the frustration of waking up way too early. "The fuck?"

"You're going to go clean up my apartment for your mom and dad, dipshit," Vaughn hissed at me. "You're going to go grocery shopping for them and play a good host to make sure there's nothing in there that I'll have to explain to Kelli when I see her."

I blinked at him, "You want me to hide your porn?"

"No," Vaughn snapped. "Just make sure we don't have any of her panties on the floor or anything," he growled as he turned to walk away. "What I have in the fridge probably isn't edible by her standards either. Get off your ass and make sure your parents are taken care of."

"Fine," I grumped as I got out of bed. I took the time to pull the sheet up and over Naddy. She was still naked and while she didn't sleep like that often I wasn't going to give her a reason to not do it again. It was always nice to be able to get a handful of titty without a shirt in the way. With that thought in mind, I pulled the blanket over her, tucking her in.

Satisfied, I walked out into the kitchen to see Vaughn with a thermos in hand, standing at the door. "If you go back to bed," he said to me. "I'm going to beat your ass."

"I'm up," I huffed at him as I went to the coffee maker. It was empty. What Austin had made this morning was in the thermos Vaughn had in his hand. "Greedy bastard."

"I'll make more," Austin offered from the table. He had cut fruit on the tray in front of Landon and it looked like he was trying to encourage the baby to eat it but there was more smashed fruit on the tray and on the baby's face than could've ended up in his mouth. "Just give me a minute," he made a face as he tried to scoop up what might've been pineapple, but could have also been a banana. "Go take a shower and it'll probably be ready then."

"He's making me clean up his apartment," I pointed out as I went to find my tennis shoes. "I might as well wait for a shower and just pick up something from Starbucks." I tugged them on, balancing by the couch. "I think we can try to use him as a means to keep my mom from losing her shit when we introduce Naddy to them."

"Are you wanting to do that today?" Austin asked, brows up. "Because you might want to warn her about it."

"Not today," I took a minute to find my keys. "Mom and dad are gonna need to decompress and relax after flying in." I nodded then put on a funny face when I noticed I had caught the attention of Landon. I stepped out the door and grimaced at the idea that I was going to spend the majority of the day cleaning.

Fortunately, after I got to Vaughn's apartment, I realized there wasn't really much to do. He wasn't a slob. He didn't leave clothes on the floor. After checking the bedside table and under the mattress I decided to not make any effort to look for titty magazines. I'd already been in his closet, which was well organized with his suits and shirts. There hadn't been any stash of skanky videos that might make my mom clutch her pearls.

I was a little disappointed. I don't know why I expected something, we weren't teenagers anymore. There wasn't any reason to hide dirty magazines, he didn't really need them with the internet.

I got into the kitchen and marveled at the size of his fridge. It was twice the size of Austin's. When I cracked it open I noticed it was damn near barren. He told me to go shopping and this was why. This also explained why he never really bothered to come back here. The only thing that was here was a few overpriced suits.

I walked through the living room, ready to make a run to the store when I remembered something important. I eyed the couch. I went to it and gave it a cursory sniff. It didn't smell like sex. I jerked the cushion off of it, not seeing anything that could be considered a questionable stain. He must've cleaned it. Was this what he wanted me to check out?

I fixed the seat cushion and tried not to think too hard about how it felt to walk in on them together. Knowing that I had Nadia in his bathroom, on the counter and pressed against the mirror, made me swallow any bit of jealousy that began to rear up.

I didn't have the right to be jealous, not with all the things that Nadia let me do to her when it was just the two of us. Or I guess I should say what I encouraged her to do to me. So far, she'd been more than willing to entertain my experiments.

I was gonna have to find time for her to do that again. She didn't have her apartment anymore and Austin was home all the damn time. I huffed as I stepped out of the apartment, I would have to figure something out.

It took me about an hour to get food that I knew my parents would appreciate. I loaded up the fridge and made sure there would be things like coffee, milk, and sugar. I covered the major food groups. I got cold cuts, chicken, and the basic things I saw Austin using often when he prepared dinner for us.

Satisfied that I was finished with the chores Vaughn gave me I went back to the house. There was something about Vaughn's apartment that just seemed way too empty. Mom and dad were gonna hate it, but they needed to stay somewhere until I got them into a house.

When I pulled up I was surprised to see Naddy's car gone. What did she have to do if her boss was in the hospital? Maybe she was just out running the roads like I was. The only reason why it bothered me was I had gotten sex in my head and now I wanted it.

I walked into the house to see Austin holding Landon with the infant's feet on the floor mimicking as if the baby were walking. He was cheering in a way that I honestly would've never expected to see the other man do. I guess he was a better father than I would ever be able to anticipate.

Then he looked up at me and I realized that he was really close to cracking. I guess he'd been left by himself doing all the work with no help and it was wearing on him. Sex last night had only been a bandaid on the growing problem he was facing as a single parent in a house full of people that could easily help him.

"How's it going?" I asked and I came up behind the baby, carefully grasping his little wrists so I could take up the reins of giving him the illusion of walking. The baby didn't protest and I took that as a win.

Austin flopped back onto the floor. He released a sigh, "Realizing the reason why they haven't been able to find Lauren is because she can't hack this." He gestured to Landon and me where we had carefully toddled to the kitchen. "She wanted a lot of money so she could get a nanny because she didn't have it in her to devote all of her attention to someone other than herself."

"And you stayed with her long enough to knock her up," I pointed out.

"I'm mentioning it because Nadia wants us to fuck without protection," he sat up and rubbed his hands over his face. "And I don't want this to happen again."

"Don't be stupid," I began, straightening and picking up Landon at the same time. He fit against my chest with his butt seated against my forearm. There was a little bit of squish and I had the horrifying thought that I might have to change the diaper because I picked him up. Could I pretend he didn't need a diaper change and give him back to Austin without it being suspicious? "Nadia and Lauren are two different women. Plus, Naddy has a support system that would help her. That's what we are. Plus her parents." I made a face, if we got Naddy pregnant her mother would definitely murder us. I shook my head and looked down at him, "You have a support system, too. We're just dicks and not helping you like we should."

The baby against me started to smell and I grimaced. I was going to have to change his diaper or suffer through the rancid smell. Was it because he had solid food? Or did formula just make baby shit smell worse?

"He needs to be changed," Austin summarized and he got to his feet, coming to take the baby from me. "All you had to do is say so, man."

"Pam said we need to help you," I reminded him and shifted so he couldn't take Landon from me. "So, I'll change him. I just need you to supervise." I led the way to the nursery, "Because I have no idea how to do it."

Changing a diaper took longer than I wanted it to. I might've gagged, I'm not proud of it but Austin did it so I don't feel bad. Landon ended up peeing on the both of us and I think the little guy found it to be hilarious. Because he cackled. A baby cackled. I guess he was smarter than I assumed him to be.

After we finally got him cleaned up and the mess he made up we came back into the living room. "You get used to it," Austin said. "Your gag reflex eventually stops and you focus more on keeping the mess contained as you clean it up."

I let Austin carry him, "He peed on me and he laughed. At this point I feel like he should be potty trained."

"I don't think he has the coordination to stay seated on the toilet much less get up there," Austin said as he put Landon down onto his blanket. "Plus, I think he's not really crawling so that eliminates that idea." While he spoke, the baby pushed himself up onto his hands and knees. We both watched him for a minute to see if he was going to make an attempt to escape, but he just rocked back and forth.

"Thought he'd prove you wrong."

"Honestly, I'm kind of relieved because it would mean I have to do more baby proofing," he sighed. "Have your parents landed yet?"

"Shit, I don't know. I figured Vaughn would let me know if I needed to pick them up," I said as I pulled my phone out. I sent him a text to ask about it. "He said they were flying in, he just didn't say when."

"You didn't bother to ask?"

I shrugged at him, as my phone buzzed. 'I'm trying to get out of the office now so I can go pick them up. If you want to be helpful, you can offer your truck to them so they're not stuck in my apartment.'

I groaned, "He's gonna make me give up my truck."

"What have you been doing lately? Staying at home being lazy," Austin pointed out.

"Vaughn said something about the bar opening soon," I protested. "It shouldn't be long before we're working at it. I plan on working behind the bar, I'm gonna need my truck. I thought you were gonna work in the kitchen."

"That was the plan," he admitted, then looked down at Landon, where he was still rocking. "But I don't think it's something I can keep to. Or at least not full time. Who is gonna watch him while I'm at work?" He looked up at me, "I'm expecting us to be on the same type of schedule Nadia is on. How the hell am I supposed to make that work and be a parent?"

"Plenty of people do it," I tried to sound comforting as I said it. "Single parents do it all the time. I don't know how they do it, but they do." I shrugged and I looked down at my phone, sending my mom a text just in case she'd give me a clue as to when they were rolling in. "We'll figure it out." I ran out of things to say and it was apparent with the way he flopped back against his chair that they weren't much comfort.

16

Vaughn

I was so ready to walk out the door the moment Kelli messaged me about their arrival that I dropped everything and stalked out to my car without a concern towards my own father. I didn't even consider how odd it was that I was excited about someone else's family coming home. Though if I was honest Kelli and Dave were more paternal to me than my own parents. Though in my mother's defense she spent the majority of my childhood struggling with my father. Once they divorced and found my stepfather, I was at that age that I was so angry I didn't want to give anyone a chance.

Now, I know better. But back then it wouldn't have kept me from being angry or a shitty person. And Nadia caught damn near all of my grief.

I wasn't going to reflect too much. Though it may have had something to do with the money I dropped on the phone I intended to give to Naddy. Gifts didn't soothe bruised egos, but I knew for a fact that after I got both her and her friend squared away with jobs she wouldn't be as standoffish with me.

I wasn't going to hold my breath, but after last night I wasn't feeling like I was on the outside of their little group. It was a relief, like I got pulled from the second string to starting. It was the one time in a relationship that I was eager for it to last, while before any woman I 'committed' to was just a means to an end.

When I got home I was surprised to see that she wasn't there. I had intended to give her the new phone immediately even though I hadn't gotten into contact with her coworker. I made attempts, but she never answered her phone. Hopefully, that wouldn't be held against me.

We didn't have time to wait around for Naddy to decide to come home. I didn't know whether or not she would accept a new phone from me, if it would be okay for me to give her gifts. I left it on the bedside table, not saying a word to Austin but knowing he would be smart enough to know who it was for.

"I don't know why you said I needed to clean your apartment," Gavin spoke up as he drove us to the airport. "The couch didn't even have a funky smell to it like I expected it to."

"I had it cleaned," I assured him. "I was more worried about there being something in the fridge for them."

"I thought I would find some sort of weird porn you left out or something," he sighed. "Maybe I'd find a whip or some cuffs." He shrugged a little as he pulled us into the parking lot. "Maybe a butt plug at least."

"I leave the strange stuff to you," I said, not reacting to his assumptions. "The strangest thing I've done is what you've seen because you were there."

"Ugh," he got out of the truck. He didn't wait for me as he started towards the terminal. But when I caught up to him I got a look of disapproval. "Vanilla is boring. I think the least thing you could do is try pulling hair here and there."

I hummed, "I thought that was something you might've done in the heat of the moment. She didn't protest."

"Try having her pull your hair," he suggested, smirking at me. "Gotta get down there between her thighs and lick it until she can't take it anymore."

"I've done that," I blinked at him. She had pulled my hair then, tugging because she had gotten overly sensitive.

"It didn't get you going?" he asked, surprised as we found our way up to the security guarded gate. The view of the concourse showed just a few people milling about, no sign of Kelli or Dave. They had just landed when they texted me. They should at least be in the baggage claim by now.

I rolled a shoulder, "There were other things going on. I was a little distracted by making sure I got her off enough. At the time we had made a deal. I was trying to make sure I would get the opportunity to fuck her again, with or without you." I rubbed my jaw as I considered that first time I had been involved with the three of them. There had been excitement due to the anticipation of being included. There was the rush from kissing her, tasting her cunt and getting intimately familiar with her scent. Her nails scraping against my scalp added to it. "I'll need to give her a reason to pull my hair again."

"She left marks on you," he eyed me. "How'd that feel?"

I put a hand to my chest, there was a trail of little bruises she'd left on my skin. I had given hickeys before, but it wasn't often that I received them. The older I got the less women had been interested in the idea of me leaving a mark on them, especially if it was something that wasn't easily covered. Naddy had left marks around my collar bone and on my pec, all of them easily covered by my shirt. I didn't know how to word an answer to his question, so I just shrugged.

Gavin snorted like he understood. Maybe he did, I wasn't entirely privy to what they did before I joined the group. "You should try experimenting with her," he said after a beat. "Whatever she's willing to do, of course."

"Experimenting outside of what we're already doing?" I asked as I eyed him. "What's next? You want to bring another woman into this? I thought we had already done something like that."

Gavin paused visibly, looked at me then redirected his attention back down the concourse where we could see a group of people filtering down to pass shops. "I've done the three way with two girls," he admitted. "And there's nothing wrong with it. It either goes one of two ways, you gotta get both girls off or they end up ignoring you in favor of exploring their own curiosities." He frowned a little at that, "Which is fine, great to watch. I can't really complain about it. But could you imagine us bringing another girl into bed and Naddy being all over it?"

"You're afraid she'll decide she likes girls instead?" I asked, surprised. I didn't expect him to have that insecurity.

"She didn't have college to get all that stuff out of her system," he pointed out.

"I don't think you have to go to college to experiment with things you're curious about," I said evenly. "Nadia wasn't a virgin when you first slept with her, was she?"

"No," he said after a beat. His hand went into his hair, tangling in the curls as his dad came into view, the man a head taller than his mother. "I guess you have a point. But does that mean she's ready to settle down with the three of us?"

"Don't you think last night was a sign of that?" I asked just as Kelli and Dave crossed the security barrier.

"Gavin!" his mother cried out in delight and engulfed him in a hug. "Oh, my baby boy!" she squealed, even though Gavin wasn't the youngest. "I've missed you so much!" She gave him a big kiss on his cheek and I didn't make any attempt to hide my amusement.

Dave patted his son heavily on the back before he came to me. He gave my shoulder the same heavy handed treatment, "Vaughn! You look good, I gotta say it's been way too long since we've heard from you. When

Gavin insisted we move with him when he was first drafted we couldn't deny the boy. I'm really glad you made quick work of selling *that* house."

"You didn't like living in luxury?" I asked, hoping that they wouldn't consider my apartment to be the same thing. "That house he had you in was pretty posh."

"When you don't grow up with it all it looks like is a bigger chore of keeping it looking good," he released a breath. "I am more than happy to go back to the house I bought with her."

I grimaced at that, "Someone was pretty quick to buy it when you guys left. They're not interested in selling it, I've asked. But I can get you close to the same neighborhood."

"That's not important," Kelli said as she let go of Gavin and came to me. "What's important is we're home!" She didn't hesitate to pull me down into a hug, her arms went around my shoulder and she rubbed my back like she was comforting a small child. I was surprised by what it did to me. I hugged her back and just took comfort in it. It was like I was hugging my own mother, I spent enough time with Gavin that Kelli definitely had a hand in raising me. "I am so glad to see you two getting back together again," she hummed in my ear. Then she pulled away and smiled up at me, "Even if it just means you're getting into trouble."

"We're too old to get into trouble," I argued.

"You're not thirty, yet," Dave said as he started to direct us to baggage claim. "You're not even close to being old, much less old enough for a mid-life crisis."

I just hoped he held onto that energy when he looked at my apartment. When we got to my building both he and Kelli whistled. "Are you sure we're not putting you out?" Kelli asked. "Because this looked like this is some sort of high end hotel," she said as she boarded the elevator. "Are we going to have to deal with housekeeping?"

"I have a housekeeper that comes through once a week," I admitted. "But I can let her know that I need her for an extra day if you think that's necessary." I hit the button for my floor before I twisted my apartment key off the ring. When I lived there regularly my cleaning lady would come in twice a week, I was sure she wouldn't have any issues doing that again.

"I can keep it clean," Kelli reassured me. "Dad's is housebroken, I promise."

I laughed when Dave proceeded to shake his head, like he was disagreeing with her assessment. I let them into my apartment after I gave Dave my key. I decided to give them a short tour. Despite the square footage the only rooms off of the living space was my bedroom and the bathroom. The rest of it was vast and open.

Gavin's parents looked amazed and impressed. It felt good to see the pride on their faces. It was more recognition than I would ever get from my own father. It felt good, what my surrogate family gave me.

That's not to say my mother didn't give me what I needed. She always marveled at what I had accomplished and she was never shy about giving me praise. But my old man was always critical and it was never anything I could shake. I wasn't good enough for him.

At least, not yet. As soon as the bar was finished, something that wasn't that far from being done, I would be out from under his shadow and be able to stand with my own success. It was a freedom I craved almost as much as I craved Nadia.

I sat heavily on the couch, wondering if she would be home by now. It was almost time for dinner. Would she be cooking tonight? Or had Austin already beat her to the punch? She was more inclined to cook less healthy options, using more fats and carbs. It was good even when things were a tad over cooked. Austin had mastered cooking far better than Naddy had but still there was something extra.

I was biased when I shouldn't be. My bias should be in favor of my friend instead of the girl we liked in high school. But things evidently weren't going to work that way.

"So," Kelli came to sit next to me, "Where are we going for dinner?"

17

Nadia

I ignored the box on the bedside table. It still had plastic on it making it all the more shiny and distracting. He followed through and got me a new phone. I hadn't bothered to ask Deidre if he had gotten in touch with her. Was it safe to trust Vaughn? I wanted to, he didn't really have a good reason to lie and say he was finding her a new job at his own expense.

I looked at the box, not wanting to pick it up. The brand was familiar but the model itself wasn't. My own phone was five years old and I had lost touch with the technological advances that they had made with phones. I figured that since I didn't have a flip phone and could search things up on the internet, I was fine. From the wide screen pictured on the box, I was sure now I was wrong.

It looked expensive. I pulled out my current phone to do a quick search on the phone he bought for me. I immediately regretted it.

Did this mean I owed him something? There was no way I would be able to pay him back, especially if the diner was going to be closed the entire time Freddy recovered. If Freddy even had the desire to reopen it at all.

I ended up drowning in a pit of despair. I ended up juggling between the prospect of finding a new job and what Vaughn could possibly demand of me in exchange for a phone that cost way too much money. It left me lying face down on the bed, listening to Austin play with his son in the living room. If I was a good person, I would be in there with the two of them trying to build a relationship with Landon. And that just made me spiral out further.

My phone went off, it echoed through the living room. I heard him get up and a squeal from the baby before he came into the bedroom. "Everything okay?" he asked as he sat on the bed by my hip.

"They're moving him out of the ICU," I reported. "We're not even sure how long he's going to be out and unable to work." I rolled onto my side to see him and Landon both watching me with a similar expression. Concern.

Were babies able to feel that kind of emotion?

Landon reached for me and without thinking I opened my arms to him. Austin set him carefully on my chest. He managed to find a way to keep himself balanced on his little hands and knees, eyeing my face with those bottomless blue eyes. I struggled for a moment, trying to decide where I should put my hands. They hovered on either side of Landon as he seemed to find balance on me. He looked like he might go sliding onto my side.

"Did the nurse or doctor say anything?" Austin asked, watching me with something that I couldn't define on his face now.

"They aren't going to," I sighed, making Landon shift precariously on me. He blinked widely at me like he hadn't expected that to happen. He suddenly dropped onto his belly on my chest. His arms and legs splayed onto me, his head followed suit only to shoot upward again so that he could look down at me. "We're not family," I continued carefully, watching the baby on me.

Austin hummed, his attention on the baby that was on me. "If they're going to move him out of ICU, that has to be a good thing. Maybe they're sure he'll recover from it."

Landon's head dropped on my chest again and I blinked, trying to figure out what I should do. I put a hand to his back and rubbed gently, somewhat awkwardly. "Is he okay?"

"Tired, probably," Austin smirked a little bit as he said it. "I figured I would go on his cues for naps. It seems like every time I try to put him down for one he fights it so I figured we'd try this out." He slouched a little as Landon became a little heavier on me, "It seems like every time I try to do it he just gets so fussy that I'm pretty sure if I keep trying that method I'm going to go crazy." There was a wild look in his eye that suggested that he was pretty close to it already.

"Have you had a shower, yet?" I asked, hoping the question would distract him.

He shook his head and picked up his phone, "Vaughn messaged me a little while ago about going out to dinner." He looked a little sheepish, "That was why I came in here. To see if you could watch him while I did that."

"I think he's down for the count," I assured him. "Take your time. I'd ask if you wanted a glass of wine or a beer to take with you, but I doubt Vaughn is going to give you that kind of luxury."

Austin looked relieved and he stood, "If you need anything I'll keep the door unlocked. Just holler at me."

"You're lucky that this guy has me pinned," I said as he backed toward the bathroom. "Otherwise I would take advantage of you in the shower."

Austin just released a groan as he turned to go into the bathroom. The shower cut on and I was distracted briefly by the idea of a wet, naked man in such a close vicinity. And Austin was a man that looked absolutely delicious with nothing on and I knew it would only be improved by him being wet.

I wasn't going to look too hard at the fact that even after last night. I was going to chalk it up to the fact that anyone would be intrigued by a wet naked man.

Landon shifted on me, startling my mind out of the gutter. He stretched out a little bit, his head knocking lightly against my chin.

He made me see stars but once he settled I relaxed. There was something about the heaviness of a baby on my chest that made fatigue start to set in. It had been a long day. Couple that with the noise from the shower and the heavy breaths on the body on me and it was only a matter of time before I dozed off.

I couldn't say how long I slept, but I woke up enough to see the ceiling overhead. There was a creak of the house, the shower had been cut off. But at this point I felt like I could nod right back off.

"That's dangerous," Austin said. He was standing just inside the bedroom, a towel wrapped around his waist and his attention fully on me. Or, because of his words, maybe it was on Landon.

"Sorry," I said, putting a hand on the infant's back. He was still breathing heavily, still asleep. "I didn't think, he just kind of put me to sleep, too."

"Not what I meant," he said as he came closer to the bed. He stood over us, looking down at me. "Seeing you hold him like that," he began to explain before he seemed to think better of it. He shook his head, "Let me get dressed and I'll get him so you can get ready, too."

He went to a dresser and pulled out a fresh pair of boxers. He threw the towel onto his shoulder, giving me a nice view of his bare ass. I'll admit I watched him dress like a perv and when he looked back at me it didn't seem to bother him. "Are you trying to get it two nights in a row?"

"Depends if we can get lucky with him again," I said while waving a hand at the baby that was still on me. "Because if I get to see a show like that again, but in reverse there's a good chance I won't be able to say no."

He chuckled but the front door opening seemed to break off anything he might've said in response. He opened up the bedroom door to see who was home and it let in more noise than I expected.

"Austin!" a woman cried out and I wished I didn't have Landon on me so I could see what was going on. "Look at you! I haven't seen you since high school graduation!"

"Mrs. Stockton," Austin didn't mirror her excitement but he sounded just as pleased to see her. "I had no idea you and Mr. Stockton were coming to visit just after you got in."

I took that as a warning, but I was still stuck under Landon. Could I sit up without waking the baby? If I did wake him up was there a way that I could sneak away without being spotted? There wasn't a chance that they pulled up without noticing my car. What was I supposed to do?

Vaughn came into the bedroom, he came to the bed and opened his mouth to speak but stalled out. He eyed me and the position that Landon was on me. He didn't say a word as he carefully, gently scooped up the sleeping infant. He shushed him lightly, like I'd seen mom do, and transferred him to his own chest. "You probably have about ten minutes to clean yourself up if you want to meet them, otherwise you might want to hide."

I sat up, now that I could, watching as he gently juggled Landon into getting back to sleep. "What do you think I should do?"

Vaughn looked mildly surprised that I asked. "You're not bound to get any grief out of this," he said after a beat. "After all, it was all Gavin's idea. I wouldn't let him put the blame on you. If this is something he wants you to do and you're open to it, might as well rip off the bandaid."

He had a good point, "Give me a minute so I don't look like I just rolled out of bed." I stood and started towards the bathroom before I paused, "Does this mean I'm invited to dinner, too?"

He gave me a slight smirk, "If you weren't then consider this your invitation." He didn't say anything after that, he took the baby out into the living room and from the squeal of delight that echoed through the house Gavin's mother was happy to see him.

I ran a brush through my hair and after a little bit of struggling decided the best thing I could do with it was pull it into a ponytail. I cleaned my face, making sure there weren't any trails of drool hanging out around my chin. After that I realized I should put a little makeup on, I was about to meet Gavin's parents and they had no clue about him being in a relationship, much less the mess we were in.

I needed to make a good impression. I needed to make it look like he hadn't brought home the girl from the poor side of town. I needed to look like I had my shit together even though God knew I didn't.

I didn't bother with foundation, even though there was more than enough redness on my face. Instead, I just put a little eyeliner on and mascara. I stepped back from the mirror and eyed my reflection. Where was the improvement? I still looked like a mess. Maybe I should just hide and hope that I wouldn't catch too much crap for chickening out.

I took a deep breath, listening to the voices coming from the other room. It had to go better than it did with mom. Right? It would be awkward to meet his parents and be threatened with violence. Granted, I couldn't really think of anything that I did to the three of them that would warrant that.

Let's rip the bandaid off.

I tried to brush out the wrinkles in my shirt and had a brief moment where I considered changing. Austin walked out of the room in a shirt and shorts that weren't what I would call impression making. But he knew these people, he didn't have to work for anything.

Men had it way too easy.

I decided against changing and walked out of the bedroom, trying to appear as natural as possible. They had grouped up in the living room, a woman held a sleepy looking Landon and an unfamiliar man sat back in Austin's arm chair.

It was so easy to see that Gavin was a mixture of the two of them. The woman had similar coloring to him, but he got his height and curls from his father. The man looked like he might've even taken the same route to life that Gav did, his build was athletic though it looked like age had caught up to him.

Gavin sat beside his mother and Austin was on her other side, nervously watching Landon as he looked like he was on the verge of a meltdown. He hadn't slept long enough and that was something I felt, I could've gone with a longer nap. Vaughn was in the kitchen, from the sound of it preparing a bottle for the baby.

"Who's this?" The woman asked, seeing me. She gave me a pleasant open smile, making her look more like Gavin.

I looked at Gavin, waiting a beat to see if he would introduce me before I decided I should be forward. "I'm Nadia Evans," I offered her a hand, reaching over the table.

She readily took my hand and shook it, "Kelli Stockton. That over there is mine, Dave Stockton." She took the reins as she introduced her husband, who I offered my hand to. He gave me a reassuring nod.

I awkwardly, the situation left me to clarify who I was in the house outside of my name. I eyed Gavin helplessly, was he going to make me tell them? He didn't look like he had a grasp of what to do. "I'm the girlfriend," I offered her uneasily. I hoped that the fact that I didn't say whose girlfriend I was wouldn't be noticed.

"It's nice to meet you," Dave said from the chair. He didn't seem to notice, or he was just going to let it fly.

Kelli didn't seem like she would. She blinked at me then looked at each of the men in the living room. I wasn't standing close to any of them, so I couldn't make the claim by proxy. She looked down at Landon then to Austin only to come back to me. "Is he yours?" she asked, unsure.

I guess it was an easy assumption, even though Landon looked nothing like me he carried enough of Austin's facial structure and traits where it could just be assumed that he got all the good genes from his dad. Something I was secretly hoping was the case after meeting Lauren.

"Um," I put my hands behind my back as I struggled to think of a way to break it to her. "No. He's not mine."

"She's my girlfriend," Gavin spoke up finally. It appeared that he realized the position he put me in by not saying anything sooner.

Austin didn't say a word, he just raised an eyebrow at his friend. Was he going to object or correct him? I guess there wasn't anything really to correct, more like clarify.

"Oh!" Kelli's eyes lit up and she gave me a harder eyeing. "Is this a girlfriend, girlfriend?" she asked her son, "Or is this just a minute?"

Damn. Harsh. Gavin didn't even look fazed.

"She's my girlfriend," Vaughn said from behind me. He stepped around me and offered the bottle to Kelli. I felt relief for a brief second until he kept going.

"And his," he nodded towards Austin. Then he looked at Gavin expectantly.

Gavin looked from me to Vaughn. He seemed to realize this was what he wanted and he quickly added, "All three of ours."

Kelli looked confused for a beat, taking the bottle and offering it to Landon. The baby readily took it, holding onto it as his eyes began to droop. He wasn't concerned about the conversation at all.

"All three of you?" she asked.

"It was my idea," Gavin said with a bit of heat. It was almost like he expected her to object. "If anyone is here to blame it's me." She didn't sound accusing when she said it but I didn't know her. There might have been something there that Gav knew better than I did. Or maybe he belted that out because he was nervous, which was a vast change from when he met mom.

"It usually is, yeah," Vaughn agreed with a snort. I didn't know if he was answering Kelli or supporting what Gav said. From the smirk he had left me clueless.

Kelli sat back a little, still holding Landon close as she took each of us in. "This is more than I really needed to know," she said to her son. "I can't say I'm surprised that it was your idea," she looked down at Landon. She looked up at me, "I can't even begin to imagine why. The three of them together were a handful."

"There's a lot of questions that I don't know that I want the answers to," Dave said from the chair. He looked at Kelli, "Best thing, he's settled down. Worst thing, he hasn't. He'll have to deal with the consequences of what happens with his friends."

Kelli's mouth opened then closed, like she wasn't quite ready to give up whatever thought she was having. She shook her head then looked at the sleeping bundle in her arms. "Where are we going for dinner?"

***

"I didn't intend for it to go like that," Gavin began from beside me. "The way I saw it going was we went over to their place for dinner or a cook out or something." He was laying on his back, attention focused on the ceiling. "I would know what to say when they asked who you were and there wouldn't have been any of the strange or strained talk. Mom wouldn't have looked so damn judging."

"Landon kept her distracted," Austin pointed out, stretching on my other side. "At least she had a mellower reaction than Nadia's mother did." He shifted closer to me, nudging my shoulder with his, "Would your dad act like that, too?"

"Dad's patient where mom is hot tempered," I told him evenly. "I don't think he'd make threats but if mom followed through, he'd help her hide the bodies."

"I guess that's somewhat comforting," Austin said, surprising me with the amount of sarcasm he laid into it. He went quiet and when Gavin didn't make any attempt to add his opinion to the matter I thought maybe it was because they went to sleep. "I would like to think if I was in the same position as Mrs. Stockton that I'd take the same stance. You can't really control who your kids fall for. All you can do is hope for the best and be there if it falls apart."

"Hopefully," Gavin began in response, picking up my hand. He brought it to his lips, kissing my knuckles. "Hopefully, this isn't something that falls apart."

That made my chest ache. "As long as we're all working together I don't see why it would," I tried to soothe.

"Why are you still awake?" Vaughn asked as he came into the room. He set the baby monitor on the side table. "I would figure that at least two of you would be passed out by now. Unless you're not put off by tonight."

He paused and eyed the three of us, "If you're wanting sex I want a raincheck and I'm not willing to go sleep in that other bed. Save it for another day."

"We could've just been waiting for you," Gavin said as he urged me onto my side. He settled against my back, wrapping his arm around me. "I don't know that I want to have sex after the weird looks mom gave me all night." He winced, "I don't want to know what was going through her head. What else she might've been assuming."

"I hate to ask, but what are the chances that anything she could assume would be wrong?" Vaughn asked as he sat on the edge of the bed. He took off his shoes then paused, looking over a shoulder at us. "You have encouraged some … untraditional things. More than just this," he waved a hand at the three of us.

"You were worried about parents giving you shit," Gavin said to me. "Now I'm worried about disappointment and judgment that I'm gonna see on my mom's face every time I see her." He made a disgruntled noise, "This was probably the worst idea I've ever had. Why did I think this could go well?"

"What did you want to happen?" I asked curiously.

"I don't know," he huffed out.

"Don't worry about it," Vaughn said evenly. He stood and turned, eyeing the three of us. It was a position he faced often in the beginning.

Neither man on either side of me seemed to be willing to move. Gavin was molded to my back and Austin was lost in the screen of his phone. I sighed and elbowed the man behind me so I could shift onto my back. Once that was done I gave Vaughn a look and then opened my arms to him.

He hesitated, looking as if he weren't sure he should take that route. He pushed his slacks off and tugged the button down over his head, the undershirt following it into a pile of clothes on the floor. Before he moved onto the bed I made sure I tugged the sheet and blanket down, ignoring Gavin's protest. It earned me a smirk as Vaughn prowled up the bed and onto me. He didn't shift to my side like I half expected him to, he just pressed me into the bed.

"Was this what you had in mind?" he asked, his hips pressed into mine.

He didn't have an erection, but I could feel his interest going that way. I considered immediately shooting him down, after all we were just together last night. And while things might not ache now, I wasn't willing to find out if doing that multiple days in a row with the three of them would cause discomfort.

It was a shame. I reached behind him so I could grab a handful of his butt, earning a narrow eyed look from him. He had been bluffing though he seemed all the more willing to crawl onto me, to press against me. Why hesitate when I am being forward?

"I thought we were supposed to take breaks when it was all three of us," Gavin objected. "If you're gonna fuck her while the two of us are still in bed you can't expect us to not participate. Plus he said he wanted a raincheck."

"I'm not instigating anything," I said pointedly even though I didn't remove my hand from his butt. "Just if you're going to try to push me one way I'm going to push back."

Vaughn snorted as he looked down at me, his hands framing my face. I couldn't tell if he was intending to push it or if he was just enjoying the feel of my hand on his ass. It felt like I'd been in this position with Gavin before and on a whim, I decided to see if Vaughn came with the same quirks. I released the cheek I'd been holding and I slapped his ass hard enough for it to make a sound.

The expression went from cocky to shocked in a blink of an eye. Vaughn stared at me like he was at a loss for words. And I had a brief moment where I questioned what I'd done. Was he going to freak out on me? Was I going to have to deal with him blowing up because I'd crossed a line he wasn't prepared for? Was my curiosity going to get me into trouble?

"Did she just do what I think she did?" Austin asked, looking between us.

Vaughn still didn't say a word. He just blinked rapidly then glared at Gavin. "This is your doing," he accused.

"I didn't tell her to do that to you," Gavin shot back.

Austin broke out with a laugh, earning the attention of the other two men. "Was it you?" Vaughn growled in response. I couldn't tell if he was angry. The beginnings of an erection had definitely perked further up, he was getting hard. But that could have easily been written off due to the fact that our lower bodies were still pressed together.

Maybe this was a bruised ego? It wasn't just shock, I imagine if it had been just me and him I probably would get a different response. But because his friends witnessed his ass get slapped it was producing this. Would Gavin act the same way if I had done it to him?

"No," Austin said with a chuckle. "I just thought it was funny that the first person you would blame would be Gavin." He put his phone onto the bedside table. "What if this is just something *she* came up with on her own?" He grinned a little, "You can blame Gavin because we both know he's gotten into some things that are questionable. And some of the ideas he's had here are something that I wouldn't have come up with on my own." He looked at me, amusement still obvious. "But we forget that we didn't have the luxury of knowing Nadia back then or after high school. We don't know all of what she's into."

"I'm sorry," I hazard up at the man on me. "I didn't think that would bother you," I started feeling sheepish. "I figured since you were friends with him," I nodded towards Gavin who growled out an objection, "that you would be into similar things?"

"Naddy," Gavin hissed out. Then his anger fizzled out, he flopped backward with a huff, "I get blamed for all the weird things we do. It's not all me." He folded his arms over his chest and stuck out his bottom lip, "She encourages a lot, you're just not paying attention if you don't notice it."

I choked a little, "I get that I did this but I don't see how you can blame everything on me." I reached over to give Gavin a solid poke to his stomach. "You started this, it was your idea. You can't say I encouraged it."

Vaughn moved, shouldering his way between Gavin and I, "You started this, right? It wasn't Naddy's idea." He didn't cling to me like his friend did, he seemed content to just lay beside me. "It's probably just better to accept the fact that you're a bad influence."

18

Nadia

I had the house to myself. It wasn't something that happened often so I still found myself peeking through each of the rooms to make sure that none of the men I lived with were actually there. It made the house seem empty and I hadn't had this feeling since I moved in.

I needed something to do.

I decided the best way to keep myself busy was developing a list of things I could do to help Freddy while he was in the hospital. Working on getting our paychecks ready for him to sign, getting into contact with the utility and companies for both his house and the diner so he wouldn't come home without the necessities to name a few. Deidre had helped quite a bit, she knew more than I expected. It helped more than I imagined. I didn't want to be useless when it came to this situation anymore.

I know it was a sign of what she'd likely experienced in life. It was a sign that I only knew so much about her. If it wasn't something she readily offered the answers to, did I have a right to ask her about it? Would it bother her?

Overthinking about Deidre had me looking for anything else to entertain me. I was a horrible friend and I didn't need that in the forefront of my mind. That's when the unopened phone box that still sat on the bedside table got my attention. Gavin and Austin hadn't said a word about it when they left this morning with Landon in tow. Vaughn hadn't presented it to me, he hadn't made a big show of it. He just left it where he knew I'd see it.

I picked it up and tugged the plastic off of it, I opened the box and eyed the media that was shoved in with it. There was a pamphlet with all the details of the brand and instructions on how to use the phone, and underneath that was the actual phone. It was a powder coated black with the brand name down at the bottom and three camera lenses in the upper corner. I flipped it over to show a shiny black screen.

I pulled my phone out. The cracked screen looked up at me, with the battered case held together by tape. How was I supposed to feel about this gift? Were there strings attached? Should I ask or was it better to wait for him to approach me with said strings?

Looking between the two phones I decided to throw caution to the wind. I wanted the phone. While it might not necessarily be a need, I definitely wanted it. I pried the battered case off my phone, turned it off and after a little searching I had my SIM card out, in the new phone it went. I turned it on and the phone lit me up in the dark bedroom. There wasn't a crack in sight on the screen.

I hugged the device to my chest. I had gone so long without anything brand new that I forgot how good it felt to have something straight out of the box. At this point, I didn't care if this phone came with strings. I didn't care if he decided he wanted more from me.

I didn't know if I would regret this later. All that mattered was the feeling that sat in my chest now. And the fact that since he left it on the bedside table, he hadn't bragged about it once.

***

Dee sat across from me at the table, counting out what we had shoved in a deposit bag the last time we had been in the diner. I had Freddy's laptop open in front of me and I was busy adding up hours for each of us. From there I was putting the hours into the program he used to do payroll. The hard part was figuring out how it worked without screwing it up.

"I ran the report on the credit card machine and this is gonna take me a minute. I never really cared about how people tipped us until now. Now I wish everyone used cash," she sighed as she arranged signed receipts into piles. "This is one thing I don't know anything about."

"I can try to do a search for it," I said as I pulled my phone out. The bright clean screen mesmerized me for a moment before I unlocked it and found the search engine. This wasn't the first time I fished it out of my pocket, I'd already done a search to watch a video on how to use the payroll program. Now it just seemed like I was looking for any excuse to pull it out.

"You keep doing that you gonna end up dropping it," Dee said without looking up. "I think you already know for a fact that is how you do considering what your old phone looked like before you upgraded." She didn't wait for me to say anything. She put a stack of receipts beside me, "That's Jodie's. When you finish hers I'll give you mine and yours."

"It's only a matter of time," I agreed without looking up. "I'm gonna develop a habit and turn into Jodie," I tried to laugh it off as I continued through the search.

"Have you made a plan?" She asked after I started typing on the laptop again. "I've been getting my resume together and it's times like this that I realize I've not done a damn thing with my life."

I paused and looked at her, "I thought maybe we would get things taken care of and things would go back to normal." It sounded way too optimistic to my ears. I knew even after I said it that the likelihood of things going back to normal was slim, damn near impossible.

Dee reached across the table and pressed the screen of the laptop down low enough so she could look at me. She raised her eyebrow at me like she was waiting for me to do the math on my own. When I didn't do as she expected she frowned at me, "Girl. I know it would be so easy if Fred just came back to work. It would be too easy to just keep on like we've been keepin' on. But you and I both know that isn't going to."

"I'm not ready to let this place go," I admitted. "I'm not ready to go back to square one."

"Me either," she huffed out. "I've been looking at the job sites and stealing the want ads from my neighbor's paper for the last week. I can't sit and wait. I can't let my mama fit the bill while I'm out of work because my boss tried to die on me."

I winced and looked back down at my phone, still in my hand, "I gave Vaughn your number."

"Vaughn?" she echoed. "Is that one of your men?" At my nod she readjusted the screen of the laptop and sat back on the bench across from me. "What makes you think I want one of your men? Is he the curly haired one? I might consider it."

I chuckled uneasily, what was I supposed to say to that? I shook my head and took a breath, "That's Gavin you're thinking of. Vaughn is," I paused as I struggled to describe him. "He's usually well dressed, black hair," I shrugged a little. If I had a picture of him on my phone I would've shown her. But this phone was new so I didn't have any pictures of any of them. "Green eyes," I looked up at her as I continued to struggle. "Attractive but you still find yourself wanting to slap him."

I didn't specify where I wanted to slap him. I'd taken that opportunity last night and I was still waiting for the repercussions of that. Especially the conversation after it. The act itself had been satisfying though, especially the look on his face after.

Deidre cleared her throat and leaned forward so she could rest her chin in her hand. "That the number that's been calling me? Why are you giving my number to one of your men?"

"He's got connections that I can't even fathom," I admitted. I put the phone onto the table and began to twist my fingers together. "I asked him to do me a favor by helping you find a job to replace this one."

"I don't take handouts," Dee said with a little bit of heat. She sat back and returned her attention to the receipts. "I can do that all on my own. I've done it all by myself all this time."

"It's not a handout," I tried to clarify. "I'd say it's more along the lines of me returning the favor."

She frowned at me, "What favor do you owe me?"

"You made it incredibly easy for me when I first started this job," I pointed out, ticking off my list on my fingers. "Anytime I screwed up you were there to help me. When I came to you with my current situation, you showed concern without judging me." I dropped my hands into my lap, not sure what else I could say. "It's not a handout," I repeated weakly.

Her lips pursed and she looked down, "If he has any good leads on jobs I'll see what he has to say."

I don't know why I took that as 'call him now.' But I picked up my phone and found his number, I hit the icon and the next icon for it to go to the speaker phone. I knew if she hadn't answered the phone when he reached out to her then there was a good opportunity that she wouldn't now that she knew what it was about.

"I didn't mean for you to call him now, girl," Dee snapped, but she didn't take my phone.

I shrugged as Vaughn answered after the first ring. "Is the house on fire?" he asked, sounding dubious. Understandable considering that I rarely called him.

"No," I cleared my throat. "You're not busy, are you?'

"I'm showing Kelli and Dave a house," he said evenly. "Austin and Gavin are here with the baby, too. I wouldn't really call this entertaining but if you want to come along and look at houses you're more than welcome to join us."

"I'm doing a little work at the diner for Freddy. I was hoping you had gotten into contact with Deidre, like I asked." I knew he hadn't, even though Dee had admitted otherwise.

"I've reached out a few times, but she hasn't answered my calls," he said. I couldn't explain the relief I felt that he didn't lie. "I just need to get a few things from her. I have a guy that needs a bookkeeper, but that's going to need someone that has experience. I couldn't put her in there without her knowing if she could handle it."

"I can't do bookkeeping," Dee responded. "What we're doing now is figuring things out as we go. I've not got any formal training and it wouldn't be a good idea to put me into something like that." She made a noise and covered her face with her hands, "I ain't done anything that required education. I got my high school diploma, but I haven't done anything else."

Vaughn was quiet for a beat. I guess he wasn't expecting that I would have him on speaker phone. I would have to apologize later. "Just a high school diploma isn't a bad thing. I can work with that. Do you know how to use a computer? I mean, excel and things like that?"

"I know how to do internet searches, spend too much money on Amazon, and write emails," Dee answered after making a face. "It usually doesn't take me long to get things figured out."

"How do you feel about working as a receptionist? It would be more along the lines of business casual, but I think we could get you trained pretty quickly. You would have to answer phones, take messages, keep track of realtor schedules, and show clients to the office of the realtor they had a meeting with. Things like that."

"You said receptionist?" Dee asked. "That sounds like a secretary to me."

"You're right," he said easily. But he didn't linger on the idea long. "We do have coffee that we keep fresh in the front room, that would be something you would be responsible for. That is if this was a job you were interested in."

She peaked at me through her fingers then her shoulders slumped, "You have my attention. I think this is something I would have to get back to you on."

"I'll text you my email so you can forward your resume to me and we can discuss pay and benefits, as well as hours," Vaughn's tone was all business. It was almost like I was listening to a different person for this conversation. "If this isn't something that's going to work for you let me know. Naddy said to look for positions that gave you nights off. I'm assuming that's something that I should stick to?"

"Yeah," she agreed. "I have two kids. I don't want to take advantage of you even though you just had the audacity to call my friend Naddy. Girl, don't tell me these men don't appreciate how good a name you got. Nadia is a beautiful name, boy."

I don't know why that surprised me. Vaughn let out a guffaw, clearly surprised, too. With a chuckle, he answered her. "It's a childhood nickname that I haven't been able to let go of. I promise, I fully appreciate Nadia's name."

"Good," Dee sniffed. "I look forward to speaking with you privately and I appreciate your willingness to help your girlfriend's friend."

"I look forward to working with you," he said. "Nadia," he addressed me, saying my name with a purpose. "Call me when you two are finished up. I think we're going to meet up for dinner again tonight and I know that I would appreciate your company."

"I will," I said before ending the call. I could feel the heat rushing to my face and I could feel Deidre's scrutiny. "Thanks for at least entertaining that for me."

"Girl if the money is there I'll do more than entertain it for you," she nodded towards the table top that was between us. "But we need to get this finished so you can have a date night with your boys. He gets me a good job and I'll overlook that God awful name he called you."

19

Gavin

I stayed in bed with Naddy after Austin got up and got Landon breakfast. I didn't bother to help because I knew the other man wouldn't be staying. He got a call from his attorney and while he didn't go into the details, I heard most of it on the way to meet Vaughn and my parents at a house. They had found Lauren. I figured this meeting would be the deciding factor on what would happen with Landon.

He didn't say what he wanted to do. I could guess. But I wasn't going to call out my boy playing mommy. After having Naddy's mom call me out for not helping I knew it would be counterproductive.

It made me feel like a shitty friend. They already called me the bad influence and I wasn't so sure they were wrong. I always thought my ideas were great. Look at where they led us. Could Vaughn or Austin really complain?

I shifted onto my side, eyeing Naddy where she slept. What were Vaughn's chances with this if it hadn't been for me? I had my doubts that she would've given me a chance if it weren't for Austin. He was really the bad influence here.

Her lashes fanned out against her cheeks, shifting slightly as she slept. She wasn't snoring like usual, giving me a clue that it probably was long before she would wake up. She had one arm twisted up and over her head, while the other flailed out to one side like she was aware there were people missing from the bed.

I leaned into her. Taking in her scent and enjoying the feel of her soft body against mine. This was my favorite way to wake up. There wasn't any snark coming at me, no grumpy noises, just her deep breaths and her warm body.

I brushed my fingers against her cheek, being careful to be as light as possible. I couldn't lay here without touching her. Her lashes fluttered and she stretched, arching up so the sheet that was bunched around her breasts. It made me wish she wasn't wearing the shirt she was sleeping in.

She squinted at me before reaching up to curl her fingers through my hair. She snagged a knot tugging my hair gently before the strands gave way. I melted against her, nuzzling her cheek before I followed it down to her ear. She hummed and turned to me, her other arm curling around my side. She rubbed my back gently even as she kept combing her fingers through my hair.

I closed my eyes and just let her pet me. I didn't resist the temptation of nibbling at her ear. When her head tilted, I followed the motion, kissing my way down her throat. I didn't intend to do this, I wasn't going for this but if she wasn't going to stop me I wouldn't object to morning sex.

I tugged the collar of her shirt down so I could get access to more skin. She made a noise, something low in her throat. It sounded encouraging so I reached down to find her hip and I followed it down until I got to her knee. I hooked my fingers under it and pulled her leg up over my hip. I rolled my hips against her, giving her a good feel of just what she did to me.

I expected her to pull away, for her to stop me because that was the way it had been the last few times I tried to get fresh. There was always something that interrupted the fun. Always something that gave her a reason to pull away.

This time, she didn't seem to be in any hurry to pull away. It seemed like reason enough to get myself a handful. I slipped my hand into her shirt and cupped her bare breast, the fact that it took no effort to get her nipple into a stiffened peak was promising. I tracked my way back upward, hungry for a kiss. I did it without thinking but I got a solid taste of stale morning breath.

When Naddy tugged away from me I knew mine was just as bad. She stuck her tongue out, "Ugh."

"Got caught up in the moment," I admitted as I grimaced. I eyed her, trying to decide if I could forge forward again and avoid kissing her. There was no reason for us to stop now, was there? I rocked up so I was between her thighs better and I could feel the heat of her even through my boxers. "It put you off that bad?"

"Not put off," she said as she drifted away just a little. "But it's enough to make me want to brush my teeth." She sat up and twisted to eye me, "You gonna get up and brush yours, too?"

"If I do, are we going to end back up in bed?" I asked, hopeful.

She shook her head with a slight eyeroll and went for the bottom of the bed, giving me a view of her ass. Her panties covered her cheeks pretty well because this girl wasn't one for wearing sexy lingerie. The little blue flowers didn't detract from the obvious dampness I could see between her thighs. Was that a no? The view she afforded me suggested something else.

That got me out of bed and had me following her into the bathroom. Naddy didn't look bothered, she went straight into brushing her teeth. This bathroom didn't have the same kind of counter that the bathroom in Vaughn's apartment did. While there was a double sink, the counter was set a little lower and if I was gonna try anything I wouldn't be able to fuck her against the counter.

There was no reliving fucking her in front of the mirror here and that was a crying ass shame.

I gave the shower a hard look over as I scrubbed my own teeth with my toothbrush. Could I make it work in the tub? Standing things would be a little precarious and for it to even work I would have to pick her up. That wasn't too much of an issue, but I knew from experience that she had a habit of making my knees weak.

"What are you doing?" she asked.

"Trying to decide if I want to take the risk of breaking our necks just so I could fuck you in the shower," I told her. I glanced at her to gage her reaction.

Her brows were together as she eyed the bathtub in the little alcove that was surrounded by brown tiles that were older than the both of us. She looked up at me with a frown, like she was trying to decide if the mechanics were possible. "I feel like if we were going to have sex in the shower we should've taken advantage of the bathroom in Vaughn's apartment when we had the chance."

I sighed and nodded, "We'll have to wait until we get mom and dad out of there before we can take advantage of that."

"I guess that means we just have to be old fashion and fuck in a bed," she said as she turned to go back into the bedroom. "Unless you changed your mind?"

I grinned and I spat the suds from my mouth. I gave my mouth a quick rinse and made quick work with washing my face. I went to follow her as I considered just what I wanted to do to the woman in front of me. I narrowed my eyes, "I didn't change my mind." I rubbed my jaw as I eyed her. "I'm just trying to decide how I'm gonna get back at you for exposing me to Austin and Vaughn."

Naddy had sat on the bed and she looked a little surprised when I said that. "I exposed you?"

"When you slapped Vaughn's butt," I reminded her. "And they knew immediately where you got that from."

"That's your reputation that you've built for yourself," she said slowly like it was something she expected me to know. "I slapped Vaughn's ass because it felt like he was trying to one up me and I felt like it would give me the upper hand." She paused then shrugged, "And I thought maybe he might be into the same stuff you are."

I frowned down at her, "What about Vaughn says adventurous? Dude is all about caution and taking well thought out risks." I drug my hands through my hair only to tug them down to rub my face, "I don't want them to know some of the specifics as to what I'm into. I don't want to answer questions or get weird looks from them. Anything that is," I paused as I considered how to say it. I drummed my fingers against my chin before deciding the best route was to be direct, "Anything that isn't normal or traditional, shit you might consider weird but are still down to do to me are things I want to remain between us."

Naddy looked at me, "I didn't mean for it to cause a problem, Gavin." Her gaze dropped and her expression showed remorse, "I'm sorry."

It came out of her so easily. There wasn't anything demeaning in her voice, she didn't call me names or roll her eyes at me. There was nothing that suggested that she didn't mean her words.

I edged closer to her, my chest felt tight and I couldn't find words. I dropped down to my knees and easily pressed myself between hers. I wrapped my arms around her waist and just leaned my cheek against her thighs. Her fingers were in my hair again, I closed my eyes and just rested there.

I could remember all the times where I'd seen Austin ready to drop the L word on the girl petting me. I could remember the feeling I got when I found out she knew and reciprocated the feeling to him. The only thing that kept the word from falling out of my mouth now was that I had my mouth pressed against her bare thigh. My teeth sank into the skin when it was almost too much to hold in.

Naddy squealed and tried to shove my head off my lap. "Gavin!" she barked my name out when I didn't let her go. She fell backwards onto the bed and made another attempt at prying me off, but failed.

That's when I decided to take advantage of the situation. I let go of her thigh only to shove both of them onto my shoulder. I pressed my lips against the crotch of her panties, they weren't as damp as I would hope they would be. But that was something I could easily change. I just arched a brow at her to see if she was still wanting to push me away.

"If you bite me again or even think about biting me there," she began, her tone threatening, "I will knock your teeth out."

I considered it, digging my teeth into the fabric. I gave it a slight tug, pulling the fabric away from her skin. I waited to see if she was going to stop me after that, but she didn't move. She'd propped herself up on her elbows so she could watch me and glare at me like she was daring me to bite her again.

I was tempted, but I didn't want to see if she'd legitimately attempt to knock out my teeth. I could see the anticipation on her face though. She wanted me to go further. She wanted me to bury my face between her legs. Lucky for her that's what I intended to do.

I tugged her panties down her thighs just enough to get them out of the way. My eyes connected with hers and I pointedly stuck my tongue out at her. Then I swept it out along her outer lips, tracing it slowly. She took a breath and watched as I pressed my tongue between her lips, using the same teasing manner until I felt the top of her slit.

At first, I didn't bother to spread her. I wasn't focusing so much on the act of tonguing her sex. I was focused more on her expression, the way anticipation and hunger flitted over her face. "Pull your shirt up," I demanded before I got a real mouth full of her.

"Quit teasing me," she shot back, not bothering to do what I asked.

"Gimme what I want and I'll give you what you want."

She looked like she wanted to argue but she flopped backwards, wiggling as she tugged her shirt up and over her head. She tossed it aside then sat up a little back on her elbows. It gave me the perfect view of her tits.

In response, I spread her lower lips and flattened my tongue so I could brush it against the length of her opening. I paused at her clit, flicking it against the little bundle of nerves. Her thighs tightened minutely on my shoulders and I shifted to make sure she wouldn't be able to hinder me as I pressed two fingers into her.

Her hips rocked up and she mewled. When I began to thrust my fingers in and out of her, she flopped backward onto the bed. I didn't obscure my view of her breasts too much, but at that point I didn't really care. I was too caught up in the act. I twisted so that I could hook my fingers upward and with a bit of searching I found the raised bit of skin inside her. I knew I hit the right spot as her hips bucked upward against my face and hand.

A hand tangled in my hair and tugged at the strands just as my lips closed around her clit. I moaned, unable to resist the slight burn. Her back arched up and she keened in response, letting me know that the noise I made affected her. Encouraged I didn't hold back as I worked her into a fervor.

Her legs flexed on my shoulders, struggling to close only to flail out as she got closer to a completion. I could feel it, just how close she was. Her inner muscles clenched and spasmed around my fingers. If I hadn't been teasing that spot in her while I sucked on her clit it would be likely that this wouldn't be enough.

I found just enough time to process a thought to be grateful to Vaughn for showing me this little bit of her just as Naddy cried out. She bucked against my face then stiffened, arching her hips off the bed as she flooded my mouth. There was a salty sweetness to the taste of her that had me swiping my tongue along her dripping cunt so I could savor the flavor. She twitched each time, squeezing my fingers hard until I had to pull them out.

"Trying to crush my knuckles?' I asked her as I licked my fingers clean.

"Trying to get you to give me a little relief," she murmured.

"Was it too much?" I asked as I sat back on my heels, eyeing her open thighs. Her chest still heaved with breath and it caught my eye. "If I'm pressing too hard on something you gotta say."

She hummed and it didn't sound pained. Instead it sounded drunk, "Was just a little sensitive." Naddy looked down at me, gaze glazed but hungry. "You're not done. Just give me two seconds." She pushed herself up into a seated position then reached for me.

I stood and started to lean down to kiss her, but her hands found the waistband of my boxers. She tugged me forward and I followed until my knees hit the bed. She had my cock out and her lips wrapped around the head of me before I could even tangle my hands into her hair. I tilted my head back and just reveled in the feel of her hot mouth. She used her teeth to skim over my skin, using her tongue to soothe my skin at the same time. I wasn't afraid of her taking a bite out of me, even after all the times I dug my teeth into her. She was better than me.

It was when I hit the back of her throat that I knew I wouldn't be able to fuck her mouth long if I wanted to do anything else. I tugged on her hair, getting a moan that I echoed because it felt so good. "You keep doing that," I gritted out. "And you'll have me coming down your throat. It'll take me a little while to get up and running again."

She released me, pulling my cock out of her mouth and gave me a look that I could've swore left a mark. "Where do you want to come?" she asked.

I like to think it's not often that I get struck silent, but she got me there. I pushed her back on the bed and I was ready to climb on it before I pulled up short. I needed to get a condom. I needed to use protection. But the last time we were together she had said she wanted to go without, she wanted to throw caution to the wind.

Now was the perfect opportunity to do that.

Now was the perfect opportunity to see what had Austin so ready to drop out the L word. Why was I hesitating? It wasn't that I was afraid of expressing feelings I had to her, it was the fear of what she would say. I knew Nadia cared about me, but I doubted what she felt involved the L word.

"Come here," she said.

I think she could see me struggling with what I wanted. She tugged me onto the bed, crawling backward until we were near the middle. My boxers were down around my ass while she was naked, a quick tug of her panties had them off but I couldn't do the same thing with my own underwear. If I took them off it felt like it made the decision for me. It felt like it left me too vulnerable.

I think she saw it, because she laid back and just looked at me like she was waiting for me to decide. There was no rush. The fact that she was patient enough to wait for me just added to my indecision.

She reached up and cupped my face, "What's wrong?"

"This is a bad idea," I said as I rested back on my heels between her thighs. I could see every bit of her that I wanted to touch, that I wanted to kiss and taste. Places that I'd like nothing more than to bury myself into.

"Sex is a bad idea?" She asked, looking mildly surprised. "Why is it a bad idea?"

"Unprotected sex is a bad idea," I clarified.

Naddy's lower lip poked out. "I just had my period before Landon got here and got stuck," she began evenly. "If there's a safe time to have unprotected sex its now, even with me being on birth control." Then she sighed, almost visibly letting go of her argument. "But if you would rather be careful, Gavin. That's fine. I don't want to make you do anything you don't want to do."

She thought I was being cautious out of concern for an accident happening. She didn't have any idea what I was really afraid of. I didn't know if I should brave it or just tell her the truth. I really didn't want to reach for a condom in the bedside table.

I leaned down against her, pressing the length of me against her opening. I could feel the dampness of her sex against mine and I knew there was no chance that I could resist sliding into her bare. *I am so fucking stupid when it comes to this girl.*

I was careful to keep my weight on my knees and elbows, but for the most part I pressed her into the bed. I kissed her, trying to put everything I felt into it. Hoping that nothing stupid would come out of my mouth when this was all said in done. Nadia sighed against me, wrapping her arms around my waist and her legs around my hips. She figured out what I decided but she didn't make any attempt to push me into her.

She was giving me control.

All it would take would be a slight adjustment of my hips, a careful roll and the head of my cock would slide down her slit until it found her opening. Just a little shift in positioning to make sure I had my aim right. I could feel her muscles flexing, like she needed me in her. Like she couldn't wait for me to take that leap.

I eased my way in, even when every nerve ending screamed for me to just thrust my way home. Every cell wanted me to pump every ounce into her, to fill her like it would give me some sort of claim on her. It wouldn't and that knowledge was probably what kept me from going on instinct.

Nadia's hips bucked forward, impatience wearing on her just enough to cause my cock to slip forward further. That control wore thin, the heat of her was something I was used to, the tight grip around my cock something I enjoyed regularly. But without the thin barrier everything seemed to be hyper focused.

"Don't rush me," I croaked against her hips.

Her nails dug into my back but she didn't move against me again. Her legs tightened around me and she made an impatient noise. I couldn't, I couldn't let this go. I wanted to draw it out as long as possible. But when I became fully seated in her, her tightness fully wrapped around my dick I figured this was as close to heaven as I was going to get.

I started at a slow pace, thrusting shallowly. When her teeth dug into my lip I knew it wasn't enough, she wasn't going to be able to get anything out of this if I didn't stop trying to take my time. The beauty of this was Nadia would want more, she would still want me.

Even if I did something stupid like admitting how I felt.

I tugged my lip from between her teeth and buried my face against her neck. I quickened my pace and she moaned in approval as I did. The longer I thrust into her the harder her nails dug into my back. I was so intent on just being in her that I had lost track of time, from the way she throbbed around me it was almost as if she were close.

I rolled my hips and she gasped into my ear. It wouldn't take much to get her erupting around me but I knew if I did that I wouldn't be lasting much longer. I couldn't ignore the building pressure, the tightening in my balls that had my driving harder into her.

Her hands moved up my back, shifting to cling to my shoulders. Nails bit right back into my skin. I didn't let up, putting more force behind my hips. She arched against me, her breasts pressing into my chest. I almost regretted not being able to put my face between them.

There was always another time.

Her breath hitched and she squeezed me tightly. I couldn't resist it, I grunted as it tugged me. I couldn't manage to keep it together. I erupted before I could make sure she came first. It was sudden, almost a shock I wasn't prepared for.

I stiffened, unable to hold back the groan that ripped through me. Every effort I made to stay above her was gone in favor of wrapping my arms around her and clinging to her as I emptied myself out. I couldn't tell if she had come, too.

I drowned in the feeling, blind and drunk. The only thing I was aware of was the fingers combing through my hair. I was still buried ball deep in her and she held onto me tightly. I couldn't tell anything outside the burning residue of the orgasm that still rocked through my brain.

"I love you," came out of me in a breath. At first I didn't realize I said it until I felt the brush of fingers against the back of my neck. I was so dazed I thought it might've been a dream.

"I know," she said in a soft tone. "I know."

She left me waiting. My heart in my throat. Fear of rejection leaving me quiet. Nadia wasn't going to say it back.

My stomach twisted up and I leaned on her, clenching my eyes closed and wishing I wasn't so fucking dumb. There wasn't any going back from this. There wasn't any chance of making it better.

Her lips touched my cheek. They brushed their way to my ear. "I love you, too," it sounded small and unsure. But she still said it.

20

Nadia

Freddy being in a regular patient room made things easier. I could bring him things, like a couple of fresh changes of underwear and a clean shirt. Even if he wasn't able to wear them because he wasn't able to go to the bathroom. I was happy to see a few bouquets of flowers in his room, relief that other people cared about his wellbeing made me feel a little better.

There was even a teddy bear with a heart that said 'Get Well Soon.' It seemed odd and out of place, like it was meant for a child. Maybe it was bought by one. Did he have kids? When I walked into the room there was no one else there.

He was sleeping, tucked in securely with wires and tubes still everywhere. There was a heart monitor beeping quietly beside the bed. It had a steady tempo that was a relief. I sat down in the plastic lined chair, not sure what to do. Should I wait for him to wake up? Or was it better to just come back?

Gavin was on the first floor of the hospital, poking around the gift shop. I could probably get something practical and useful or we could go to the cafeteria. I peeked into the bathroom, hoping to see he had toiletries. I hadn't thought about getting him soap or anything. Was he able to brush his teeth? I'd never had to stay in the hospital so I had no idea how things like this worked.

I stepped out of the bathroom, debating on whether or not I should message the man waiting down stairs to pick up a toothbrush for me. Maybe I could ask one of the nurses outside? I didn't want to bother them because I knew they had to be busy. I pulled out my phone and fidgeted with the lock screen, trying to figure out what I should do.

"What're you doing?" Freddy asked, sounding tired.

It came out of nowhere, it felt like I jumped a mile into the air. I had my phone hit the floor with a deafening crack. "Shit! Fred!" I huffed and bent down to pick up my phone. "I was checking to make sure you had everything you needed. Do you need a toothbrush?" I asked as I picked up my phone, grimacing as I turned it over to see the damage.

There wasn't a crack on the screen but it looked like there was a scuff mark on the corner. My luck never worked out like this. I stood up and shoved my phone into my pocket, deciding if it weren't in my hand I couldn't drop it again. "How are you?"

"I'm in the hospital," he said as he squinted at me. "I had a heart attack. Things are shit." He looked away and adjusted the blanket around himself. "They have me on a special diet and everything tastes bland as hell," he coughed a little. "They want me to quit smoking and I haven't seen the list of shit they want me to give up but I'm sure it's pretty fucking long."

"I've been telling you to quit smoking for months," I pointed out as I went back to the chair. "I brought you some things from home. Clean underwear and some shirts. You didn't have any pajamas otherwise I would've brought that, too. I didn't think about bathroom stuff. Do you need me to go down to the store and get you a toothbrush and a razor?"

Fred squinted at me again. "I ain't worried about growing a beard. They got me a toothbrush that probably cost me fifty bucks." He rubbed his hand over his face. "What are you doing here, Nadia?"

"Checking on you," I said like it should've been obvious.

He grunted, "You need to find yourself a new job. Give me a piece of paper, I'll write you a recommendation." He paused to think about it, "I'm gonna tell them that you're a bossy ass."

"Why are you telling me to find a new job?" I asked, struck. "You're going to get better and after a little while you'll open the diner backup. You're going to need waitresses for that."

"I had one of the doctors tell me I'm probably going to be out of work for three months, if not longer depending how I heal and whether or not I do what they recommend," he said as he waved a hand dismissively. "It's insane to wait for me to get better. File for unemployment and get another job. Be smart, Nadia."

"Why wouldn't you do what they recommend?" I shot back at him. "Do you not want to get better?"

"I do what the hell I want to do," he snapped back. The beeping of the heart monitor spiked for a moment. He took a breath, "After I'm released I'm probably gonna have to sell the diner. There's no reason for you to stick around hoping I get better."

I quieted. I wanted to argue with him, but I could see a stubborn streak in him that I had seen on a number of occasions. But I wasn't prepared for it, I wasn't prepared for him to give up. What was I supposed to do? I looked down at my shoes. "Please don't put on a letter of recommendation that I'm a bossy ass."

"It was a joke," he said after a beat. He released a noise, "Kid, stop worrying about me. I've run the diner on my own for longer than I can remember. I have money put away and I'm sure I can sell the building for a decent amount." His eyes closed, "Did you get payroll figured out?"

"Yeah. We got the diner and your house clean," I reported. It got his attention and he looked at me. "We counted out and evened out the till. We have the bank deposit ready, but I wanted to make sure you were okay with it before I took it to the bank. We didn't fill out the checks because," I paused as I struggled to come up with a reason. "I guess I wanted to give you the opportunity to check it so you didn't have to worry we were going to screw you over."

"Just fill them out for me," he said without blinking. "I'll sign them so you and Dee and the little girl can get on with your lives."

I opened my mouth to argue, but he loosely folded his arms over his chest. Everything about the man in the hospital bed said that he was done with the conversation. It hurt, but I couldn't push to get more out of him. He looked fragile, though I knew it was the situation that created the image. The tubes, the heart monitor. It sent home the image that he wasn't unbreakable.

"I'll finish up the checks," I began. "We didn't rob you blind." I took a deep breath and turned to the door. "If you need anything you have my number."

I didn't wait for him to respond. I walked out of his room and found my way to the bank of elevators. I couldn't define the feeling that sat in my gut as I wandered through the hospital's lower floor. I was looking for Gavin, but I wasn't at the same time. Going from hallway to hallway aimlessly fed the growing numbness inside me. I wasn't prepared for the finality Fred had with how to move forward after having a heart attack.

I wasn't thinking as I walked, I didn't really see anything. I just moved forward. That was the only option, wasn't it? Moving forward. I was a little surprised when I ran into Gavin. Somehow I ended up by the cafeteria, where he had apparently decided to hang out while he waited for me.

"Are you okay?" he asked, eyeing me in a way I wasn't really prepared for.

This was what I got for telling him I loved him. He was more attentive than I would ever expect him to be. Usually he was all the sexual innuendo and that was something that I equated to be Gavin. I didn't know how to deal with him on a level like this. He took my hand as he drew close enough and while he was someone that wasn't afraid to touch me this felt different. But I couldn't think of any time where he pointedly went for my hand with the intention of just holding it.

I let him because this seemed like a fragile new place that I had moved us into by acknowledging his feelings. I didn't want to hurt him because I wasn't all there. I swallowed and let him tangle his fingers with mine. "Yeah," I lied. "But I need to get back to the diner. You don't mind driving my car do you?"

"Sure," he gave me his usual easy going smile. "I'm gonna mess up your seat though, because you are way too short for me to be able to drive your car without sliding it back."

I didn't protest as I led the way to the parking lot. I wasn't really paying attention to the route I took, I just followed the tug of his hand. I gave him my keys when I saw the beater and I let him put me in the passenger seat.

As soon as I sat down I had my phone in my hand, I started a text thread with Deidre. I let her know everything, how Fred looked and what he said. How he mentioned selling the diner. I unloaded everything onto her. And it took a minute for me to realize that I dumped a little too much because after the third wall of text Dee called.

"You gotta calm down," she said after I answered the call.

"I am calm," I argued.

"No, no you're not. You might feel like you're not having a meltdown, but if you look at the texts you just sent me. Girl," she released a breath. "People react to things, like heart attacks, differently. There's not a lot you can do if he wants to shut down the diner and keep it closed. All we can do is take care of ourselves while he recovers. Getting another job is taking care of yourself." She paused for a moment, "I emailed your boyfriend my resume and he has me starting next week."

"Did he tell you what you'd be starting at?" I asked, hoping that he wouldn't force her to take a pay cut.

"More than he should considering that I have no idea what I'll be doing and they're gonna have to train me like I haven't been working since I was sixteen," she said in a quick puff of breath. "I didn't mean to distract you," she began again. "I'm just trying to get you to see that he's got to cope with what he has going on. And his method of coping isn't going to help your situation at all. You need to take care of yourself. You gotta eat and you got bills to pay." She was starting to sound worried, "You can worry about Fred. You can keep track of him when he's being a crabby asshole all you want. But you've got to take care of you, too. Don't make me message this man that just gave me a job. If he's not paying attention I will cut him loose for you."

"It just seems like it's one more thing falling apart," I admitted, my voice cracking slightly. "First the book store, now Fred in the hospital. What's next?"

"Don't you do that," she snapped at me. "Don't you put yourself into that funk. Things happen and sometimes it's more than one thing, sometimes it's several in a row. But you know what you got?" She asked, but then she didn't wait for me to answer. "You got three good things waiting for you at home. Three things that are there to lift you up and keep you grounded."

My chin quivered against my will and I struggled against the sudden burn in my throat. I closed my eyes because I really didn't need Gavin to see my crying. I bit my lip, trying to think of what I could say that would keep me together. I cleared my throat, "Do you mind taking the checks up there for him to sign?"

"I'll be more than happy to get my check first, yes," she said easily. "I need to go shopping for something that I can wear to work. Because I have to dress professionally. I have to make an impression." She paused for a beat, "I'll get Jodie her check, too. You can meet up with me for yours. I won't spend your money and make you get lunch with me. But I could use your company and opinion. Okay?"

"Okay," I replied and I ended the call. When I put the phone down in my lap Gavin reached over for my hand. He tangled our fingers together and rested our hands on the gearshift.

He didn't say a word. Just held my hand and took me to work. Today is the last day I would do anything that I could call work for the diner.

***

We were making a trend of going out to dinner. I think this had to be the third or fourth time we had gone out since Gavin's parents had come into town. I had no idea who was paying for all of them and I felt guilty about the fact that I hadn't made any offer to pay for at least one meal.

I just didn't have the money for it.

We sat around a large table that accommodated six people, there was just enough room for Landon's highchair positioned between Kelli and Austin. Near empty plates were spread over the table top and for the most part dinner had been pleasant. I felt awkward and while Kelli wasn't necessarily sending disapproving vibes my way, there was definitely something she didn't like about our situation.

"So," she began as she offered the baby a french fry. "What happens when you have a baby? How do you figure out who it belongs to?"

There was a hand on my thigh, Gavin still being especially touchy but he wasn't pushing the line of inappropriate. He clenched his hand into a fist, clearly bothered by Kelli's question. "Why does it matter?" he asked, a little bit of bite behind his words. "We're making things work with Landon and the only person he belongs to, really, is Austin. Why would another kid change the dynamic?"

"I think we're assuming too much," Vaughn spoke up from across from me. He was sitting between Dave and Gavin, he didn't look nearly as bothered as the man that sat between us. He had a placid look on his face as he addressed his best friend's mother. "Not to make decisions for Nadia," he said, sparing me only a glance. "But this isn't a discussion we've even had. There's a very good chance that she's not even interested in having kids. Either way, it's a conversation that we should have on our own."

"I want grandchildren," Kelli said, though it sounded more like a demand.

"You have two other children," Gavin pointed out beside me. "Let Rob or Ted give you grandkids." He put his elbows up on the table and covered his face for a beat before he finally dropped his hands to glare at his mother. "Why even bring that up? You just met her. Is 'when am I gonna get a grandbaby' really something you want to put on a new relationship?"

"I'm asking because you chose to introduce her to me," Kelli said, there was something false about the cheerfulness in her tone. It may have had something to do with the fact that she had Landon's full attention. "I didn't get the luxury to meet any of the women I knew you went through while you were playing. The last girlfriend of yours I met was in high school. I knew then she wasn't going to stick around for longer than the two weeks you had until graduation." She sat back in her chair and looked at me. There wasn't anything cold about her expression. It was just clear she didn't get it. "How long should I give this?"

"Longer without you questioning it," Vaughn broke in before Gavin could. "Longer if there's not the added pressure from you or your judgment."

"Vaughn," Dave objected from beside him. Apparently, he didn't like the other man's tone. "I get it. But let her say her peace. Let her get her concerns out of the way now otherwise this is what we're looking at for the unforeseen future."

"Are you on their side?" Kelli asked, voice raised like she couldn't believe her husband.

"I see the reasoning behind it," he said evenly. "I think you forgot how we got together." He leaned closer to her, his voice lowering as he said something that he didn't want the rest of us to hear. Kelli's expression showed that he was reminding her of something that might not have matched what facade she was wearing. He tilted his head back, nodding it towards their son. "You're assuming that this is a passing fancy. But you're not watching him. You're thinking back to all the girls that would pass through the house for gatherings." Dave shook his head, "It hasn't even been a week and you've passed judgment."

"I already told you it was my fault," Gavin said as he threw his arm over the back of my chair. He leaned into me. "All of this was my idea," he gestured around the table. "From what we're doing to you knowing about it." He shrugged a little bit, jostling me. "I could've saved myself the headache by not saying a word to you. I could've kept her a secret and the only time there would have been any reason for you to meet her was if," he met my gaze, "if something like that were to happen."

Kelli looked at her son. She seemed consumed by his words until her gaze moved to me. Her brows drew together, she nodded slowly. "I'll let it go. This," her eyes bounced between Gavin and I, "this isn't something I really get to have an opinion on, is it? It doesn't matter what I say, does it?"

"Your concern is appreciated," Austin answered for Gavin. Likely trying to soften whatever blow she felt from this. "It does matter."

"But it's not going to change anything," Gavin finished.

"The only people that should have a say involving the relationship are the people involved," Dave said with a finality. He directed his attention to me, "And as long as there is consent and everyone involved is happy, there's nothing we need to worry about."

It felt like the first time I was acknowledged the whole night. After the day I had, I wasn't going to complain. Only now I had to say something. I nodded uneasily, not shaking Gavin off and trying my best not to feel like I was stuck under his arm.

"It didn't start off as my idea," I admitted. I looked away, not sure I wanted to admit at the table how I felt. "It wasn't something I would've decided to get into on my own. And this is certainly something I wouldn't have expected to go on for as long as it has," I met Kelli's gaze as I said it. "But," I looked at the man on my left then to the man on my right. Both seemed to be listening intently. Then I saw Vaughn. "But it fits."

Kelli seemed to relax, whatever idea she had about me hopefully dissolved. She nodded and turned her attention back to the baby at her side. "I'll let it go," she said after a beat. "But that doesn't mean you get to walk away from the conversation thinking I'll let go of the idea of you giving me grandbabies. You're my first born. I demand it."

"Landon is available any time you need a baby to spoil," Austin said easily. "Especially if I can get you to agree to watch him occasionally."

21

Nadia

"He didn't need to buy my lunch," Deidre said as she shoved clothes along the rack in front of her. We were in a department store, pursuing the marked down section. I knew we both were hoping to find something that fell into the elusive business casual description. All I had was a pair of faded slacks and a fitted button down that was a little too tight.

We were looking for Deidre, she was starting her new job Monday and she seemed to be buzzing with excitement when we first met up at the mall. She didn't protest Gavin coming along up until now. Granted, I hadn't brought him with me on purpose. He came along because he didn't want to be stuck at home.

"He tries to call me stubborn, but situations like this are one where he just proves me wrong," I said as I pulled a blouse off the rack. I turned towards her and held the blouse in front of myself, waiting for her opinion.

"Girl," she frowned at me as she eyed the black fabric I had in front of me. "No," she took the hanger from me and put it back on the rack. "Just no. Also," she paused and pulled a blouse off and held it against me, "go for colors that are going to look good for you. We ain't in middle school for you to be having a goth phase. Plus if a man is calling you stubborn, he's only saying that because you ain't doing what he wants you to do."

"Lies and deception," Gavin said from behind us. He had his phone in hand.

"Boy," Dee gave him a look, something that I could only call a mom face. "Don't even try to play me."

Gav's bottom lip stuck out and I couldn't contain the laugh that bubbled up in my chest. "I would be terrible if I didn't admit to being a little stubborn," I said, trying to give him a break. I looked down at the blouse and grimaced, "This has shoulder pads?"

"Girl, you can rip those out. Don't tell me your mama never taught you how to sew?" She looked at me doubtfully. "I know you grew up like I did. Sometimes you have to buy something that doesn't suit you and fix it so it does."

"It wasn't something I was really good with," I admitted. "I guess that's why I always look bad." I shrugged as I put the blouse she had pulled out back on the rack. "Probably why I'll always be stuck in a dead-end."

"You don't look bad," Gavin immediately protested. He drifted closer, one hand went to my shoulder and the other went to my waist. "You're beautiful," he said before kissing my cheek.

Deidre just smiled sweetly at Gav. "That's sweet, hunny. Why don't you go find something you need? Let us have some girl talk," she said as she waved a hand in an aimless direction. "I promise," she held up her hand as she spoke. "I will not be a bad influence."

Gavin looked doubtful, almost like he didn't want to do as she asked. But he gave me another kiss on my cheek before he left my side. We both watched as he followed the tiled pathway out of the apparel section. I watched him until he veered off of the path.

Once he was out of sight and obviously out of earshot I looked back to Dee and was confronted with the way she took me in. Her gaze didn't meet mine, it just drifted over my face before she glanced back down the way Gavin had gone. "I didn't peg him to be a puppy dog," she finally said. "You either got him hypnotized or he is so blinded by love he has to be attached. Those other boys that way, too?"

I opened my mouth to argue with her then I thought better of it. Gavin wasn't what I would call clingy by any means. Up until I told him I loved him. That changed things. "Austin isn't," I told her thinking of the man we left at the house. Something I felt bad about, "He's got a son so he's not really able to focus on me like Gav does." I redirected my attention to the clothes we had been pursuing. "I've not got him hypnotized."

"Uh huh," she sounded doubtful as she went to the other side of the rack. She pushed a few hangers aside before she looked up at me. "If we go look for him, what are the chances we will find him at a jewelry counter?"

"No," I shot down. I shook my head and picked up a button down that was a mint color. There weren't any shoulder pads or embellishment. I held it up to my chest and looked at her for approval. Hoping that it would distract her from the train of thought she was cruising on.

Her lips twisted up to one side as she eyed me. Was she even looking at the shirt I held? She shook her head, "Is it gonna bother you if I call you on your denial?" She paused and pulled back, "How would that even work? That ain't legal, is it?"

"What?" My voice raised a little at the end. I knew what she was alluding to. "It's not even been long enough to suggest something like that," I said, struggling to keep a cap on my emotions.

Suggesting marriage just seemed to be way too fast.

Deidre just gave me a blank face, "Why are you losing your mind about my question?" She put both her arms onto the racks of clothes in front of her. "I asked if it's legal for the four of you to get married. *If*, girl. If. I didn't say he was gonna pop the question on you," she took a step back and returned to looking at the clothes in front of her. "I was just curious." She pursed her lips and didn't look back up at me, "That's a good color for you. It's not dark and it looks feminine. It'll make you look friendly."

I considered the button down again, eyeing the price tag before I decided to drape it over my arm. We moved through the clothing in front of us, quietly. I guess my reaction was probably harsher than it should've been. "This is new," I admitted to her as she stepped out from between two racks of blouses to a larger rack that held dresses. "I don't really think about a goal as to what could happen between the four of us. I feel like making that conclusion, like that's where it could end up is scary."

"Your parents divorced?" she asked as she eyed a simple slip of a dress. It was a royal purple that seemed to pop, with the light brown shade of her skin I was sure it would look lovely on her. She turned to me, holding the dress up to her chin. "What d'ya think?"

"Definitely," I said as I eyed the dress. Would I be able to pull off that color? Why would I even need a dress? I shook my head, "My parents are still together."

"Then why does it scare you?" she asked. "My daddy didn't even bother to stay after my mama had me. Cedric's daddy was the same type of useless ass man," she put the dress over her arm and went back to the rack as she spoke. "There are way too many useless ass men in this world and I get you being weary of the men you are with. If they aren't asking you for money and they aren't just looking at you for sex," she paused to look at me. There was a seriousness in her expression as she took me in. "What's the problem?"

"I'm afraid of not measuring up," I admitted.

"Are you still on that?" she asked, pulling a face. "Is it because of the baby, still?"

"No," I shook my head immediately then paused to reconsider it. I drifted to the same sales rack she was standing in front of and decided to use the different colored fabrics to distract me. “Kind of. But it's not necessarily just Landon. Gav had me meet his parents.” I found a slate gray dress in my size and I picked it up. It looked safe, something that could easily be dressed up, but professional. ”And while he claimed the blame for all of it, I still got the vibe that his mom thought I’m,” I paused and gave the area around us a cursory look. When I was sure we didn’t have anyone in ear shot, I lowered my voice, “I’m a slut because I’m with all of them. Or worse, I’m only there because they have money.”

“Do they have money?” Dee asked curiously.

“I assume,” I admitted. “But I don’t look at their bank accounts because that doesn’t really matter. It's not really my business and I don’t want them looking in my bank account.” Mostly because I knew mine was a whole lot emptier. “It’s an insecurity that popped up when he first mentioned meeting his parents. I think, to him, this is a step in making things....” I paused to consider my words, “last?”

Deidre snorted and rolled her eyes pointedly, “If you feel that way you need to let go of what other people think.” She put another dress over her arm without showing it to me. “What you need to worry about is you and what goes on in your house. If no one else approves, it doesn’t matter. If you’re happy at home with these three boys then let it be.” She gestured to the load she had in her arms, “Don’t let nosy people mess you up if you got a good thing going. I’m gonna try these on before I spend money I don’t have.”

I don’t have an argument with that. I was going to have to let it go because Dee was right. If we were happy, why should I let other people’s opinions drag me down?

After I paid for the few things that seemed to fit well enough and make me look something like a professional, I found Gavin. I was relieved when I found him in the electronic section in front of the televisions. After Dee's suggestion that he would be looking at jewelry I had been scared. He wasn't reacting the same way Austin did when I admitted my feelings to him.

He didn't have the stress of finding out about an unexpected child. Would things have been different if Lauren never reached out to him? Would I feel just as uneasy and unsure about the future if Austin was reacting the same way as Gavin?

When Gav's fingers tangled with mine as we walked out to the store, the resentment I normally felt when I thought about Lauren drained away. As much as I cared about these men, I was still afraid of what it meant. I was afraid of how easy it was to fit in between them and how it actually felt.

I was afraid because I was moving into an area I never expected to be in. I was afraid of the loss of control I had because I cared and they knew about it. I was afraid of the unknown.

***

I was in the spare bedroom, digging through my claimed closet. I needed to find the rest of the interview clothes so I would be ready to replace my job. I didn't notice I had an audience until Landon gurgled for attention. Except Austin wasn't holding his son, in the doorway was Vaughn with the infant balanced on his arm in nothing but a diaper.

"What are you doing?" he asked. He looked between me and the pile of clothes that I dropped onto the bed. "You probably should have gone through your clothes before you moved in," he suggested. "Unless you need money?" His brows were drawn together and there wasn't anything patronizing on his face. Just concern.

"Eventually," I said as I kept digging through the box I'd purposely been avoiding since I moved in. "I'm trying to get my professional attire out so I don't look like a slob when I start applying for new jobs."

Vaughn relaxed and he looked down at the baby he held, he bounced him a little as if judging to see if Landon was paying attention. The baby blinked owlishly at him, his eyes batting particularly slowly. I could see why Vaughn had him back here.

"You can just send me your resume," he said, his voice lowered as he kept his attention on the baby he held. "And I'll have you a job by next week at the latest." It was no big deal to him, he wasn't concerned with the idea of having to do something for me. He met my gaze and it was apparent that he was waiting for me to respond.

"I don't want you to do that," I said as I waved a hand, trying to make him think it wasn't something I was worried about. "I haven't even started looking, yet. If I get desperate I'll let you know."

"Don't," he shut me down pretty quickly, "dodge me." He turned to go across the hall, taking Landon with him. "Fucking let me help."

Irritation bubbled through me and I dropped the jeans I had in hand onto the bed. I hit the light switch and I followed him into the nursery. "I'm perfectly capable of finding myself a job. There's no reason for me to ask you for help," I threw out my hands as I spoke. "I've done it all on my own for the last ten years. I'm good."

Vaughn gave me a dark look as he pulled a onesie from the dresser. He didn't make any further attempt to argue with me as he carefully put the baby on the changing table and began to dress him. I watched, looking between them as a realization hit me.

I didn't do enough. I let Gavin and Vaughn help Austin without actually making any attempt myself. I needed to change that, especially if I wanted to shake the insecurities of me not measuring up. I needed to step up more.

I shifted beside Vaughn and pulled out a tiny pair of socks. With some wiggling and a little wrestling I was able to get both of them on Landon. I could feel the attention of the man beside me but I didn't let it stop me. I picked up the infant from the changing table, found the stash of extra pacifiers that I knew were shoved in a tote and offered it to him.

"I can put the baby to bed," I said to Vaughn after Landon took the pacifier. I didn't wait for him to say anything, I went to the tan glider and sat down, I propped Landon up on my shoulder and looked up at the man still standing at the changing table. "You worked all day. Go relax."

While the frustration was evident in the tense set of his shoulders, he didn't argue. But he turned and leaned back against the table, folding his arms over his chest as he watched me start rocking. "I can find something that pays well," he said after a beat. "Something that doesn't make you feel like you have to work yourself to death just to pay your bills."

I bristled a little, but I bit my tongue. While Landon felt heavy against my shoulder I could tell from the subtle shift of his body against me he wasn't asleep. He was listening. While it was unlikely he knew what we were talking about, our tones said enough.

I took a breath and released it slowly, trying to force myself to relax. "I don't have the education and experience you do," I said evenly. "I'm in a similar boat Dee is in where all I have to my name is a string of jobs that went nowhere. Fast food, cashier, and waitress. What can you do with that?"

Vaughn lifted his chin, his brow raising as he digested my words. He looked away from me and I could see a slight tick in his jaw. "Won't know unless you let me try."

I nodded but I didn't have anything else to say to that. I kept rocking and resting a hand on Landon's back to steady him. This was something I was going to have to get used to. What was I supposed to say in the face of seeing someone wanting to go out of their way to help me?

22

Nadia

I don't know when I fell asleep but after Vaughn left the room I couldn't account the minutes after Landon felt heavy against me. Was there some sort of magic to the kid that put me to sleep? This was the second time and he didn't seem to be bothered by it at all. Maybe it was because he was so close to my ear, so his little breaths lulled me to sleep, too.

I didn't have an answer but I didn't even realize I had nodded off until someone pulled the baby from my arms. I moved with him, not wanting to give up the little bundle. I didn't settle back in the rocking chair until I heard a gruff, "I'm putting him in the crib."

"What happened?" I asked, dazed because I had been sleeping harder than I first realized.

"You weren't in bed and Vaughn started complaining when I got too close to him." It was Gav. He shushed and there was a grumpy protest from Landon. "It's okay buddy," he said as he continued to shush in the same manner he'd seen Austin do it.

I watched blurrily as he tried to settle the baby again before he set him into the crib. He kept shushing him and even went as far to pat the baby gently on his belly. While there was a little whimper from the crib, there weren't any further complaints from him.

"I didn't mean to fall asleep," I whispered to him.

"Don't worry about it," he whispered back as he grabbed the baby monitor from its charger. "Let's go to bed," he said to me as he turned to go out the door.

Then Landon made a noise. A whimper mixed with a sigh. We both froze, waiting to see if it was going to lead to more. The baby was splayed out on his back, his little arms fell back against the bed and one sock had scrunched up to show his heel. Should I fix it?

"Naddy," Gav got my attention. "C'mon. Let's go to bed."

I let him lead me through the dark house to our bedroom. Austin is stretched out under the covers, his attention on his phone. He didn't look up until Gavin placed the baby monitor on the bedside table. "He's asleep in bed. He got a little bit fussy when I picked him up," he reported as he went to his side of the bed. "But as far as I could tell he's down for the count."

"What was she doing?" Vaughn asked, he was positioned between Austin and Gavin. He didn't even look at me as he asked the question, he genuinely appeared curious.

"Found 'em snuggled up in the rocker, both out," he said with a snort. "Seems like the baby put her to sleep instead of the other way around."

I stalled out at the end of the bed, "Pretty sure he was asleep before I nodded off." I looked between the three of them, trying to decide where I would fit. Where did I want to be? It feels like the safest place for me to go would be in the middle of everyone.

No one would feel left out or jealous.

Vaughn was in the middle, his arms were behind his head and while he didn't look like he was on the verge of sleep. He looked relaxed. His gaze connected with mine and he raised an eyebrow, like he was waiting on me to make my decision. Maybe there was something a little daring there, too.

I shoved my pajama pants off and with a little maneuvering, I got my bra off without taking off my shirt. From there, I crawled up the bed. I was careful not to trample over Vaughn's legs or ankles. His brows went up as I tugged the blanket and sheet down so I would be able to cover up.

"Are you serious?" he asked, his hands coming from behind his head like he might ward me off.

On a whim, while hovering above him, I decided to straddle his hips. It wasn't an exact mirror of the last time we were like this but it felt similar enough. I leaned down, planting my hands on the bed just above his shoulders. I tilted my head as I looked down at him, "Don't you do this to me?"

Vaughn's hands fell on my hips and I could feel that I had his interest. He looked like he was struggling to come up with an argument for me being on him like this. Then, and I saw it when it happened, something seemed to occur to him. "Are you sure you want to do this?" he asked, a slight smirk tugging up one side of his mouth.

Gavin was on his side, watching the exchange and he didn't seem to be on the same page as the man beside him. Austin had put down his phone, paying attention to the exchange. "What's the problem?"

"No problem," Vaughn said, his smirk growing into a grin.

That's when I felt one hand release my hip. I didn't get much more of a warning before his hand fell hard against my butt. I jerked forward onto him and my eyes went wide. Aside from the sound that echoed through the room it was quiet.

No one said a word.

Vaughn quirked an eyebrow up and his hand, now on my ass, rubbed the offended cheek. "That makes us even," he said after a beat. When I didn't move off of him, his hand squeezed. "Do I do it again?"

Before I could say a word, Austin reached over and slapped me hard on my other cheek. I jumped with that and I looked at him, barking out his name. He didn't seem to be deterred by it, he just looked at Gavin. "This your doing?"

"I'm pretty sure you just did that while I sat here and watched," Gavin argued. "You can't really blame me for the two of you having the idea to do that to her." He shrugged, like he was unbothered by the accusation. "You're assuming that she was into that, you didn't ask. Like she did to you," he said to Vaughn. "So she might not be into it."

That got the attention of both men and I was grateful Gavin had made that connection. Granted, it was tit for tat when it came to Vaughn. I had done the same thing to him a few nights ago without having any repercussions before now. If anything, Vaughn had been polite and eager to help.

The three of them were looking at me like they were waiting on me to confirm or deny Gavin's thoughts. I honestly didn't know how to feel. I swallowed and looked between each of them before I shrugged, "I don't know."

A hand went into my panties, squeezing my butt and hip. Fingers drummed against the crack of my ass and for some reason it was like pushing a button. I hadn't intended, really, for this to go down this path but since Vaughn was going to tease me I might as well take advantage of the position I was in.

I rolled my hips against his and his brows went up. "Is it going to be like that?" He asked, voice hoarse. "Is that what it did to you?"

I took a breath and straightened above him. How was I supposed to answer that? Did I want to? I pulled my shirt upward and over my head, I hadn't planned this but the chances of me going to sleep now was slim.

Austin seemed to be on the same page. He didn't wait for either of the other two men to react to my state of undress. He cupped my breast and closed his mouth around the tip hungrily. It saved me from having to make any attempt at being sexy from there.

"Naddy," Gavin spoke up as he sat up, too. "You gotta tell him if you liked him slapping your ass."

Austin's mouth distracted me, the pull igniting things in me far better than the sting in my butt. "Why does it matter?" I asked, reaching for Gavin. I wanted him to touch me, too.

"Because," he began but didn't wait for me to answer him. He just pulled the back of my panties down, found some free real estate on my ass and gave me a solid slap that had me gasping. "If you're into it, it's going to happen again." There was something about his gaze that was daring, like he was waiting for me to balk at the idea or maybe ask for more.

"I don't know," I snapped at him. "It hurts and I'm turned on, but," I waved a hand at the man under me and the man beside me. "There are a few things that are also contributing to that. I'm not gonna say that it's what got me going. I'm not gonna come to you and ask you to spank me."

"But if it's in the heat of the moment?" Gavin prompted, and I could see in his eyes he wasn't going to let it go. This was something he enjoyed. I should've known this was where things were going to go when I first agreed to this in Vaughn's bathroom.

"I don't know," I repeated. "If you hit me again, you're not gonna like how I react."

That seemed to get the attention of all three of them. Austin let go of my breast and he drew closer. "Do we need to stop?" he asked. His erection was to the point where the fabric of his boxers was barely containing him. He wouldn't want to stop. But I knew without saying anything that if I said stop, Austin wouldn't question it and we'd all lay down to go to bed.

I didn't want to do that. I didn't want to give up the burn that was easing through me. I didn't want to test the limitations on just how hard they were going to spank me. Or how I would feel while we were in the thick of it.

There was something defensive about it. Like the shock from the first few slaps were wearing off and I knew if Gavin were to swat at me again I'd throw a hand back at him. All the teasing they did with him the last time we were in this position didn't entirely expose what he and I had done in Vaughn's apartment. But if he was going to test me he'd just be making it difficult to keep my mouth shut.

"No," I said to Austin. "We're just done with that. No more slapping my ass unless someone wants to lose a finger." I threatened as much as I could without growling.

"It's fair to assume that goes all the way around?" Vaughn asked from under me.

I took a breath and slowly released it, trying to get my nerves to settle down. "Unless you ask for it I won't be slapping your ass again," I assured the man under me.

He chuckled and arched upward, "Get her panties off so we can have fun before someone changes her mind."

I didn't want to argue with him even though I wasn't the one that was likely to change my mind. I shifted where appropriate, so that my panties could be removed. There wasn't any talk of who would go where. Gavin didn't give the opportunity for arguments to be made, he pressed me down until my chest was flush with Vaughn's.

Austin was behind me with Gavin and I shot a worried look over my shoulder. With all the things I let them do to me should I really be afraid? They haven't hurt me so far. This was just a little experiment that escalated from something I had done. I would learn to not be so impulsive.

The line of thought I was on immediately derailed when two hands spread me, exposing every inch of me. There was no hesitation, no wait for me to adjust to it. Fingers began to prod my inner folds, tracing the length of my slit until they found my clit and began circling it. Another set of fingers, thicker fingers, pressed into me at the same time and worked in tandem with the other teasing fingers.

"I'm just supposed to lay here while you two have all the fun?" Vaughn asked.

"Play with her tits," Gavin suggested before I felt a tongue come into play. He traced his tongue from the bottom of my opening up to the little circle of clenched muscles.

Vaughn grumbled and he pulled me up so that I wasn't lying against his chest. It forced me to raise myself up on my hands so he could find where he wanted to start. His mouth started at my shoulder, his teeth and tongue began to move down until he found my collar bone. Hand cupped my breasts, pressing them upward and together so he could follow the line he created.

"Train," Austin spoke up. "Let's do that. I call first."

Gavin pulled away from me, the teasing he had been doing at my anus. "How's that fair? Maybe I want to go first," he huffed out.

"Are we moving things around?" Vaughn asked against my skin. "Because I can be right here," he rubbed his face between my breasts, "while you two fight it out."

There was a brief exchange between Austin and Gavin, like each man was trying to test the other as to what they wanted to do with me. "If you're hitting this," a finger tapped at my rear opening, "you can prep it yourself."

"That's not where I want to be," Austin shot back as he stood. He went to the bedside table and I watched slightly dazed as he pulled out condoms, tossed several on the bed, and the bottle of lube. "So if that's where you're planning on going you can take advantage of the position she's in so as soon as I'm done you can take over."

Gavin didn't argue. He didn't say a word as Austin ripped open the foil package of the condom. None of them was going to object to the fact that after the last time the three of us were together I had admitted that I didn't think this piece was necessary. While Vaughn and Gavin both seemed to be on that page, or in agreement with giving me what I wanted, Austin wasn't.

Austin being assertive and demanding was a small saving grace. He didn't even wait for the other man to argue as he pressed the head of his cock against my opening. He eased into me, spreading me slowly and drawing a whine from me.

He suggested a train, meaning they'd each take turns with fucking me instead of all at once. I don't want to admit that I had a preference. I definitely enjoyed any moments that I had with each of them, but with each of my three men right here I didn't see a reason why I couldn't have all three of them in me at once. If I was going to have all three of them in right after the other, wouldn't it take longer?

I didn't get the chance to voice my thoughts, because Austin didn't hold back. He took advantage of the position I was in, ass in the air, and thrust into me with a force that shook me. He hit things in me that I was so used to them exploiting before we got to this step. It was like my body expected them to play with it after so often that it was sensitive to the fact it didn't get the attention it was used to.

It felt like he triggered me into an orgasm a whole lot faster than he should've. It blew through me in a way that I couldn't hold myself up and I was left smothering

Vaughn against my breasts. He didn't protest but he did shift so I could hear his gasp of breath, "Damn that was quick."

"I'm not done," Austin grunted as he threw his hips into mine more solidly. The sound of it echoed through the room. There wasn't much difference between the sound of his fucking me and when they had slapped my ass. It didn't dampen until Austin's hand landed on my shoulder and his thrust became shallower.

"That was a wet one," Gavin announced, he had laid on his hand pressed between Vaughn and me. His fingers cut through my curls and teased my flesh where it was spread around Austin's cock. It just added to the buzzing nerves that Austin had already induced. "Think we can get more like it?"

"Help me out and we might," Austin grunted as he kept up the shallow, hard thrusts into me.

"If I help I call dibs on going in second," Gavin called as he found my clit and began to assault it as Austin continued to move in me.

"Does this mean you're going to be fucking her pussy, too?" Vaughn asked, his attention was on my throat now. "Or are you going to tap her ass?"

"Haven't decided yet," Gavin admitted. "I figure by the time he finishes I'll make a decision then."

"Are you going to wrap it up, too?" Vaughn asked as he nibbled along the column of my neck.

I was dazed and at first it didn't connect to what he was talking about. Then Austin made a strained noise, "You should." I could feel a tremor go through him, hinting at the fact that he was close. "Don't. Be. Stupid," he gritted it out and punctuated each word with a solid thrust into me.

They were speaking like I wasn't there. Like I wasn't something they were all three focused on. There was a good chance the reason behind that was because I wasn't entirely coherent to add my two cents. I didn't have any arguments planned. Even after the talk I had with Austin on the matter I didn't really think there was anything I could say that would change his mind.

Gavin on the other hand, I wasn't sure about. He didn't look like he was sure what he wanted to do now. He was still teasing my clit while Austin railed me from behind, he didn't make any move to tease the free hole I had.

"I don't want to wait my turn," Vaughn admitted. "Decide where you're going to be because as soon as he finishes up and pulls out, I'm going to get where's open."

Gavin made an irritated noise and pulled his hand from me. It didn't deter from the burn of nerves or the high of endorphins I was cruising on. Austin had kept moving like he hadn't heard their exchange, the bite of his hands on my hip and shoulder suggested that he was barely holding it together himself. I had no complaints, I'd be lucky if I had any working brain cells after they were done with me.

"Take my place," Gavin said to Vaughn. "The sooner he busts a nut the sooner we can get a turn."

"Should stay with the train idea," Austin gasped out. "When was the last time it was just the two of you?" he heaved as he thrust into me, "I haven't been with her on my own since before he got involved."

"The last time it was just me and her was before she moved in," Vaughn admitted. "And that fucker ended up walking in on us." He didn't point out the fact that he knocked me for a loop during that encounter. Literally. I was lucky the bruise he gave me was something that had been easy to cover.

"I watched her suck you off," Gavin argued.

Vaughn shifted from under me, looking confused. "Not me," he shot back.

"Him," Gav pointed at Austin with the bottle of lube. "I got to watch. I haven't come in on you and her going at it since the time you nearly knocked her out with your head." He squirted lube into one hand and went about spreading the liquid between my ass cheeks, not at all deterred by how Austin was still moving in me.

"What you're saying," Vaughn began, "was this was supposed to be an opportunity for each of us to have a piece on our own while the rest of us watched?" It was clear he wasn't sure what to make of it, "How long did you think we'd be able to keep our hands to ourselves?"

A curse erupted from Austin and I felt him stiffen. Any chance Gavin would've had to press his fingers into my rear hole were foiled by the hips crushed against my butt. Austin didn't make any attempt to move, leaning heavily against me and made me press against the man beneath me.

"Do what the fuck you want to do," Austin wheezed as he seemed to struggle to get himself back together. He pulled his softening cock from me and pressed kisses between my shoulder blades. "This was what I wanted." He pushed himself back from me, giving Gavin some room. "You do what you want," he flopped on the bed. "As long as she's cool with it I'll sit and watch."

Vaughn looked speculative, not making any move to do as he said he was going to. His eyes were narrowed and he had his full attention on the man behind me, who seemed to be making extra sure that the lube was spread adequately between my cheeks before he even considered toying with the clenched ring of muscle.

"When was the last time you were with her by yourself?" Vaughn asked.

Gavin tensed, his finger easing into me stiffly, there was no finesse to it. No teasing. He was caught up in the other man's question and when I cast a blurry look at Austin, I could tell he had everyone's full attention. "Uh," he began, his voice at a higher pitch than usual. "What was it? A couple of days ago?" He didn't sound sure and there was a good chance he was going for nonchalance.

"I'm not in a position where I can remember," I rasped as he worked that single finger into me.

"You had every opportunity to say something," Vaughn growled. "And you didn't."

"Are we supposed to report when we're together one on one? I just figured it would be something that could happen without there being any sort of problem," Gavin huffed. "I mean if you're butt hurt about it, I think you should reconsider the fact that when I walked in on the two of you, you hadn't said a word about intending to get in her pants when I left."

"Stop," I barked. I didn't make any attempt to push myself up, I couldn't. My thighs were trembling and my knees didn't feel like they would be able to hold me up if I were to attempt to even stand. "You're not supposed to be jealous of each other," I pressed my hands into the bed, on either side of Vaughn I pushed myself up enough to look down at him. "It's not gonna work if you are. There are going to be moments between all four of us and moments when it may be one or more of you with me. That's what happens when we do things on the spur of the moment."

The man beneath me frowned at me, a tick in his jaw. He turned his attention to Austin, like he expected him to be on his side. Austin was just stretched out beside him, watching the situation with hooded eyes. He didn't look like he had a care in the world. There was no concern at the prospect that I was having a sexual relationship with each of them, not just all of them together.

Austin just shrugged, "You had to realize that this was the way things were going to be when you were first with her by yourself. If you're going to keep a tally of who is with her then it's going to make things get shitty real quick."

"If you want to go next go ahead," Gavin offered. "I'll just be back here," he pressed another finger into me. "Playing with her butt."

I didn't know if that was a fix for Vaughn. Did that make things okay? Or was this going to be another problem that would crop up later?

I could see Vaughn swallowing. Did he realize he was the cause of it or was he just surprised that no one else was bothered by the same thing he was? "I'm not trying to cause problems," he said lowly. "It's not something that I would expect to be cool." He arched upward a little, taking advantage of the position I was in, hovering over him. "We've made this work before I knew about it, there's no reason why it shouldn't keep working." He cupped my face with both hands and he tugged me down to him, kissing me with a little more hunger than I would've expected.

Gavin's fingers began to spread me and he didn't speak, perhaps feeling guilty for something he shouldn't. He took his time, distracting me with how focused he was on it. It was to the point that I was moving with the slow pace he had set with his hand. I think to encourage more, the stretch of his fingers weren't enough and he didn't give me the depth that I needed.

"So, I'm guessing you want to go solo?" Gavin prompted when Vaughn seemed to be caught up in tasting me.

The man kissing me didn't immediately pull away from me, he slowly teased his tongue around mine. He reached between us and arched up, pushing down his boxers. I felt his erection against my stomach until he fell back against the bed.

"Fuck it," he growled against my lips. "I don't want to wait anymore. I'll just have to find time to get time one on one on my own." His hands tangled in my hair, keeping me close so that he could whisper to me, "I'm going to get the chance to fuck you on my own again."

I didn't argue, I didn't have one readily available with the man behind me now thrusting three fingers into me. I figured the best way to convey that I heard Vaughn was to find his erection and shift so I could line him up with my dripping sex. Fortunately, he moved with me, encouraged so he could easily sink into me.

He moaned and I froze, I didn't give him the opportunity to put a condom on. Would that be a problem for him? One hand that had been tangled in my hair fell down to my hip, he didn't make any attempt to pull out of me. He arched upward into me and began to thrust into me. He was going slow, almost like he was savoring the moment.

"Hold up just a sec," Gavin said from behind me. "Let me get in, too."

The bed dipped a little and while the man under me stopped thrusting I could feel the man behind me pressing against my rear entrance. As far as I could tell, Gavin hadn't put a condom on either. I could feel every ridge of his cock as he spread me. I throbbed until he was fully seated into my ass.

"Slow, go slow," became a mantra to me.

"Does it hurt?" Austin asked.

I shook my head, because it didn't. Gavin had made extra sure I was ready for him. Just the feeling of both of them in me, with no barriers hadn't been something I was prepared for. The feeling of both of them in me was overwhelming, but even more so because I felt everything.

I was almost afraid that I'd break.

Vaughn didn't listen to me and he began moving at a pace that I wasn't prepared for. He struggled to stay close, like he wanted to maintain the kiss that he started before he pressed into me but he couldn't. He let go of my hair and wrapped his arm around my shoulders, keeping me close. He groaned against my temple.

"I should've warned you," Gavin said from behind me. His hands dug into my hips, his pace matching Vaughn's while being more restrained. His hips still bounced off my ass but he was gentler.

It didn't matter. Their combined movements and how I felt everything was too much. I choked and fell against Vaughn, I couldn't hold myself up anymore. A wail broke out of me, drawing out as Gavin's hips started hitting my ass with more force. A tremor went through him, desperation spread from him to the man beneath me.

It seemed like we just started, that Austin had suggested that we go one at a time. And while I had definitely lost count since the beginning of all of it, I was sure I'd gotten to the point where it couldn't get better. There was no outlasting either of them when they were working together to push me over the edge.

A string of curses came from under me, I felt Vaughn straining before he erupted in me. It was almost as if he were burning me as he filled me up. He grunted, holding me tight to him even as Gavin kept up behind me. It just expended everything, leaving me in a pool of buzzing nerves.

Then Gavin set me on fire. He choked out a groan, his hands dug into my hips. He stiffened and the heat of his come seared me. All of Austin's warnings came screaming through my head, but none of them revolved around what they should. He worried about pregnancy. Where was the warning about losing myself between the three of them?

If they burned themselves into me, were there any chances that I would be able to go without them? I knew they ruined sex for me, it just never occurred to me that they would ruin me for anyone else. Gavin had joked that I would be stuck with them, I could hope that he meant it.

After this I doubted I would be able to go without any of them.

23

Nadia

A noise cut through the darkest, just loud enough to carry over the snores and heavy breathing of three men. At first, I just blinked my eyes open and looked at the ceiling. Low light was streaming in from the shaded window giving me an idea that it was morning, but no clue at the time. I normally didn't wake up this early and it was clear that there were still three bodies in the bed with me.

What woke me up? I closed my eyes, while my bladder wasn't screaming at me nature was calling. It probably would have waited another hour or so. But I was awake so I wiggled my way out from between two bodies to relieve myself.

I tried my best to stay quiet, feeling my way through the bathroom without turning on a light. After I finished and came back to the bed, I was no longer worried about what had woken me. Until I heard the noise again.

It was a quiet, puny little cry. The baby monitor sat on the bedside table, but the little green light that showed that it was on was dark. That meant the baby could've been crying for a while now and no one heard it because we were all asleep.

I found a shirt on the floor and threw it on, hurrying to the other end of the house. "Oh buddy," I tried my best to sound as soothing as I could as I reached for him over the rail of the crib. "Baby," I shushed as I hefted him up.

He was mid melt down, hiccupping with tears and burying his face against my shoulder. There was no telling how long he had been crying and we hadn't heard.

I tried my best to comfort him, patting his back and struggling with what I should do next.

Why would a baby cry? I put my hand on his diaper and that was telling enough. It was full and I took him to the changing table. He didn't fight me to change him fortunately, it helped because I didn't change nearly enough of his diapers.

I thought for a minute that I might be able to get him back to sleep, but his hand went into his mouth and it was clear he had amped himself up a little too much. There was no going back to sleep now. I tried not to groan, because I could definitely stand to go back to bed. Hopefully, I'd be able to figure out the chemistry to make his bottle.

I picked him up and went to the kitchen, having quieted down Landon now seemed to be fully invested in what I was doing. He was propped on my hip and watching as I found a clean bottle and the can of formula. I squinted at the directions, "How does he do this every morning?"

"Sometimes he gets help," Vaughn said sleepily. "It's one of the reasons why he always has coffee made in the morning. I make the bottle, he makes the coffee." He was standing in the doorway of the bedroom, he hadn't bothered to dress so I'm assuming there was a good chance he wasn't entirely awake.

Landon wasn't fazed by it, gurgling at the man as he came to the counter to take over the bottle making for me. I decided I'd take up the coffee making chore. Not thinking about waking up Austin. I had the coffee maker percolating by the time Vaughn handed Landon the bottle.

"Gonna go get in the shower," he said, still vaguely tired. "If you need help, wake him up." He started to walk back into the bedroom before he paused to look at me. "Put him in the high chair otherwise you're going to spoil him."

I blinked, "What? How?"

"You hold a baby too much he's going to end up spoiled," he said, not bothering to see if I was going to listen.

"That sounds like a lie," I huffed after him, turning to look down at Landon. "You? Spoiled? Sounds like a load of crap to me. Would you agree?"

Landon just looked at me with those big blue eyes. I took that as an affirmative. I got comfortable in Austin's chair. At this point I wasn't quite sure what to do with Landon. I rocked a little bit and he leaned against me then he rocked upward into a seated position only to fall back against me, holding the bottle aloft as he drank from it. He repeated the act of rocking before I took the hint.

"Don't throw up on me, please," I whispered to him, "and I'll rock you all you want."

"You doing this is going to mean you're gonna find him reaching for you more often," Vaughn spoke up from the doorway of the bedroom. "Are you going to be okay with that?"

"Are you questioning whether or not I'd be willing to help with him more?" I asked. "Just because I'm holding him?" I rolled my eyes and directed my attention down to Landon, where he fit against my side. He looked up at me. "How do I talk sense into this guy?"

Landon made a noise, like he was offering me some sort of baby insight to Vaughn. Formula dribbled down his chin and I wished I had thought to grab a burp cloth or a bib. I'd seen him wearing them before, why didn't I grab one?

A towel landed on my head, like he had realized the problem I had and thrown it at me. I wasn't going to complain, I took it up to clean Landon up. He kicked his feet and made a noise I could only call disgruntled. When he didn't start fussing I released a breath. "I'll figure it out, I promise," I said to him.

"Good," Vaughn spoke up and I found him standing beside us. "Seal the deal and make it permanent." He paused to sip at a mug, "Take some time today to get your resume together and email it to me."

I opened my mouth to argue but the look he gave me stalled me out. "Consider it me making up for the bookstore closing, which it is," he turned away to go back into the kitchen. "Plus I'm going to look for something that will bring you home earlier instead of you coming home late."

I guess as long as it paid well enough I couldn't complain. I grimaced, unable to shake the feeling that came with handing over that control to him. Even if it was something he felt he owed me. I was so used to doing things myself, it felt like I was giving up a piece of me to him. I was going to have to let it go.

"I have the same kind of skill set Deidre does," I admitted to him. "Expecting me to be able to fit into an office job is probably expecting too much."

"I'll let you know how that works out," he said as he came back to him. He bent down to press a kiss against my brow, followed shortly after by pressing one to Landon's brow. "I'll see you later."

The baby gurgled again, bottle still in place and formula dribbling down his chin. It made it clear that any time I picked Landon up I was going to have to make sure I had a towel ready. I knew kids had a tendency to be messy, but having one in my lap making a mess was definitely eye opening.

And I let two men come in me last night. The chance of me getting pregnant after that was pretty slim, thank you birth control, but holding the consequences of unprotected sex was terrifying. Almost as terrifying as just how close I'd let them become, how fast I had let it happen.

I wanted to question how I got here, how I let all this happen. How did I overlook four years of hell to get here? I twisted my lips up as I continued to rock slightly. I was being forced to change the views I had of them back then from the moment all of this started. I looked down at Landon and he met my gaze, "I'm in trouble."

He made an answering noise. That was quickly overshadowed by a barked out, "Fuck!" Austin came barreling out of the bedroom, tugging up a pair of boxers, and racing down the hall. "Landon, buddy," he began as he got to the nursery's door. Then he pulled up short, noticing it was empty. "I overslept," he muttered as he turned to come back down the hall. He spotted us easily and looked embarrassed, "You haven't been up long have you?"

I just shook my head, "I heard him crying when I got up to pee. It's not a big deal, he's been fine since then." A little white lie. "You probably needed the sleep if you just now noticed Gavin cuddling with you."

He made a noise then looked at the baby monitor that he held in his hand. He turned it on then back off, "I guess the batteries died in it." He sighed in defeat and looked back down at the two of us, "I guess it could've been worse. I'll put this on charge and start breakfast." He turned to go back down the hall, the set of his shoulders drooping a little.

He was more wore down than I expected. How was I supposed to help with this? I looked down at Landon and he seemed to be focused on where his father was going more than me. Was the stress just because of the baby? Or did it factor back to Lauren? I didn't know if I had a right to ask.

I picked up one pudgy little foot, counting the round little toes. "We're gonna give Daddy the day off today," I told Landon. He wiggled his toes then giggled, entertained by the attention. "I'm just gonna ask you to be gentle, okay?"

It was a solid hour after breakfast before I could get around to pulling my laptop out to get to work on my resume. I wished it took me that long to get it put together. My job history was sorely lacking and was a list of retail and serving jobs. Terrible compared to Vaughn's work as a realtor, especially considering the apartment he lived in. And the fact that he was able to buy the building that the bookstore had been in.

It gave him a string of connections that I could never hope to have. People that were more than willing to do him a favor by hiring under-qualified folks like Deidre and me. That was assuming he'd find a job that he saw as appropriate for me.

The easiest thing to do would be to have me work at the bar, the likelihood that he'd be there all the time was pretty slim. How often did Vaughn even get his hands dirty with manual labor? Probably not since his football career ended.

I sent the email, sparing Landon a glance where he rocked on his hands and knees on the floor. Austin was taking his turn in the shower and Gavin was out in the garage, getting a run in before he came to take baby duty. It seemed like a good idea, taking turns to keep an eye on the baby.

"We could do this," I said to him as I opened up a career board by force of habit. I even applied to a few that I knew I would be able to do. There weren't any worries about whether or not I had experience running a register, waiting tables, or doing customer service. Jobs that I knew how to do. They were things I was familiar with.

I figured if I could find a job before Vaughn could it would fix the problem. Then the sense that I owed him something wouldn't be there. It might piss him off, but that was a risk I was willing to take.

I was in the midst of filling out the application to another career board when my phone went off in a quick series of chimes. I almost thought I'd gotten lucky super quick before I realized it had to be someone I knew. I deflated and decided to use the fact that Landon looked like he had inched forward a little to ignore my phone.

"Are you gonna crawl?" I asked the baby, closing up my laptop and moving so I could get a look at his face. "Where are you gonna go?"

Landon babbled at me, his attention firmly on the floor directly in front of him. He rocked forward, a hand went upward and then slapped against the floor. He didn't move far, he was still trying to figure out the mechanics, but he definitely inched forward.

"What's going on?" Austin called from the bedroom. He didn't wait for my answer. He came into the living room in nothing but his boxers, a towel draped over his shoulders. It was a delicious picture that I couldn't really appreciate.

"Somebody's trying to go places," I told him with a grin.

"Oh no!" Austin started in mock distress. "We can't do that, yet," he bent down and picked his son up, holding him aloft. "You get any more mobile there'll be no holding you back!"

Landon squealed in delight. No fussing for the man that held him. I watched as he took him back to the nursery, sure he was going back there to change him.

I should take the opportunity to get in the shower, especially before Gavin could commandeer it. But I let my phone distract me, hoping that it would be Dee with a report on how her first day was going. Or that Freddy came to his senses and decided he wasn't going to close the diner after all.

Instead, there was an address from Vaughn. 'Meet me here. Dress professionally. I've got a cover letter and resume already printed so all you need to do is be presentable.'

How had he found something that quickly? I groaned and sent him a message in return. 'I need time, I haven't even had a shower.'

'I'm going up there for my lunch. I still have an hour before I can do that. That gives you plenty of time to get ready, doesn't it?'

Of course a man would assume I could be professional and ready to go in just an hour. I got up and trotted into the nursery. "Vaughn wants me to meet him," I said to Austin as I entered the room. "I'm gonna go jump in the shower. That'll leave you here with Gavin. Is that okay?" I asked the question, hoping he'd say no.

"Go ahead," Austin said with a nonchalant shrug. "We got this handled. I was just thinking we'd both go out back and lift some weights."

"That doesn't sound like a good idea to do with a baby," I winced a little as I said it. It didn't occur to me until after I did that he was joking. "Alright. Get swole."

Dejected, I went about getting ready as Vaughn had advised. I didn't drag my feet out of curiosity. What did he find? Would it be something that would work? My stomach knotted up as I put makeup on. Was there a right amount to use? Was less is more a good position to be in for an impromptu interview?

I struggled with eyeliner and mascara before I decided that would have to be enough. I pulled my hair up into what I hoped was a delicate but professional look. I gave myself a final look before I went to the spare room, wearing just my underwear, the fact that all the men were in the backyard made it so I didn't feel self-conscious about walking through the house nearly naked.

I decided that the simple, gray dress that I picked up when I went shopping with Deidre was close enough to being professional. I found a light purple cardigan and threw that on over it, for a pop of color. The dig for shoes had me running out the door with just half an hour to get there.

I might've appeared like I was ready to go. I might look something close to the word professional. But from the way my stomach knotted up, I knew it was all a lie. I'd never fit in whatever job he intended to thrust me into.

24

Vaughn

I left the door to my office open with the intent on keeping an ear out for Naddy. I was sure there'd be noise when she saw her friend at the front desk. So far today, Deidre showed up early and had coffee made and waiting for me when I walked in the door. It was made to perfection, better than anything I could've bought from a chain.

Dad had raised his eyebrow at her, but he didn't say a word after drinking the coffee. He just went into his office and shut the door. I didn't hire people often, it wasn't something that I really bothered with. Everyone in the office was hired and vetted by him, that meant a lot of beautiful women came in and out of our office for notable reasons.

I just hoped he would decide that Deidre wasn't his type. I might have to encourage her to bring pictures of her kids to put on her desk that would be a decent deterrent. I was sure that was one less problem she'd prefer to deal with.

It left me questioning how we didn't face regular sexual harassment law suits. As far as I knew, we didn't. It might've been something he kept swept under the rug or he might've just avoided it simply because he had enough attorneys in his pocket.

"Hey girl!" I heard Deidre announce from the front room.

It was enough to get me out of my chair and to my office door. I could see my father's office door was open, but I didn't see him at his desk. Hopefully, he was in his private bathroom and not catching the exchange happening in the lobby.

"Wow," Naddy sounded amazed. "This is where he got you hired on at? How's that going?"

"I'm getting used to it," she admitted. "So far, it's not been that different from working at the diner. I'm just not waiting on as many tables and I'm not gonna get tips for babysitting clients and realtors."

It was amusing that she referred to it as babysitting. But, unfortunately, dad came into view. He stood just inside his office, his eyes narrowed as he focused on what was being said. He eyed me like he was suspicious of me. Granted, loitering in my office just out of sight from the lobby might not give me the best of appearances.

What struck me was that he didn't say a word. He stepped out of his office, adjusted the front of his jacket and moved into the lobby. Damn him. I started to step out when I heard him speak, "Deidre, who is this?"

"This is my friend," she said easily. "She was coming to join me on my lunch break, but she's about twenty minutes early," she explained and I couldn't see her face to see if the lie was obvious. "But," she typed at a keyboard, "I just got a message from the delivery driver. Your lunch is on its way, should be here before it's time for me to take mine." She sounded placating, giving him a good distraction away from Naddy. I was going to have to make sure that I bumped her salary up with payroll before it was time for her to get her first paycheck. "Did you need anything? Maybe some more coffee?"

"No, that's fine," he said, sounding slightly unsure. The fact that Deidre could knock some of the confidence out of my father's voice instantly made me like her. That made hiring her all the more worth it. Dad retreated back into his office, closing the door behind him.

I took that as my opportunity to leave the office and see Naddy in what she decided fitted the professional definition. She wore a gray dress that went down to her knees, an a-line skirt flared just around her hips without giving much to the imagination. She had a lavender cardigan over it and the only thing she needed to complete her librarian look was a pair of glasses.

It was professional. Just boring. I shouldn't complain because Naddy dressed like this meant she was less likely to get the attention of other men, hopefully. I was having a hard enough time sharing her with Austin and Gavin, I didn't like the idea of other men looking at her and wanting her, too.

I tapped on the reception desk and gave Deidre a nod, "Remind me that I owe you a raise."

"Boy," she cocked her head to one side and eyed me speculatively. "I just started. Don't think I won't hold you to that."

I didn't fight the grin as I turned to Naddy. "I've got an errand to run that I need you to come with me on," I said to her. "Let me grab something from my desk then we'll go." I didn't leave her there long, because even if dad didn't know how to handle Deidre I didn't want to run the risk he was going to come back out of his office. "It won't be long, if you need me," I began as I passed reception, "You've got my number."

"You have a client in an hour and a half," she reported back to me. She went as far as wagging a finger at me, almost like she was chastising me.

"I'll be here, don't worry," I assured her as I guided Naddy out of the office and into the parking lot. "You should have told me that she has this bad habit of mothering people."

"I wouldn't call her doing her job mothering," Nadia huffed out. "Especially considering how you put her into a position she's not familiar with." She looked worried as I opened the passenger side door for her. She didn't immediately get into my car, she just looked at me.

"She might be over compensating, don't take advantage of her."

"As long as she makes my dad uncomfortable I'll have a job for her as long as she wants it," I assured her. "As far as I'm concerned she can just make coffee for me. Are you going to get in or not?" I drummed my fingers against the door. "You heard her, I've got other things to do."

That seemed to satisfy her, or at least she was accepting it because she sat down. When I came around to the driver side, I was met with a confused expression. "How is she making your dad uncomfortable?"

That gave me pause. There wasn't a good way to answer it that didn't make me look bad. Honesty would probably be the best route. But it would likely garner judgment by proxy. A lie would be something I could easily cover as long as she never actually met him. I used the need to drive to draw out answering her, I paid a little too much attention to it.

"It's embarrassing to admit," I began carefully. "But anyone he considers to be beneath him is off putting.' I grimaced a little, struggling to admit that he was a racist, classist man. His shortcomings were reflected on me, he was part of the reason why I was where I was at. "I didn't hire Deidre there with the intent of making my father uncomfortable. There was a spot that needed to be filled and I thought she would fit into it."

"If she complains to me about it I get to kick your ass," she said without missing a beat. "I sincerely hope you didn't put her into a position that she's going to be taken advantage of."

"For my father, business is a priority," I told her easily. It was true, to a point. His first priority was closer to getting laid without strings. Business was a close second. "He's going to do anything and everything he can to protect his dollar." I shook my head, "The only thing Deidre is in danger of around my father is him deciding that he's attracted to her."

As soon as the words were out of my mouth I realized I said the wrong thing.

"Tell me you're kidding," she said after a length. When I didn't immediately answer her, she reached over the center console and swatted my shoulder. It wasn't something she was going to let go.

"Deidre is smart," I pointed out to her. "She's not going to let anyone pressure her into doing something she doesn't want to do." I spotted the high rise that Henri's office was in and began to shift lanes so I could easily turn into it. "I didn't put her into a position where she wouldn't be able to thrive and take care of her family."

That seemed to satisfy her. I didn't feel her scrutiny and after a glance I saw her gazing out the window. It should've been a relief. But I knew there wasn't any chance that I would walk away from this conversation and still be appealing to her. I could only hope that today would make up for it.

When I pulled into the parking lot I found the folder containing her resume and the cover letter I wrote up for her. I did everything I could to make her stand out for the few jobs I knew that could be entry level. Bringing her with me to pay Henri was going out on a limb.

I got out of the car and came around to help her out. She didn't wait for me to open the door but she didn't shake off my offered hand. The distance that I felt with Naddy in the beginning was starting to dwindle. Or so I hoped.

Naddy followed me readily into the lobby. She didn't question me as I led her into the elevators, but from the way she fidgeted I could see the anxiety in her.

"It will be fine," I said, trying to reassure her. "Let me do all the talking."

"What is this and why am I here?" She asked, her voice steeled a little. It did little to cover the way she shifted from foot to foot and soothed a hand over her hair. She had it pulled back from her face with bobby pins, but every time she worried with it one of the pins slid further out of place.

"I have to pay a bill," I explained lightly. I wasn't going to go into the fact that it was something that could've easily been done from my office and she didn't need to be here. But I had more to do. When I stepped off the elevator, I waited just long enough to make sure she was following me.

I found Henri's secretary at her desk and I pulled a cashier's check from my inner jacket pocket. "Mr. Price," she stood up, clearly surprised to see me. "We don't have you on the calendar. Is everything alright with Mr. Fowler?"

"Everything is fine," I told her as I offered her the check. "I'm just here to cover the rest of his outstanding bill where his ex is concerned. But, since I'm here," I began eyeing the door. This was a chance that I was taking. "Is he free?"

She opened her mouth then closed it, shaking her head. She took the check from me, confusion written on her face, "He's not with a client at the moment. But he's technically on a working lunch so he's going to object to an interruption."

"I'll handle that," I said, easily stepping forward and through the door before she could protest further. I held the door open, standing just inside the elaborately decorated office. I looked at Naddy expecting, "Come on."

"Excuse me," Henri said from his desk. He didn't bother to stand and he didn't look pleased as his secretary warned. He wasn't going to be happy with me anyway. "Mr. Price, if you need to speak with me you need to make an appointment," he growled with a little frustration. "Mr. Fowler is well aware that any sort of meetings like this need to be set in advance so that I can make sure I have all the appropriate files ready to answer any of his questions."

"This," I said with more confidence than I felt, "is not a meeting that is connected with Austin by any means." I turned to see his secretary had followed us into the office. I sat down, in the event she was going to ask both of us to leave.

Naddy just lingered behind the chair that I sat in. She looked unsure and curious at the same time. This was a position she was unfamiliar with and I knew that. I was putting her somewhere she would feel like she didn't belong. But I was determined to throw all my cards onto the table for this woman.

"I have settled his account though," I told the man in front of me. "So there shouldn't be any issues with his ex anymore."

"The only issues we have concerning her is that I can't get him to agree to the logical route," Henri said irritably. "Her abandoning her son is reason enough for him to seek full custody. There wouldn't be a judge that would rule in her favor after she was found in customs when she decided to take an extended vacation without informing anyone else." He folded his arms over his chest, the meal he had been picking as was forgotten. "But Mr. Fowler doesn't want to do that. He doesn't want to cut off access to Landon like he should, given the situation."

"I'll talk to him when I see him," I raised a hand. "But that's not what I'm here for." I put the manila folder with Naddy's resume onto his desk. "I'm here to call in a favor."

Henri looked down at the folder I placed on his desk then back up to me. His brow raised and disdain overtook his expression. "I do not owe you anything," he said simply. "I have been incredibly honest with your friend and have not taken advantage of the situation he is in financially when I can tell you any other attorney that was in my position would have." He didn't touch the folder, "If you have paid the remainder you have seen that I have been quite light with the fees that I charged."

I knew he would consider himself absolved of sins, helping someone that was in a dire situation and not screwing people wasn't something he was known for. It was the reason why my father kept his number close to heart. Because he knew how to play the system to the advantage of his high paying clients.

I relaxed back into the chair and folded my arms over my chest. I just looked at the man across from me, waiting to get under his skin. I didn't even need to say a word. I was a product of what he did. I had trauma and a number of other issues throughout my life that this man had a hand in.

I highly doubted he wasn't aware of it. I doubted I wasn't the only one that suffered thanks to him. The only reason why I wasn't bothered by employing his services was because I knew he would keep an unhinged woman from taking advantage of my friend, and keep him from bending to whatever she wanted from him.

I raised an eyebrow at him, "I don't really need to explain, do I?"

Nothing showed on his face. He didn't so much as twitch. "What do you want?"

"This," I gestured over my shoulder, where I could feel Naddy hovering. "This is someone I'm dating. Austin Fowler also has invested interest in her. She needs employment."

For the first time since we walked into his office, Henri glanced at Nadia. His brows raised before he turned his attention to the folder I had placed on his desk. "I have run things just fine with just Vanessa. I don't need any more employees," he paused as he picked up the folder to look in it. His brows drew down and he gave me a glare, "Unqualified employees."

"Paralegals don't necessarily need to have degrees," I said, waving a hand before Naddy could even protest. I knew she would. "I'm sure it would make it easier on her, and if she was interested in it, I wouldn't deter her from studying it to be a more valuable asset to you. But for that to happen, she would need to be employed first."

"I could use help with filing," his secretary spoke up. "If she's able to handle the little things like fetching coffee and making sure clients are comfortable I could do more for cases."

I didn't expect that. If Henri wasn't compassionate, Vanessa was. I gave her a nod, deciding the next time I had to come in here I would make sure I was more polite.

"No," Henri said after a length. His attention was focused on Nadia, eyeing her up and down. "She hardly looks as if she would be appropriate in an office environment, that was even before I looked at her resume. Perhaps she should consider teachers as a line of work? She certainly looks as if she would be at home in a classroom."

He was reaching. "She needs a tailor," I agreed with him as I turned to look at her. "I can get her on par with your style demands easily."

"That's not necessary," Naddy spoke, putting her hand on my shoulder. "He said no."

"He doesn't have room to say no," I snapped at her. It surprised the both of us. I hadn't expected that to come out of me. It wasn't because he was declining, I could see the reasoning. Hiring someone uneducated was a risk. But I wouldn't suggest this if I didn't think Naddy would fit. I turned to glare at the man across the desk. "She's hard working and dedicated. I am twisting her arm to be here as you can tell," I took a breath and slowly released it.

"I have room to say no," Henri said stubbornly. "Just as I have reason to end my professional relationship with you and your friend simply because you are trying to guilt me into this." He stood up, adjusting the cuffs of his suit and smoothing down the material of the light blue button down he wore. "I've heard enough. You can leave. I will forward you Mr. Fowler's file."

"Do you really want to do that?" I asked. "Because I had just made him even with you. I'm sure that would look extremely unprofessional. I imagine a judge would agree with me and if I had access to you, you know I have access to every flavor of attorney that my father has done business with." I scratched casually at my chin, "That's not even going through his contacts and finding all the people he's referred to you. People I see regularly. Who's to trust you? The guy that makes knocked up mistresses disappear?"

The hand on my shoulder tightened. "That's enough," Nadia began lowly. "This is too much and I really don't need you to go out on a limb like this." She let go of me, "Let's go so you're not late for that meeting."

"Henri," Vanessa said with a hint of warning. She either didn't hear Naddy or she was ignoring what she said.

I'd like to think that I intimidated the man across from me enough for him to cave. But I knew it was likely his secretary being the voice of reason. The glare I received was answer enough, I didn't resist the urge to smirk at him. "When does she start?"

***

After we got back to the office, I caught her wrist to keep her from going to her car. I couldn't tell if she was angry with me. I could decipher her expression and outside of the tension in her shoulders I couldn't figure out how she handled everything.

I couldn't wait until I got home later to find out how she felt.

I pulled her into the office, casting a worried glance at Deidre. She watched us, eyes widening slightly but she didn't say a word. She didn't even greet us in the same way she did when Naddy first entered the office.

I closed my door behind her and I pressed her against the wall. I didn't intend to press for anything, but I was afraid of just how she'd see me. I dropped my brow against her shoulder and waited for the day to come back and bite me in the ass.

She was tense, but she didn't push me away. It felt like it took her forever to relax. Her hand pressed against my chest without pushing me away. Could she feel how hard my heart was beating?

"Don't you have a meeting?" It came out of her in a whisper.

"It was something I put on the schedule because I expected this to take a while," I admitted. "If I had something on the schedule I wouldn't get flack for having an opening on it."

"Who would you catch flak from?"

"I work for my father," I said without moving away from her. "Any free time I have while I'm 'on the clock' is money lost. I sometimes schedule fake people for meetings when I just need to be alone."

"Do you need me to leave?"

"I would prefer it if you didn't."

"What do you need me to do?" She asked.

I didn't know what to say. There was the temptation to ask her to feel for me what she does for Austin. I wanted to ask her to care about me, to need me. But I didn't know how to put it into words. It should be easy, but I knew I couldn't make the demands of her like I did Henri.

The hand against my chest moved down to open my suit jacket then wrapped around my waist. She pressed her palm against the small of my back, ushering me closer to her. Her other arm wound around my sounders and her fingers curled up along the back of my neck, tracing my hair line.

She didn't say anything else. She just held me. Instead of making me feel better it felt like my heart was lodged in my throat.

I didn't deserve to be here.

25

Nadia

I was off kilter on the way home. I didn't know how to process the side of Vaughn. His guarded exterior was something I had gotten used to. It left me feeling more things about him than I was prepared for. The fact that this wasn't the only time he's done this to me was more than a little frustrating.

I needed to pin him down and just see what all there was to him so he would stop taking me by surprise. After having each of them smack my ass I wasn't sure I would be able to do that. Especially if Austin or Gavin was around. I would need to get Vaughn alone.

Just the thought of that was a little intimidating.

My phone rang, startling me out of the turmoil that Vaughn had created. After swerving a little, I managed to dig it out of my pocket. I didn't look at the number, I hit accept and put the call on speaker. "Hello?"

"Okay," mom's voice filled the car. "I'm more than willing to accept your choices. I will not judge. But I feel like I need to have a conversation with you."

I didn't resist the urge to groan. Of course this would happen at the worst possible time. "Mom," I said after a whine. "It's been a long day." It was just after three and I only had a few hours to formulate any sort of plan as to what to do about Vaughn.

"You don't think I've had a long day? I've had a long ass week. I've had a couple of long ass weeks waiting to see if I was going to hear anything else from you and your harem about that baby," she snapped over the line. "You introduced this thing you're doing plus a baby to your mother and don't call me. For how long has it been, Nadia? I've driven past the diner, I know that it's closed.

I haven't heard a word from you at all. I just want to talk to you one on one without some boys to influence your answers."

"They wouldn't have," I assured her as I started to steer towards her house instead of my own. "At this point, I don't think Austin has any capabilities of being manipulative and I doubt that Gavin would stand the chance at being able to persuade you into anything."

"I'm not someone that can be persuaded into anything," she grumped into the phone. "Your father would like you to tell him how this works."

"I don't know that he really wants to know how this works," I said offhandedly as I found the neighborhood I grew up in. "I don't know what you're worried about. If I was in a bad situation you would know about it."

"You say that," she began evenly, "we both know that's not the truth. Just because things don't look like they're wrong doesn't mean there isn't an issue. I know you probably don't remember the problems we've had, but I can assure you that this is something both your father and I need to be concerned about." She paused to take a breath and I could hear food frying in a pan, she was cooking already. "I just want to make sure you are fine and I don't need to take a weekend off to handle them."

As soon as I rolled to a stop, I dropped my brow against the steering wheel. "Mom, I think you're seeing something there that isn't."

"Well, how about you come over here and clarify things for me," she huffed into the line. "Your father will be home in about thirty minutes. You can answer his questions and I'll judge whether or not I need to clean out the trunk of my car." She paused, "I'll have to use your father's truck. I'm not going to be able to fit those three boys in the trunk of my car."

"You're willingness to commit murder is a little terrifying."

"Baby," she made a noise. I could hear the faucet cut on then off. "When you have a daughter you will understand. You will be willing to put a man six feet under for hurting her, or at least I hope you would be."

She had a point. "Okay," I relented. "I'm already here. Do I need to call them to come over?"

"Honestly, I'd rather not," she paused and when I looked up at the house I could see her peeking through the blinds. "You might as well come inside. The house isn't clean, but I've been working all week and so has your father."

I turned off the car and got out. I walked into the house and went straight to the kitchen. I sat at the table I had spent the majority of my life at with dinner, homework, and countless lectures from both of them. It seemed natural to sit down here and prepare for the worse.

"You're dressed up," she noted, not turning from the stove.

"I guess I had an interview today," I told her. If that's what it was, it definitely didn't seem like it was. I barely said a word during it and I knew the man that I would be working for just glanced at my resume. I could only hope that Vaughn wasn't setting me up for failure.

"How did that go?" she asked, giving me the once over.

I didn't know what to tell her. I definitely didn't want to tell her that my boyfriend had strong-armed another man into hiring me, someone that was completely unqualified for the job. "It went pretty well," I cleared my throat. "I'm pretty positive I got the job." That wasn't really a question, the real question was how I felt about getting a job I didn't earn.

Mom made a pleased noise, but didn't look back at me. "Where is it at?"

"At an attorney's office," I admitted. I waited for the question of how, or why, I got hired there because it wasn't a job I've had before. "A friend helped me get the job," I clarified, hoping it would stave off any further inquiries.

"By friend you mean one of your boys?" she asked. She didn't even look over her shoulder at me. How the hell did she know?

I didn't answer her, I just slumped against the table and wished there was a way I could speed through this. I rubbed my face, knowing I was smearing make up and probably making myself look like a hot mess. "Where's Dad at?"

"He's on his way home," she said as she transferred chicken out of the pan she had been cooking. "How's your boyfriend's baby?"

"Landon is good," I said as I straightened and shifted in the chair. "He's adapted to being at the house with all of us very well. Any time I've noticed that he's fussy, he's either gnawing on his hand or obviously sleepy." I shrugged a little as I considered what I knew about Austin's son. I didn't even know that he was affected by the fact that Lauren had disappeared. Did he even realize she was gone?

"Kids are resilient," she said as she directed her attention to a pot that she stirred. "They handle more than they should and keep going," her voice wavered and she cleared her throat. "There's a good chance he'll end up as a well-adjusted adult assuming he has someone that cares about him."

"I'm well adjusted," I said, trying to sound reassuring. I didn't know if I believed it. Sometimes it looked like I had my shit together, at least if we kept the bar low.

Mom was kind enough to not comment. Though that was probably because my position in life was a reflection of hers. While my grandparents were alive when I was a kid, I didn't know them well enough to be able to judge how either of my parents had grown up. I assumed their situation had been similar to mine.

I watched her as she drained what turned out to be potatoes. She took her time seasoning what was in the pot before stirring it in again. "I only want what's best for you," she said after a length. "Are you sure what you've gotten yourself into is what's best?"

I shook my head, it took her long enough. "How do you figure out what's best?" I asked. "How do you figure out if you've made a massive mistake? I feel like if I cut and run now it would probably be a massive mistake," I looked down at the table top. There were years at this table that were detailed in every scratch, in the fade of the Formica, and at the rough edges. "I don't want to. I don't want to go back to where I started. Even if it ends horribly, I don't want to go back to just," I paused. What had Mara said I was doing? "Just existing."

The backdoor opened and dad stepped into the house with a long groan that suggested he had a day. His ball cap was on his head, but it didn't do anything to cover the sweat that accumulated in his hair. He looked at mom, took a deep breath and looked relieved, "What's for dinner?"

"I've got some Lowry chicken, potatoes, and zucchini," mom reported. "But before you go park yourself in front of the TV I thought we would have dinner around the table."

Dad's gaze connected with mine. He dropped his lunchbox onto the counter before he came to the table and sat across from me. "I tried to tell her that this wasn't something I wanted to be in on," he said to me. "I figured it would go one of two ways. You'd be fine. You can take care of yourself, you've done that so far on your own just fine. Or you wouldn't be." He shrugged a little, "If it was going to go that way I would just do damage control like I'm supposed to."

"And help me hide bodies when it's necessary," Mom supplied. "Set the table, Nadia."

Of course she would tell me to do that now, not before I sat down. I pushed myself to my feet and went about getting the plates from the cabinet. I hadn't planned on staying for dinner, but it was clear that I wasn't going to escape any time soon. I didn't mention anything to Austin or Gavin where I was going when I left the house and I was willing to bet that I would be missed if Vaughn got home before I did.

After I laid the plates on the table mom was quick to start putting food on them. "You want tea?" I asked dad.

"Water," he answered gratefully. "If I have caffeine this late I won't get to sleep."

"What about you, mom?"

"I'm in the same boat as the old man," she answered me. "You'll figure that out the older you get."

I didn't want to say anything as I got them both water from the faucet, with ice. I elected to drink mom's sweet tea. I already figured I wouldn't get much sleep after the way the day started. Mom was making sure that I was going to stress about the future from here.

When I sat back down we started eating in silence. I didn't think about what this meant, whether or not they were giving their approval or were just admitting to the fact that they weren't in control of my decisions. That last part seemed wrong. Growing up my parents didn't try to control me.

"Do you want to meet them?" I asked, mildly afraid of what their answer might be.

Dad just looked up at Mom, like he was waiting for her to make the call. That was probably the case. He wasn't one to put pressure on me. It was like he said, he was here for damage control. From fixing my car to hugging me tight without judgment when I cried after a long day at school. He wasn't the type to create friction.

Mom, on the other hand, would raise hell and he would be right there beside her. "I wouldn't mind speaking to each of them and developing my own opinion," she said as she cut into her chicken. "I'm not pressuring you for children. I'm not going to tell you to pick one. You are perfectly capable of making your own choices, as your father pointed out." She took a bite. "If any of them lay their hands on you, or this was all some sort of ploy for the three of them to take advantage of you. You don't get to argue with me about what happens next."

I snorted and didn't hide the fact that I rolled my eyes. "I think you've already struck fear into Gavin and Austin. I doubt they would do anything that would cause you to rain wrath upon them."

"I can only hope so for their sakes," Dad said as he directed his attention to his plate. "Tell me about what's got you all dressed up."

***

I hadn't intended to stay at my parents' house as late as I did. I missed dinner at the house and after a few worried texts from Gavin, I made sure I sent the three of them messages to let them know where I had been. The best way to break to them the fact that my parents wanted a more in-depth meeting didn't involve a text message.

Especially, when I didn't know what had been said to Vaughn about them. Did he even care to meet my mom and dad? He hadn't said a word about introducing me to his dad. When I saw him at the office earlier, I knew the older well-dressed man had to be his father.

Vaughn was the spitting image of the senior Price. Same dark hair, peppered with gray at the temples and eyes that could pin a person with just a look. He had looked at me while I stood in the lobby with Deidre and I had been struck silent. The air of intimidation was so thick that I was surprised Dee hadn't complained to me about it.

That was Vaughn's father. My own dad wouldn't have looked at me like that, much less a stranger. It filled in a lot of blanks as to why Vaughn was the way he was.

I came into the house surprised to find it quiet. Had they already gone to bed? The kitchen light was still on and so was the bedroom, there was soft light leaking from down the hall but that suggested that the baby was likely already asleep. That should be a relief.

I came into the bedroom to see a movie on the screen. Austin was only partially paying attention to the television and the rest of his attention on his phone. Gavin was laying on the opposite side of the bed, his arms behind his head and his complete attention on the movie. Vaughn wasn't in sight and the bathroom didn't look like it was occupied.

"What's the verdict?" Gavin asked as he sat up. He propped his elbows on his knees, eyeing me. It was like he was expecting bad news.

I blinked at him, "I got a job?"

"You went to your parents," Austin pointed out. He held up his phone like he was referring to the text I had sent him earlier. "I don't expect that went well considering how your mother handled meeting us last time."

"Mom wants Dad to meet you," I said evenly. I crossed my arms over my stomach. "Dad isn't as trigger happy as mom is. That's a bright side to the situation. I think she wanted to make sure that this wasn't something I was being forced into."

Gavin deflated back onto the bed. "I'm fucked."

Austin only spared him a glance. "Have you discussed how to do that? I could cook dinner or something if you think that would make an impression?" he looked hopeful at me, his brows up and his phone was in his lap but I could see him fidgeting with it. I bet he was already considering what to do for my parents to win them over.

He didn't do that when we met Dave and Kelli.

"I don't think that's necessary--" I started to say.

"I have an idea," Vaughn said from behind me. I turned to see him lingering just out of reach in the doorway of the bedroom. "Instead of having them over and throwing the way we do things in their face, I think it would be better to show what we offer her," he nodded towards me.

"Bragging isn't going to win my mom over," I protested.

"Not what I was intending," he said evenly. "Bar is ready to go. I'm pretty positive I've got it staffed enough that we can do a dry run. Basically a party where we just invite friends and people we know." He looked at Gavin and Austin. "It gives us plenty of time to make sure we have all the bases covered for opening night as well as how the bar will run and what I need from you." He looked at me, "Your parents could come to that."

"I don't know if this is a better idea than Austin cooking dinner," I tried to warn him. "We're not fancy people."

"I'm trying to kill two birds with one stone. The more people we have the better it will be," he said to me without missing a beat. "I can already guess how meeting your parents is going to go. There's no chance of looking good to them," he shrugged like it was something that didn't bother him. "I'm not really concerned with their opinion. If I meet any parents it's not going to be for my benefit."

"I'll ask them," I offered. Fighting him wasn't something I wanted to do. The mention of opening night made me reflect on just how much work Vaughn had been doing. He had the office he worked at, he was helping Gavin's parents find a house and he came home to spend time with Landon.

How had he managed all of it?

When I didn't offer him further protests he looked momentarily confused. "It's going to be simple," he said to me. "Nothing to get dressed up over. I figured we could do a sampling of the different foods we have on the menu, that way we can get feedback on what's good and what we can leave out."

"Almost sounds like fun," Gavin offered.

That seemed to get Vaughn to focus. He shook his head and he stepped around me to get to the closet. He kicked off his shoes and began to make quick work of his button down. "We'll be working," he said evenly.

"I don't know what to do about Landon to be able to manage him as well as work at the bar," Austin spoke up. "Even if I were able to put him into daycare there isn't one in town that would be open to accommodate the hours we would be working."

"We'll figure something out," Vaughn said. "Bring him for this at least and then I'll see if I can't figure out a way that at least one of us is home to make sure he's taken care of." He dropped his shirt and continued to undress, "This is assuming that Lauren won't rear her ugly head again."

The offhanded way he said it surprised me. I wasn't aware of just how much it bothered me until my thoughts came out of me unfiltered, "She doesn't get to take him back." I shook my head, casting a wary look at Austin. "She doesn't get to have him back."

"I don't have a say in that," Austin said suddenly, he got up from the bed and he raised his hands up like he could placate me. I hadn't been angry at the suggestion of Lauren, but now I couldn't say that. "Lauren is his mother, there's no taking away from that."

"No," Gavin spoke up from the bed. "She doesn't get to fuck off like that then come back like nothing happened. That is not how reality works."

"That is exactly how reality works," Vaughn spoke up. "She is completely capable of coming back from wherever the hell she's been and petitioning to take Landon back." He sat heavily on the bed, not looking at anyone. "You're not at so much of a disadvantage anymore. You have someone in your pocket that's going to make sure you're not fucked over."

"I think all of this has proven that she's not fit," Gavin argued, he sounded angry. "Fuck her."

"I don't want to keep him from his mother," Austin said with finality. "I don't want to be the reason why he doesn't see her. If she decides to take that route, that's on her. But it won't be on me." He went for the bedroom door. "This isn't an option that I want to discuss. I have this bullshit in my head constantly. I don't need to argue about what the possible outcomes might be with you." He paused, taking a breath. His hand went through his hair and he looked back at the bed, "I appreciate that you're invested and I appreciate that you care. But all I can do is wait and see what she wants from me and go from there."

He didn't wait for anyone else to respond, he turned and walked out of the room. There wasn't so much as anger trailing him, it was more him fleeing. I was sure the conversation just added to the building stress.

26

Nadia

I started my first professional job with an email. It was simple; hours that I would work and my starting salary. It was way too much money considering I was entry level. I made sure to text Vaughn to tell him that, but the asshole just left me on read. I shouldn't look a gift horse in the mouth but it always seemed like Vaughn left me in a state of being overwhelmed.

I felt inadequate as I rode the elevator up. I wore a pair of faded gray slacks and the blouse I had bought when I went shopping with Deidre. It didn't feel like enough to wear for my first day as a secretary. Or was it an assistant? I didn't even know what my job title was.

Things were a whole lot easier just waiting tables. Often there was a uniform or a dress code that was simple. All I had to worry about the diner was having my apron on, no one really judged what I was wearing.

When I walked up to the desk Vanessa sat at, I saw her eye me. I wasn't sure if she was judging my appearance or if it was just that I made a horrible impression right off the lift. I straightened the hem of the blouse… maybe I looked wrinkled? I took my time this morning, trying to do more with my appearance than I usually did. I thought I did a decent job, Vaughn had given me a once over without saying a word.

It left me questioning whether or not he would set me up for failure.

"Nadia," she greeted me politely, standing from her desk. "I'm Vanessa. There wasn't really the opportunity for us to formally meet each other the other day. Plus on top of the tension Mr. Price likes to bring into the office, it didn't really seem appropriate for me to do that." She offered me her hand, her nails were manicured but without the acrylic tips. She wore a muted crimson dress with silver accents. She looked classy and well put together.

The comparison made me feel all the more inadequate. "It's nice to meet you," I offered meekly.

"We don't really have time to chat, we've got to get things started before Henri gets in the office. I'll start by showing you how to clock in, then we'll go make coffee," she said easily. She waved me around her desk and gestured for me to sit down. "I've got you a computer on order, it will be here next week so in the meantime you'll have to use mine when necessary."

It made it so much more obvious that they didn't need me and Vaughn was taking advantage of the situation. I cleared my throat, "If I'm putting you out I don't need to be here."

"While I'm sure Henri would adore to hear that," Vanessa said with a smile, reaching over to wiggle her mouse. "I could use the help. So, unless you're going to run for the hills before I make the effort, let me take advantage of the fact that he caved." She directed me to an application on the desktop and I followed the prompts to create an account. "Henri doesn't like change so he's probably going to be grouchy or pretend you're not here." She shrugged, "But he'll have to get used to it."

"If I don't have a computer to work from, what am I going to do?" I asked her. "Please don't tell me I'm just going to sit at the desk."

"Oh no," she grinned. "You get to get coffee, lunch, and do filing while I do everything else."

She was too pleased by the idea, but given how much I was making now I wasn't going to complain about being a glorified waitress. I had the coffee maker going as she gave me a run down of the clients that would be in the office today. I wrote down how coffee was preferred and who favored water over anything else.

I had Mr. Lange's coffee ready for him as soon as he walked off the elevator. He only spared me a glance when I put the mug on the coaster on his desk. Any sort of impression I could make with him was shot and he didn't so much as give me a good morning. Vanessa warned me.

That was fine. It left me in a position that I was used to. The only extra thing I had to worry about was filing, but it was so easy to figure out. Vanessa was thorough and precise with everything she did in the office. It was easy enough to adapt to and I knew with her direction she would steer me in the right way.

For the first day, I was more confident that this was something I could handle. I didn't see a problem, even when I rushed to get Mr. Lange's lunch only to get a little bit lost. I still made it back to the office with ten minutes to spare.

It's when I walked into Mr. Lange's office with his lunch in tow that I faltered. All the confidence I built up throughout the day drained so fast it made my head spin. Vaughn's father sat in front of my new boss with his striking features.

"You hired someone new?" he asked, eyeing me speculatively. There was recognition in his gaze, he remembered me from that brief moment in the lobby at his office.

I waited for him to call me out, for him to say that he knew me from somewhere. To ask where Mr. Lange picked me up from. Would he connect me to his son?

"Vanessa has been complaining about how much I over work her," Mr. Lange said without giving me a glance. "She has finally twisted my arm hard enough to the point I had to give her what she wanted."

"I never imagined that I would have to tell you not to give into a woman," Mr. Price chuckled, not taking his eyes off of me. "You give in and they just keep taking."

"Employees are not the same," Mr. Lange said before looking up at me. "Did you need something?"

"I was bringing you your lunch," I said evenly. I looked at Vaughn's father and offered him a smile, trying not to be bothered. "Did you need anything, sir?"

"Edward Price," he told me, his brows rising just a little bit. He didn't offer me his hand, he didn't even stand. He just shifted so he could get a better look at me.

Yep, this was Vaughn's father.

"It's a pleasure to meet you," I said without missing a beat. "Did you need anything?" I prompted again. "Coffee, water?"

"He's not staying," Mr. Lange cut in. "He was just in for a visit. You can go on your own lunch." He sounded dismissive, but he wasn't being disrespectful.

"Thank you," I said lowly.

I turned to walk out of the room and I heard a hiss from Vaughn's father. "You sure have a knack for hiring attractive women, I was under the impression that you didn't care for them. How do you find them?"

"I attract women that prefer to not be sexually harassed. If you make either one of my employees uncomfortable you know that I will not side with you on this matter," Mr. Lange said coldly. "Now, instead of making a nuisance of yourself, why don't you get to the point?"

I left the office so I couldn't hear their conversation. I might've tripped on the way out. It made Vanessa look up at me, surprise on her face. "Sorry," she said immediately. "I should've warned you. Some of Henri's clients get so familiar with him they don't make appointments like they should. Edward is one of those clients," she pulled a face as she said it.

It called back to Vaughn barging in here and demanding Mr. Lange's time.

I didn't know what to say. "He told me to go on lunch?" I asked her, not sure if it was something I should follow. Mr. Lange might sign my checks but I was sure that my real boss was out here behind the desk next to mine.

"Go ahead," she said pleasantly. "Take an hour. That should give him enough time to get out of here."

With that long of a break I didn't know what to do with myself. I had lunch at a fast food joint that was close by and I lingered in the little dining room a little longer than I should have. I didn't know what else to do. I doubted I had enough time to go back to the house. But I did spy the building that Vaughn and Deidre worked out of. Maybe I could work in the habit of visiting at least one of them for lunch?

I was surprised when I beat Vaughn home, it was just before six. Austin had dinner on the table and Landon was in his highchair. He squealed in delight as I walked in the door and the feeling he gave me wasn't something I had words for. I didn't get to come home to this while I worked at the diner. Everyone was usually in bed.

Gavin was on the couch, a sports show on the television. He gave me a lazy smile as he got up. I was rewarded with a kiss and a loose hug before he went to the table. It was already set and Austin was putting servings onto plates.

The domestic air was comforting.

"Vaughn is running late," I observed as I came to the table.

"He stopped to get some drinks," Gavin supplied. "Figured we needed something to celebrate your new job. He shouldn't be much longer." He folded his arms on the little strip of table, "Do you want to wait on him?"

I blinked at him, surprised he would send his friend on an errand then decide to eat without him. "Yeah, especially if he's not that far out behind me. If we're all gonna sit down for dinner we all should be here."

"I'm just setting the table," Austin said as he went to the fridge. "I didn't say it was time to eat." He placed a browned chicken breast onto a bed of spinach and a mixture of other vegetables. "Don't touch it," he growled at Gavin. "Help me out by feeding him and I'll let you eat."

Gavin heaved himself back to his feet with a grumble. He went to the cabinet that held the baby bottles and formula. He took his time getting Landon's liquid dinner ready, because he had the baby's attention. Little fists hit the plastic tray he sat in, like he was demanding the man fixing his meal to hurry.

Then the front door opened and Vaughn stepped in, a six pack in hand. That's when I noticed the immediate difference between the son and the father. The man I was involved with had his cold moments, he often wore a mask of disinterest and disdain. But as Landon squealed of delight at seeing him walk through the door, Vaughn's face lit up in response.

He was an attractive man, something pretty to look at even when his features were schooled into a blank expression. But with the grin that pulled across his lips and the happiness that he reflected back at the baby as he approached him, he was startling. There was no avoiding just how beautiful he was when he looked genuinely happy.

How had I not noticed just how good he looked like this? Had I ever seen him happy? I didn't know. Even before all of this started.

Vaughn looked up at me, the expression he showed Landon still lingering on his face. "How was your first day?" he asked, taking the offered bottle from Gavin. He gave it to the baby, distracting himself from me for a beat and reigniting that smile.

Should I mention his father? Should I announce that I had met him and could see all the startling similarities between the two men? Would he already know?

Would it wipe the soft, gentle expression off of his face?

I swallowed, "It went better than I expected to." It wasn't a lie. But maybe it was better that I didn't go into all the details. I was sure that he could go without knowing that I'd met his father. "Vanessa assured me that she's going to have me trained enough so she can take a vacation within the month."

"Vanessa?" Austin echoed as he finished plating the food. His brows were drawn down and he looked at Vaughn. "That was your doing?" He didn't sound impressed as he said it. "Why does that sound like a good idea?" His voice didn't raise but from his expression it was clear he didn't think it was.

Gavin looked confused, looking between the two men. He had a fork in hand like he was waiting for the okay to eat dinner. He didn't put together the connection, or he just didn't know who Vanessa was. It showed how oblivious he could be, I was sure he had gone up to Mr. Lange's office with Austin on a number of occasions. Maybe he didn't interact with Vanessa when he had been there?

Who was I kidding? He just didn't bother to learn her name. I'm sure if I described Vanessa he would be on the same page.

"I took her to Henri's office to put pressure on him," Vaughn admitted. "I wanted to make sure he was doing everything possible to make this," he motioned towards Landon, "work in our favor. So far, it's worked. Just because you have visitation doesn't mean that Lauren can't come back for more child support or with accusations that you are hurting or mistreating Landon in some way." He raised his hand, anticipating the need to interrupt Austin, "Your current situation doesn't make the future easier. Lauren will be a wildcard in your life until he turns eighteen. Trust me, I know."

"Your mom wasn't like Lauren," Gavin protested. "There's no comparison there at all."

I wasn't going to object, or argue, because this was a subject that I wasn't entirely familiar with. This was a part of Vaughn that I was still learning. And while I should be offended that I was being used, I wasn't going to ignore just how much I was making and how I was stepping out of the endless cycle of moving from one dead end to another. That and I had a feeling Vaughn was lying.

I wasn't there to put pressure on Mr. Lange to take care of Austin's case. I was there to keep an eye on his father. I just couldn't figure out why.

"Are you bothered that she's working for a man that is handling your child custody case?" Vaughn asked after a length. "Or are you bothered that she's getting to know your attorney?"

"That's where you got hired at?" Gavin asked me, just now connecting the dots. It suggested that he hadn't been paying attention. He looked at Vaughn, "Why do you want to give her that kind of power?"

I blinked, “How is that giving me power?” I shook my head, “I get that it's a terrifying idea to suddenly find out that you’re a parent. There’s supposed to be a difference here. I hope there’s no toxicity that you feel like you need an attorney like Mr. Lange in your pocket so you’re protected against me.” I narrowed my eyes at him, “If you think me having any sort of ‘power’ in this relationship is a bad thing, then we have a whole lot more problems than me working in Austin’s lawyer’s office.”

“Dumbass,” Vaughn grumbled as he sat down at the table. “She's less likely to have people creeping on her working for Henri.” He looked at Austin expectantly, “Putting her in a place where she’s making more money will do a lot of things that don’t really work in our favor.” He shrugged and began to pass around a bottle of beer to each of us. Then he picked up the fork, beginning to eat. “Regardless as to where this all goes, putting someone into a position where they are worse off than where they started in the beginning of the relationship is shitty. I don’t intend to do that and you shouldn’t either.”

I cleared my throat, drawing the three men’s attention back to me. I didn't want to see what their reaction would be to Vaughn’s words. So I needed to play distraction. “Don’t talk about ends like they’re bound to happen soon,” I said to him. “This is just the beginning. Let’s look at this, instead, like it's the beginning.”

27

Austin

I wasn't sure how to feel about this. I walked through the airport terminal, the same one that I'd been left standing in for hours not too long ago. This time I didn't have Landon with me, it was a brief moment in the last few weeks where I was alone and I felt so anxious I was ready to get this over with just so I could get back home.

Mr. Lange had tried to deter me from doing this, he called it unnecessary. He had already done all the paperwork and after I pressed him, made sure charges weren't pressed against her. It hadn't been long enough for Lauren to see real jail time, what he was really concerned with was giving me primary custody. If she decided to fight me for it, Mr. Lange couldn't guarantee that the court wouldn't still side with Lauren.

It's why I felt the need to come out here. There hadn't been any sort of arrangements for her to get Landon back. As far as I was aware, she hadn't said a word about him. I hadn't gotten an email or a text, either before or after she disappeared. I needed to know now. I couldn't wait until she decided she was going to wreck my new found happiness.

I hit the buzzer that had her name labeled neatly by it. I didn't know if she was home, I didn't give her any sort of warning that I was coming. It probably wasn't a good idea considering the restraining order I had on her.

"Hello?" her voice called down from the speaker. It was too late for me to worry about the consequences of my actions.

"We need to talk," I said firmly. I was nowhere near as confident as I sounded.

Nerves knotted up my stomach as I waited for her response. Was she calling the police? This was going to blow up in my face and I was going to end up regretting this.

"I've gotten into enough trouble with you," she snipped back at me. "I don't need you tearing me down any further, Austin."

Something in me twitched. The memories of every volatile exchange between us flooded through me. Had I started some of them? Was I the reason why our relationship had been toxic? Did I deserve every slap and kick she gave me?

There were times where I thought it was all my fault, I shouldered the blame for all of it. If Landon wasn't involved, or at stake, I would continue to let her place blame on me. But I couldn't do that right now.

"You don't get to hide from this," I snapped at the little speaker. "I'm not going to let you get away with leaving me in the airport with our son only for you to decide a month from now that you just want to keep making me miserable by trying to take him from me again." I was yelling and I turned to see the street. It wasn't deserted and there were a few people that were looking at me.

I'd lost control. The fact that she had the power, still, to make me slip like this was concerning. I took a breath and slowly released it, counting slowly backwards from ten. I couldn't let her do this to me, if I did that she would win every time.

I closed my eyes, trying to think of a reasonable way to do this. If only I could channel Vaughn's confidence, if there was a way to put myself into his shoes I wouldn't end up in the situation ever again.

"This is something you won't be able to keep doing to me," I said the thought out loud. I didn't even care if she heard it. Saying it just felt like it was giving the thought reality, like I would be able to reclaim my manhood with everything else this woman had stolen from me.

There was a buzz, cutting through my conviction. I turned quickly, the door didn't open. No one stepped out of it. Did that mean Lauren was offering me entry?

"It would be really fucking stupid for me to come up stairs," I spared the speaker a glance before I reached forward to tug the door to her building open. There would be no telling what could happen in her apartment. I would be leaving myself vulnerable to her in a way I never wanted to do again.

"I thought you said we should talk," she spat over the little speaker.

"Out in the open," I waved my hand around the stoop I stood on. "Where there are witnesses. This would be for the safety of both of us."

The line went quiet and I wondered if she was considering the reasoning behind my words. If she ever reflected on our relationship and considered how things went with remorse. Did she regret how things went? Or was I as much a villain in her life as she was in mine?

"You can buy me coffee," she offered through the little speaker.

Relief flooded me and I let go of the door. I stepped off the stoop and I waited on the sidewalk. I looked up and down the street, checking to see how many people were present. Were they watching? There was a couple that passed me, giving me a wide berth. Neither looked back at me.

Being here was making me paranoid. I brushed both hands through my hair and took another deep breath. The door behind me buzzed and I choked as I dropped my hands. I turned to see Lauren step out on the stoop.

Her face was fresh, slightly shiny with moisturizer. Her blond hair was piled up on the top of her head in a messy bun. She gave me a glare, the eye shadow that lightly framed her eyes seemed to magnify them. I should've been set on fire where I stood with the look she gave me.

"There's a Starbucks a couple of blocks from here," she paused as she eyed me. "Unless you have a car?"

"I took a taxi here," I admitted.

She made a noise, unimpressed with me and stepped out onto the sidewalk with me. She bumped into me solidly, knocking me off kilter. She stalked down the cracked cement without waiting for me to recover. She had a purposeful sway to her hips like she thought she would get my attention with the shake of her ass. That explained the tight leggings she wore.

It wouldn't work. But I wouldn't mention it, busting her ego would do nothing for me. I followed her at a length. If there was distance between us it felt safe. There wasn't a chance that she would be able to make contact with me if she took a swing.

She led us into a Starbucks and went as far as standing in line for service. She didn't say a word to me. The fact that she made no attempt at small talk was a relief. Lauren made her order then turned to me, looking expectantly as she waited for me to make a decision.

"Just a bottle of water," I told the barista as I fished my wallet from my back pocket.

"Is that all you're getting?" Lauren asked in a disbelieving tone.

"This isn't a date," I said to her. I realized she wanted something else, likely a pastry but didn't want to order it for herself. "I'm just here for a conversation."

"A plane ticket makes for an expensive conversation," she huffed and pointed a finger at a decadent cinnamon roll that was smothered in icing and crumbled nuts.

After we received our orders, I let her pick the table where we settled. The table was way too small for me and it made the situation feel more intimate than it should have. I didn't want to sit this close to her. I didn't want to be in public with her. But this wasn't something that could be said over the phone and if I got Mr. Lange involved it would cost me more than the plane ticket to come out here.

Lauren didn't ask a question, she didn't say a word. She just began to daintily pick at the cinnamon roll in front of her while she exuded confidence I hadn't felt in over a year. She wasn't painted the bad guy in our relationship, she had been the victim all because I let her trigger me so easily.

The tables should be turned now. I should feel like I had the upper hand. I didn't. I felt nervous and afraid that I was screwing things up further by coming here.

"Are you going to have a panic attack in public?" she asked, her voice filled with disgust. "Pull yourself together," she didn't even look at me. "How the hell do you expect anyone to see you as a man?"

I took a breath. That was the shove I needed. I put both elbows up on the table and rubbed my face, "Not a panic attack. Just trying to figure out where to start."

"How about pretending you still have your balls?" her features were placid, not changing as she nibbled on the flaky confection. Beautiful as always as she said ugly things.

Something twitched and I clenched my eyes closed, I took in a slow breath and let it out. "I need you to make a choice here and now," I said steadily. I looked up at her, meeting her narrowed gaze. "You can either step back, have limited visitation where you come to us and stay in town until your visit is done. Or you just give him up completely." Somehow, I managed to say it all without buckling under her glare.

I wonder if it was her turn to make a public scene. Would her life crumble around her like mine did? Would she reflect on our relationship and her past with regret?

"I'm his mother," she said in a low serious tone. "No matter what you do or say, there's no changing that."

"Then maybe you should act like it," I managed without emotion. Even though I wanted to snap at her. But I didn't. "Maybe, when you want to take a vacation, you say something ahead of time instead of just *disappearing* on us."

"What's a matter, Austin?" her voice twisted. "Being a parent hard on you? Maybe you should've been there from the beginning when it was constant crying and shitty diapers. I did that all on my own. You having him while he's teething for a couple of weeks should've been easy."

I paused, knowing fundamentally she was right. I missed out on the first three months of Landon's life. But it wasn't by choice. Falling down that rabbit hole she offered would just make an already heated conversation into something worse.

"What you did is called abandonment," I said with finality. "If I hadn't been actively looking for you and I just waited for you to decide to get into contact with me, there's a very good chance you wouldn't have this choice. My attorney has been suggesting that I go for full custody the moment you left me hanging in the airport," I told her. Mr. Lange was sure that, after discovering her on vacation in Mexico, it wouldn't be any problem for him to suggest to a judge that Lauren was unfit.

I just needed to agree to let him do it.

I dropped my hands and watched her expression. It was carefully blank and I could see a shift in her gaze. I just couldn't read her emotions. I wouldn't be able to guess what was going through her mind. She didn't look intimidated or afraid.

And it frightened me. I wasn't sure how I was supposed to react. I struggled with the doubt, every nerve ending waiting for her to snap and put me back in my place.

"He was an accident," she admitted at last. "I didn't plan it. It just happened." She looked down at the half eaten pastry. "I wanted to do the right thing with him," she said after a beat. "There was a couple that really wanted him." She looked up at me, "But when it came to signing the papers I had to get your consent. It was the first time I thought about you since you disappeared on me."

"I won't do that," I shook my head. I had been afraid of her taking Landon from me. "I won't give him up. If you try to do that I will fight you tooth and nail on it."

"I'm not fit," she said evenly. "I don't want to give up anymore of myself to him. I want to be able to do what I want when I want without having to worry about if he's taken care of." She put down the plastic fork and leaned back in her seat. "Going to Cancun made me realize how much I missed just being me. I'm not fit to be a mom."

That admission caught me off guard. I didn't know what to say. I sat there waiting for the other shoe to drop.

"Keep him," she said to me at last. "Send me whatever paperwork I need to sign to give you complete custody of him. I'll sign them."

"Just like that?" I asked in disbelief.

Lauren shrugged. "I want to move on. And if I have to worry about you showing up randomly simply because you don't like the idea that I had a vacation it's going to ruin it for me. I've let you fuck up my life enough as it is."

Of course she would twist it into a way that made me look bad. I picked up the bottle of water I had ordered and took a healthy pull from it. It would be stupid to argue, even with the negative way she painted me. If I took the bait, she might go backwards with what she was saying.

But if she was offering me just what I wanted I would be stupid to not take it.

28

Nadia

I had just finished cleaning up the break area when I heard the ding of the elevator. I started cursing under my breath as I turned to hurry down the hallway. Vanessa went on her lunch and she promised me that there wasn't anyone on the schedule for Mr. Lange until after two.

Maybe she had been wrong. Or maybe this was a test I was failing? So far, Vanessa had been pretty nice as she let me do all the things she called 'grunt work.' It was basically getting people coffee or water, fetching Mr. Lange's lunch, and keeping the office tidy. They had a maid service that came through so I didn't get to dust or vacuum. It was basically just making sure the place stayed professional looking.

The only bad part was I didn't like sitting behind a desk waiting on Vanessa to have something for me to do. Or for her to come back from lunch. I spent a good amount of the time when she wasn't in the office staying within earshot of the phone and finding something to do. Something to do that I couldn't screw up.

Being at my desk and not watching the elevator was something I could screw up.

I made it to the desks in front of Mr. Lange's office just in time to see Austin walking into it. I didn't get the chance to object, yell at him to wait. I hit the door with more force than I intended and jerked it open to stumble in just behind him.

"What are you doing?" I gasped, out of breath. Both men looked at me, Austin's expression showing shock and Mr. Lange didn't even blink. "You don't have an appointment," I managed, struggling to pull myself together and straighten the frazzled look I achieved in my mad sprint.

"What were you doing if you were not at your desk, Ms. Evans?" Mr. Lange asked.

Oh no. I cleared my throat, my mouth dry and I saw my last day being just two weeks in on this job. What would Vaughn have to say about that?

"I finished up the filing Vanessa had me do. There was a little mess in the kitchenette so I cleaned it up," I informed him. "I know it's important that I should stay at my desk. But I can't just sit there with nothing to do." I twisted my fingers together only to shake them out, "I can't let you pay me this ridiculous amount of money just to sit there and do nothing."

The man at the desk sat back a little bit. His attention was on me, but he didn't look angry. "Fetch Mr. Fowler and I water. Stay at the desk until Vanessa gets back. Also," he pulled a face, "you are not the cleaning lady. Please stop."

I winced and nodded. I was out the door and back with water in short work. When I came back into the office the tension in the room was damn near solid. Austin hadn't sat down, he stood behind one chair that was situated in front of Mr. Lange's desk. He didn't look at me, he seemed far more interested in his shoes than me.

What was going on?

I set a bottle of water next to Mr. Lange then offered Austin his. He didn't even look at me as he took it. His face was the picture of guilt and I couldn't begin to guess why.

"What did you do?" I asked, not thinking about the fact that we were standing in my boss's office.

"Do not answer that," Mr. Lange said, perhaps in reflex. He looked between us then shook his head, waving a hand dismissively in the air. "You two are dating, nevermind. By all means, Mr. Fowler, go ahead."

"I saw Lauren," he didn't look up at me when he said it. He held the bottle of water between his hands, rolling it slightly. "I came here to put into motion what it would take for me to have full custody of Landon."

I couldn't say I was surprised. I was shocked to see him, bothered that he had taken the initiative to see Lauren without any sort of back up. It just sounded dangerous. I took a step back, looking him up and down. He looked disheveled and the shirt he wore was wrinkled and yellowing as if he had worked out in it. He was the picture of stress.

"Are you okay?" I asked him, I could only imagine how it went.

"Yeah, I think," he answered honestly. He met my gaze and took a step closer to me, "But can we discuss it when you get home?" He was unsure, it felt uncomfortable just to prod for more.

I nodded and offered him a weak smile. I turned to look at Mr. Lange. "I'm sorry for the intrusion. If you need anything I'll be right outside at my desk." Where I should've been from the beginning.

Fortunately, he didn't say a word. He didn't glance in my direction. All I saw was him pulling a legal pad from his desk drawer and directing a reproachful glare at Austin.

Should I even be grateful that it wasn't directed at me? Or should I worry? What was I supposed to do now?

I ended up just sitting there waiting for Vanessa to come back from her lunch break only to be sent on my own. She didn't let me wait around for Austin to come out of Mr. Lange's office.

"You only have an hour," she said sternly. "And if what you said is true there's a conversation we need to have when you get back." She paused as if realizing the implications she made and immediately waved both hands. "It's not a formal reprimand. Because I know I didn't say anything to you about staying at the desk. I just assumed that you would be willing to do that."

I nodded and admitted, "I don't like to be paid to sit and do nothing."

"Don't tell me that," she said with a smile. "Because I will take full advantage of it."

***

I walked into the house, relieved that my day hadn't ended with me losing another job and curious what had happened when I left Austin in Mr. Lange's office. I was hoping that I would get some enlightenment but he wasn't in the living room or the kitchen. I glanced into the bedroom and I could see him stretch out in bed, from the sound of it sleeping heavily.

Disappointment flooded me. I sat heavily on the couch beside Gavin. He had his attention on the television, a game controller in his hands that was balanced lightly on where Landon rested on his chest. The baby had his head just under Gavin's chin painting an adorable picture.

"Gonna order take out for dinner," he said to me without looking. "Already got the boy ready for bed, though he probably needs a diaper change."

"I can do that," I started to reach for him only to catch a glare from Gav.

"He's not been asleep long enough for him to go back down easily. I thought he was gonna get fussy on me and wake up Austin," he looked back at the television as he spoke. "He's been out since he got home. I thought he was going to take the reins back but he just crashed hard."

"Do you know what he did?" I asked, relaxing back beside him. "He didn't say anything about what he was planning to me."

Gavin just shook his head. "He said he needed me to watch Landon last night. He was gone when I got up." He heaved a sigh, causing the baby balanced on his chest to stir. We both froze for a beat, waiting for him to settle back down. "I've had solo baby duties all day and I'm exhausted," he gave me a look.

"You didn't go visit your parents?" I asked. "I figured your mom would be delighted to have baby time, even if it's not yours."

He nodded, "I didn't think about that. I just handled it."

I blinked at him, "When you first said you wanted me to meet your parents it was because you were close to them. When was the last time you saw them?"

He didn't look at me, if anything his attention focused more on the television. His fingers hit the buttons on the remote pad with a little bit more force. It wasn't something I expected from him then again sitting with Landon all day might've taken its toll on him.

"Gav," I began gently, not really sure what to say.

"Look," he interrupted me, his tone high and sharp. "It's not a big deal. I just didn't like the way she acted when I first told her what we were. I didn't like how every time after that there was tension and she looked down her nose at you. I didn't want you to be right about my parents." He kept going, not looking at me or seeming to notice that he was disrupting Landon's rest on him.

The baby's blue eyes opened only to squint, his features crumpled and immediately the water works began. It started light, just a few huffs as he began to work up. I guess having the person you were sleeping on suddenly wake you up deserved a proper work up to the real tears.

I didn't wait for the melt down to go further, I carefully eased Landon up and off of Gavin's chest and stood. I held him closed and shushed lightly against his temple, bouncing slightly as I had seen Vaughn do a number of times with him. Landon buried his face against my shoulder, shifting as he got comfortable against me. He whimpered and whined for a few beats more, but the light bouncing seemed to do the trick.

"Sorry," Gavin said in a lower voice. "I just didn't want you to be right."

"Only half right," I told him. "They didn't call me any names." I rocked on my feet. "What did you do all day to get him to be this tired?"

"He had fun doing pushups with me," Gavin shrugged. "I might've taken him outside with the walker. He loved it." He put the video game control onto the coffee table, "I was able to get my workout in without him giving me much issue."

The door opened behind me and I turned to see Vaughn come in. He looked tired, but still came to me without saying a word. He brushed a kiss on top of Landon's head and, much to my surprise, the baby tilted. He leaned towards the man beside me heavily, giving him no choice but to take the baby from me.

"I thought he was asleep," I whispered.

"I'll put him to bed," he whispered back. Vaughn held the baby close as he dipped in to give me a kiss.

It was brief, a brush of his lips on mine. I didn't get the opportunity to be surprised or pull back. Not that I wanted to. I blinked after him as he took the baby down the hall.

"I'm sorry," Gavin said from the couch. His attention was on the hall, too. I hadn't greeted him like that and I wondered if it bothered him, he didn't look perturbed. Just … sad. It wasn't something that sat right on his usually happy face.

"What are you sorry for?" I asked, confused.

"I think if I hadn't pressed for you to meet my parents we probably would be in a better position," he sighed then sat forward. Both of his hands covered his face, rubbing at his obvious tiredness. "I wouldn't have to worry about what your dad would say when we meet him. I wouldn't have to worry about your mom plotting to kill all of us."

I released a breath and came to sit beside him on the couch. "That's just an overprotective mother," I said, trying to downplay how things had gone when he met my mom. "I'm pretty positive she didn't mean it."

"Right," he said in a disbelieving tone. "I'm not looking forward to the test run Vaughn wants to do." He shook his head, "I don't know that I can sit around another table with my own mom looking at us with disappointment."

"It's important," Vaughn said as he came down the hall. "Almost like you helping your parents find a place is important. Except you've been ignoring that, too." He tossed the jacket of his suit onto the arm chair. "It's to settle on the menu, getting input from family and friends. It's also to get opinions on the building over all."

"So it's too late to call my parents and cancel?" Gavin asked.

Vaughn looked surprised, "Why would we do that? If anything I'm counting on Kelli to be the most vocal about what needs to be done." He shrugged, "If we can make her happy there's less of a chance that we'll have to worry about anyone asking for management. Which means we don't have to be on hand constantly and we don't have to worry about who is going to watch the kid."

"Well, I don't work nights anymore so that shouldn't really be an issue," I pointed out.

"Try telling that to him," Vaughn muttered as he went to the kitchen. He opened the fridge, his brows together. "I thought Austin was cooking tonight. What happened to that?"

"He had an errand to run and didn't get home until after four. He woke me up early this morning, too," Gavin explained, though it sounded more like a complaint. "He was gone most of the day. After I got enough coffee in me to get my day started I figured him out and got things handled."

"I'm surprised he left him with you unsupervised," Vaughn grumbled as he went to the bedroom door. "Do you want to go get something or order in?"

Austin shifted on the bed, rolling so it was clear he was awake. "Order what you want. I don't care."

For some reason, his answer seemed to quiet the rest of the conversation. The worries about seeing parents again were set aside. The impending dinner at the bar was forgotten.

Should I say something? I knew what happened, but I didn't know if it was my place. It felt like it might start an argument. Mr. Lange certainly hadn't been happy about Austin's abrupt and unadvised choice. He didn't even look at me, his attention stayed firmly on Vaughn.

"What did you do today?" Vaughn asked.

"I saw Lauren," he said simply.

"The fuck for?" Gavin asked, heaving himself up off the couch. He moved to stand beside Vaughn. "That's the reason why I got stuck babysitting? So you could go look at your ex and see what a horrible mistake that was?" Suddenly the anger that had been in his voice came roaring back. "Don't fucking tell me it was because you were suddenly deciding you wanted to go back that."

"Calm down," Vaughn said, looking puzzled.

Austin sat up in bed and turned so his feet hit the floor. He looked at his friends with an expression like exasperation. "I went to see her to make sure she knew that I was done. That I wasn't going to let her decide to show up back up and take him away only to disappear again."

"Henri pissed?" Vaughn asked.

"He wasn't happy, but he's not dropping me as a client. Though he heavily implied that if I repeated this action or anything similar without council he wouldn't hesitate to do so," Austin reported tiredly. "I can't even say that she'll follow through with the agreement. There's nothing legal to hold her to it."

"Then why bother?" Gavin asked, clearly still bothered by his choices. "If there's still a chance she wants to be a pain in the ass, she will be."

Austin just shrugged, "I know. But it was something I needed to do." He shook his head, "I want to be able to move on from everything that I can. Even if I'm stuck with her."

Vaughn nodded, putting a hand on Gavin's shoulder when the other man looked like he was about to say something more. "Let's get some dinner. There's not a lot that we can do about what he's already done."

There wasn't much protest after that. When Vaughn called a local Chinese food restaurant we were all more concerned with what we wanted and how much money we were willing to spend on it. I had my phone in hand and my attention on my banking app. I hadn't gotten my first paycheck and I really shouldn't be eating out. This was an issue I was used to and the feeling that curled through me didn't get better.

I wasn't paying attention.

I was standing close to Gavin and I didn't think he would look over my shoulder. I was wrong and when he nudged me with an elbow, I nudged him back a little harder. "Don't worry about it. No one said anything about who's paying for what."

I didn't say a word, just settled against his side and watched as Austin got plates and forks to set the table. It didn't take too long for our dinner to arrive. We gathered around the table, picking through take out boxes. Egg rolls, lo mein, fried rice, covered my plate. It had been so long since I indulged in one of my favorite foods that my eyes might've been bigger than my stomach.

"I should've cooked," Austin said as he twirled noodles with his fork.

"Whatever's left is lunch tomorrow," Gavin said around a mouth full. "I call dibs on what's left of the lo mein."

"You're gonna have to share," I said to him.

"Everyone needs a night off," Vaughn said, though he had exercised more restraint. He got up with his plate and put it in the sink. "I hope you didn't over eat too much."

I pointedly bit into an eggroll, the savory crunch coupled with the flavor of the cabbage and pork had me forgetting that I had a point somewhere. I hummed, closing my eyes as I enjoyed it.

Austin stayed at the table, though it was clear he had eaten his fill. He looked tired, but the stress was even more evident. "I am really fucking stupid," he said at last.

"You were trying to protect your kid," Gav said around a mouth full. "Trying to protect your family," he clarified, as if he needed to. "You might not have been thinking how it would go legally. I can't blame you."

"Henri probably does," Vaughn said from the sink. "I guess we'll find out what happens from here." He didn't wait for us to get seconds, he began to pack up the leftovers and store them in the fridge. He worked with a purpose that had both Gavin and I watching him curiously.

Up until he picked up my plate and Gavin's.

"What the hell?" Gavin protested, clearly not quite finished.

The look Vaughn gave me told me where he was directing this. "I don't have the patience to wait for you to eat until you're ready to pass out." He went as far as clearing the remaining food on them and began to wash them. "I don't want to hang out at the table all night."

"You haven't got to work in the morning and we haven't got plans for the weekend," Gavin grumbled. "If anything we should stay up and do damage control."

"The only person here that really has damage control to worry about is me," Austin protested. "You don't need to stress out," he rubbed at his eyes, not paying attention to anyone else. "I was fucking stupid so I should be the only one shafted with the consequences, if there are any." He took a breath and unsteadily let out a, "I hope there aren't."

"Distraction is what I was shooting for," Vaughn said. He looked at me, "As long as that's okay with you?"

Oh. That explained why he had been so quick for us to finish dinner. He was eager for us to go to bed. With Landon around, if he wanted us all to be involved in the bedroom we were on borrowed time especially if the baby had been in a fussy mood all day.

I looked between Austin and Vaughn, wondering if the idea would be shot down. I shook my head and supplied my opinion, "I wouldn't argue against it. Honestly, after the week I've had I could go for being between the three of you."

"We're talking about fucking?" Gavin asked, finally catching on. "Why didn't you just say so?"

Vaughn's shoulders twitched but he didn't stop from washing the dishes. "Nuance," he grumbled. "I was going for nuance." He put a plate in the drainer and turned to look at the three of us at the table. "It ruins the appeal to sit here and talk about having sex. I was hoping if I would just imply it you'd catch on and we could go to the bedroom without issue."

"I was hungry," Gavin huffed out as he got up. "You're gonna have to wait anyway unless you want all the weird gross noises that comes with having sex on a full stomach." He didn't wait for anyone to put their two cents in, he walked into the bedroom like he expected his advice to be ignored.

"I think I'd rather just watch a movie," Austin admitted as he got up. "It would avoid all of that and we can still have some time together."

"I'm picking the movie," Gavin hollered from the bedroom.

Vaughn stayed at the sink, even though it looked like he was done with the dishes. I got up and carefully edged closer. "He has a point," I offered carefully. "Nothing ruins the sexiness like gas and no matter what position we get into there's going to be pressure on places that's going to cause embarrassing things." I made a face, unable to help myself from envisioning how that would go.

"That definitely doesn't kill the mood," he gave me a look. "or discourage anal sex in the least." Always so sarcastic. He was irritated but tired at the same time. That was why Vaughn had been pressing for us to finish so we could go to bed.

Was the distraction for Austin? Or was it for Vaughn? He was so good at hiding things that I wasn't sure.

I stepped closer, putting my hand on his hip so I could steady myself. At my closeness, he turned just enough so I could tip up on my toes and kiss him.

Surprisingly, I caught him off guard. He drew in a breath, his lips parting in a way that was too hard to resist.

I hadn't intended for this to be more than chaste. But I was delving between his lips with my tongue as soon as I could. He moaned, his damp hand going into my hair and tugging the rubber band loose. He held me close, not making any attempt to wrestle control from me. He let me taste him at my leisure, doing nothing more than tease me and hold me against him.

I pulled back just a little so I could take a much needed breath. "Watch the movie," I said to him. "Digest. Don't fall asleep."

"All this talk about bodily functions kind of kills the mood for me," he said with a smothered smirk. "Maybe next time." He pulled away from me and started towards the bedroom. He didn't give me the opportunity to linger in the kitchen, his hand caught mine and I was tugged along to the bedroom with him.

Austin was stretched out in his usual spot, the baby monitor in hand as if he was worried about another incident of it not picking up Landon's crying. Gavin was in his usual spot, remote in hand as he scrolled through the options. He settled for something with cars and action, I rolled my eyes but didn't object.

I changed into a sleep shirt, watching Vaughn as he undressed. He took his time and I was sure it was because he knew I was watching. But outside of that he didn't make any attempt to encourage anything, there was no flirtation. I was a little disappointed when he just went to bed, climbing between Gavin and Austin.

There was just enough room for me.

29

Nadia

A hand was rubbing up and down the length of my back lazily. I was propped on a body with the heavy breaths that was coming from the man I was laying against. Was someone petting me in their sleep?

I curled into the body beside me, nuzzling into the warm chest I'd been using as a pillow. The fact there wasn't a body plastered to my back led me to believe that the body I was resting against was Gavin. He just wasn't being handsy like usual.

The toilet flushed from the bathroom, followed by the noisy whine of water through the pipes. "Fuck everyone for falling asleep," Gavin grumbled as he came back into the bedroom. The bed dipped and he pressed against my back. His arm wound around my side and he found my breast, "What are we going to do when the bar opens up? We're not gonna all be in bed like this at the same time."

"We'll figure something out," Vaughn murmured. "This is what will make or break things if you let it. If you're not able to handle working a job and a relationship, what was the point in forcing her to meet your parents and meeting hers? Why make that leap if you don't want to?"

"I thought it would go differently," he admitted. "I didn't think about the bar. I haven't since after I signed the check. Anything that revolved around it after that was just," he shrugged against me, "a distraction."

"I don't know whether or not I should be concerned by how you just throw money around or insulted," Vaughn grumbled.

"Why insulted?" I asked, it didn't feel like there was a reason to pretend to be asleep any longer.

"Insulted because even though he threw the ball long, I caught it and got to make the touchdown," Gavin said into my ear. "How awake are you?"

I turned to look at him, seeing his hopeful grin and feeling the perk of his growing erection against my ass. "I wouldn't have fallen asleep if you had picked a better movie," I pointed out. "Is Austin awake?"

"He's turned into a lighter sleeper since the kid moved in. You want him up for some fun? I'll wake him up," Gavin assured me.

I considered it, taking in the body behind me and the one I was leaning against. Did I want this to go somewhere? I did before, I shouldn't have used the need to digest as a way to relax after dinner and not give in to Vaughn's urgency. I didn't even know why I wouldn't have just given in to him.

I looked up at Vaughn, fatigue still clinging to me. I didn't see anything in his face that suggested frustration. He just looked resigned to the fact that I didn't give him what he wanted earlier.

I pushed myself up, pulling away from Gavin. I got out of bed and went into the bathroom, taking time to freshen up after I relieved myself. I looked in the mirror, seeing my tired reflection. There were dark circles under my eyes and my hair looked like a tangled mess.

There was nothing sexy about my appearance.

After I stepped out of the bathroom and moved to the end of the bed, the glow of the television at my back. Vaughn and Gavin are still relaxed, but I had their full attention. It would be really easy to just crawl between them and go back to sleep.

But … I eyed both of them before I shimmy out of my panties so that they fall to my feet. *It's always been easy to just give in and get what I want at the same time.*

Vaughn slapped a hand at Austin's chest, effectively waking him up. The other man blinked sleepily and mumbled a tired, "What the hell?" Then he turned to see me and went quiet.

The only question I was left with was where to start? Vaughn was in the middle and that seemed like the easiest place to be. I would have access to all three of them.

I climbed onto the end of the bed, careful of Vaughn's ankles as I made my way up to the three of them. I paused to tug Vaughn's boxer briefs down just enough so I could see his cock, still flaccid but there was a twitch as I exposed him.

I straddled his thighs and before anyone could reach for me I tugged my shirt up and over my head. Gavin was the first to react. He sat up and wrapped an arm around my waist, giving me a simple peck to my lips before he dipped down to engulf one breast in his mouth. The lack of hesitation suggested just how much he wanted this. His tongue swirled around my nipple before he closed his lips around it and sucked hard. I dug a hand into his hair, tugging when the pull of his mouth was a little too much.

Austin didn't sit there and watch, though he still looked tired he moved to my free side. He caught my lips in a kiss that mimicked the hunger and eagerness that Gavin displayed. His tongue tangled with mine, sweeping and caressing mine as he began to touch me.

Two of them were so distracting that I almost forgot about the man that I was on. The man that tried to orchestrate this earlier. I carefully reached down, finding his hardening cock with my fingers. I started to do what I could to encourage his erection, stroking him until his hand caught mine to stop me.

Then Vaughn sat up and found a space between Gavin and Austin to fit in. The teasing of teeth, tongues, and demanding hands melted together to the point I was having a hard time keeping up with who was where. I was so glad I didn't elect to go back to sleep.

I was pulled from Austin's lips and directed to another hungry mouth. I reached into Austin's shorts, finding his erection waiting for attention. I stroked him until he moaned against my jaw, the noise knocked me off the rhythm of my fist. I pulled away a little and took a breath, pressing my brow against Gavin's as I touched Austin. It was a rush that was so heady it made me dizzy.

Then a hand pressed under me and fingers began to prod the growing wetness found there. Fingers quickly found my clit and began to eagerly circle it as another hand unexpectedly began to spread my cheeks. Slick fingers were quick to find the other opening to tease and I found myself echoing the noises that Austin made.

The two hands worked in tandem, making it all the more difficult to keep my fist moving up and down Austin's length. A hand caught my wrist and I was saved from having to keep up the attempt. My hand was placed on Vaughn's shoulder like they knew I was going to need to steady myself.

That's when two fingers were pressed into me, in my ass and between my thighs. No matter how often they did this to me, it still made every nerve ending take notice. I gasped out, tightening the hold I had on Gavin's hair and squeezing Vaughn's shoulder. Any noise I made encouraged the hands to move.

"This is where I want to be," Vaughn rumbled, his lips against my throat. To be clear just where he was calling dibs, the fingers in my anus spread apart to prepare for something bigger to take their place. He moved his hand steadily, building up a growing burn that corresponded with the fingers that curled forward in my pussy.

"Who gets to be here?" Gavin asked, his fingers finding just the right spot in me that made me wail.

"I think I got there the last time we were here. I'll play sloppy seconds," Austin offered.

Gavin started to straddle Vaughn's wait before he spoke up. "I don't want to look at your ass while I'm fucking her… don't be right there," he huffed. "We can turn Naddy around."

"Man you have no imagination," Gavin griped before he pulled his fingers from me and got Austin to help me turn around.

I was about to protest that I didn't need help except my knees buckled ruining any argument I was about to put forth. It didn't seem like there had been enough to have me so off kilter that I couldn't hold myself up.

Austin kept me steady as they lowered me onto Vaughn's cock. It took the breath out of me as he began to stretch his way into that tight opening. It was intense and having Austin there to cling to as I sank down onto Vaughn's cock was probably the only thing that kept me from crumpling.

From the noise that came behind me, I wasn't the only one overwhelmed. Vaughn hissed out a string of curses that trailed into a groan when he was fully seated in my ass. His hands dug into my hips and I felt a fine tremble in them. Was it purely because of the tightness of that place he was in? Or was this just a power that I had cultivated over the three of them since all of this began?

A hand spread the outer lips of my sex and I focused in on where Gavin crouched in front of him. His attention was down lower, his fingers caressing then a little further down to that little strip of skin and muscle that separated the two holes. The pressure and presence of Vaughn's cock in me had me clenching, as good as this felt the anticipation of having the man in front of me inside me too left me hungry and impatient.

"Stop teasing," it came out of me in a whine.

"Sorry," he said with a grin. "I was just enjoying the view."

"I mean if all you want to do is watch I can suit up and take your spot," Austin said with a similar testiness. Maybe he was regretting the offer of letting Gavin go first.

Gavin rolled his eyes and closed the distance between us. "I never thought I'd hear you complain about foreplay." He huffed as he lazily traced his cock around my slit, up against my clit, and back down over my opening without actually pressing into me. He smeared my wetness around like he was the only one that wasn't in any hurry.

I opened my mouth to rush him, to tell him to just give it to me so I could get that blissful feeling of being completely full. Something that I never really got enough of. I didn't get the chance to say a word.

Gavin took aim, pressing the head of his cock into me without looking up. Both of us watched as he pressed forward, disappearing into me. It was an erotic sight that just threw fuel onto the fire that was burning between us.

Austin reached between Gavin and I before either of the men that were in me even started moving. He started teasing my clit just as Vaughn started to slowly ease out of me. I didn't stand a chance of keeping things together, I fell to pieces. Then Gavin began to move, gritting out curses as he pushed me through the orgasm. He made my nerves hum louder and longer, there was nothing I could do to return the favor.

"Are you gonna join in?" Gavin asked, sounding breathless. "Are you just trying to make me nut faster so you get a turn here?"

"Part of the fun is watching," Austin began as continued to tease the bit of me that was quickly becoming overly sensitized. Almost like he sensed it, he reached his hand up to cup my breast, "You can't say I'm not participating when I'm touching her, too."

"There's room," I managed, twisting so that I could reach for him without upsetting the growing rhythm of the two. I didn't want to stop the euphoria they were creating, but I needed to make sure everyone was feeling this.

Fortunately, Austin didn't fight me. He shifted so that I could wind an arm around his waist and tug his boxers down low enough to free his erection. I gave him a few shaky strokes, none of the surety I had in the beginning of all of this sticking with me. I'm careful with my grip but my hand moved in a stilted motion that couldn't possibly feel good. The only thing I could think to do was to close my lips around the head of his cock and do my best to make sure he got some sort of enjoyment.

A hand dug into my hair and Austin was quick to work towards getting his own pleasure from the situation. He began to thrust shallowly into my mouth, keeping a slow pace so I didn't choke on him. From the tightening hold on my hair, the growing persistence of the tugs of his hand, it did something for him.

Or maybe it was the moans that I had no chance of smothering. Vaughn and Gavin had found a rhythm that worked together in just making every nerve sing. It made me cling to Austin, making his hips falter for a beat before he picked back up.

I couldn't keep up with them. I didn't even try. I didn't even try to reciprocate. This was a position I had been in often enough that I knew that there wouldn't be any protest to me just laying here and allowing them to find their own pleasure from me. It seemed like a fair exchange for the growing drunk feeling I had now.

The first person to crumble was the man under me. Vaughn's arm wound around my waist and his face buried against my shoulder. I felt him stiffen beneath me as his hips stalled out. Then I felt as he erupted in me.

The burn left me choking on Austin's cock. "Christ,' he gritted as he pulled my hair, causing a lance of sparks to go through me. It felt like he was trying to withdraw but I just clung to him harder, my fingers digging into his ass. "Nadia," came out of him like a curse before I felt him explode down my throat.

It left me choking more and I didn't get any sort of reprieve until Austin pulled out of my mouth when he noticed. His semen dripped down my chin as I swallowed hard, taking several shaky breaths. It left me dazed resting back on Vaughn, with Gavin still thrusting into me.

"I fucking win," he crowed, not at all stuttering in his movements. He adjusted me, pulling my legs up so they rested against his stomach and chest. He grinned down at me, "You are lucky that there's more than one of us here to make sure you got off."

"I lost count," I slurred up to him, because I didn't have any idea just how many orgasms the three of them had pushed through me.

"One more baby," he crooned as he thrust deeper.

Vaughn twitched, making it clear that he was growing too sensitive for this to keep going. He reached between us and I felt his softening cock slide from my ass and a throb went through me. Gavin made a noise that was a little too obvious.

Another hand pressed against my stomach then slid down until it found my clit only to start teasing it ruthlessly. It wasn't Austin. He sat beside me, watching with a sleepy expression. That meant it was Vaughn trying to wring one more orgasm from me and by proxy push Gavin over the edge.

It didn't take Vaughn much effort before I was gasping. That seemed to be enough for Gavin. He started cursing before his hips slammed harder into mine then he stilled, trembling as he emptied himself into me.

All I could hear was the beat of my heart. Gavin had my knees and thighs pressed into my stomach under his weight. He didn't pull out of me, pulsing still as if he might find a second wind. I didn't know if I could take it if he decided he could keep going.

"Get up so we can clean up," Austin commanded, giving Gavin a shove. "This isn't something that we can take all night."

"I don't protest to being woken up to a good time," I said as Gavin pulled away and I was helped off of Vaughn. "Especially if I don't have to work in the morning."

"Just gotta figure out how I'm gonna do this," Vaughn admitted as he got up. He stumbled a little, having a hard time finding his footing. "Between the bar and the office," he shook his head before bending down to kiss me.

It was slow and teasing, almost like he was trying to leave a mark. Or commit the taste of me to memory. It was dazing and when he pulled away I flopped backward on the bed, content with letting them clean themselves up first before I took my turn in the bathroom.

"I thought you were going to quit working for your dad," Austin said, moving to stand next to the bedroom door. He had his shorts on and the baby monitor in hand. "What happened to that?"

"If shit goes south," Vaughn began weakly, "I don't want to leave you with nothing to show for it. What better way to screw all of this up," he motioned towards the bed. “If the bar doesn’t perform like I want it to then I’ll need to pay you back for it.”

Gavin came out of the bathroom, a washcloth in hand. He offered it to me, “Didn’t we have the talk about the risks and chances of things falling through when you first pitched this idea?”

“Yeah,” Vaughn went to the bathroom door. “But I got a little more on the line here than money. Some of it I don’t want to risk falling apart.”

Epilogue

Nadia

This wasn't the first time I had been in the bar but it was the first time that I'd been here since it was completed. Everything from shiny surfaces with warm wood paneling on the walls to the multiple big screens that would probably show every flavor of sports that was available. There was a good chance that I'd be spending a lot of time here and I couldn't resist the groan.

"Do I even want to know what that's supposed to mean?" Vaughn asked as he set a tablet onto the table he was ushering me to.

"I don't know," I admitted. "I just realized that I'm pretty much stuck with this place and all the sports themed things that's going to come from it."

"Three former football players and you're just now coming to that conclusion?" he asked, smirking slightly. "I'm trying to capitalize on the start of the football season. But if you're not into it you don't have to be here."

That felt like a trap, even though it wasn't something he had done before. "It's the girlfriend's job to be supportive, isn't it?" I said, trying to brush off my complaint. I folded my hands behind me and turned to take in the dining room part of the restaurant. "Seems pretty classy for a sports bar though, doesn't it?"

"What?" he asked, clearly confused.

"Well," I thought carefully as I tried to clarify it for him. "When was the last time you went to a sports bar? They have all kinds of stuff on the walls. You could put the jerseys you guys wore on the walls, shadowbox them. You could do the same thing with the high school and middle school," I offered to him with a shrug. "Put something from the community into this place and it might encourage the community to be here."

"That's a good idea," he murmured before leaning down to press a kiss to my brow. "You got the pick of seats and if you want a drink," he motioned towards the bar. "It's open. The bartender is getting paid but if you feel compelled to tip her she's already said she's not dumb enough to tell you no."

I started to laugh before a couple at the door caught my eye. At first, I hoped it was Austin and Gavin coming in. Given that Vaughn and I met up here from work, it left the other two guys to get ready and prepare appropriate distractions for Landon.

Unfortunately, it wasn't the two missing parts to our party. It was my parents. They were early. Something that was a fault that they passed down to me. I never thought I'd complain about that.

Both of them walked into the building, their attention on the nearly empty dining room. Dad made impressed noises at the size of the television on the wall near the door. Mom elbowed his side when she noticed me. She stepped forward even when he lingered just at the door, his hat in his hand.

"This is the one boy of yours that we didn't get the chance to meet?" she asked, suspicion heavy in her voice. She looked Vaughn up and down, like she expected him to have some sort of leash on me.

Whatever aggression she presented towards him, Vaughn didn't seem to notice. He came to stand alongside me and offered her a hand, "Vaughn Price."

Mom looked down at his hand, frowning. I thought for a beat she was going to ignore the offering and I could feel the sweat building up between my shoulder blades. "That name is a whole lot more familiar to me than the other two," she looked up at him, her expression cold. She took his hand, not hanging it but squeezing it. "Pamela Evans. That is her father, Oscar Evans, and if you thought you had to worry about him, give me a reason to correct you."

Vaughn didn't even flinch. He nodded like she hadn't just threatened him. "Any animosity that is directed my way has definitely been earned," his voice was low as he spoke to her. "I have had every opportunity to make amends for it before now and I didn't." He took a breath, not making any attempt to pry his hand out of my mother's. "They told you the truth about how we're doing this?"

Mom let go of his hand, she raised her chin a little and huffed out, "They did. Don't mistake this as approval of it. And don't think that just because I'm not saying anything about the choices she's made that you can do what you want." She paused for a beat. "All it takes is for her to say a word." She sniffed, "This doesn't count as me making judgment on all of this you have going on, either. I wanted a moment to speak with all three of you, a party isn't going to cover it."

Vaughn didn't twitch, there wasn't any fear like there had been with Gavin. But he nodded, as if he understood. "It's not in my best interest to ruin things," he admitted to her. "Not just because I don't want to be on the wrong end of whatever weapon you happen to have handy. I have more than just business invested here."

Her eyebrow raised and she didn't look like she was ready to let go of threatening him. She turned to me, "Are you caught up in this?" She gestured towards the dining room.

How was I supposed to answer that? Was it because I was dressed in a professional way? I didn't have the luxury of being able to shed a suit jacket and roll up my sleeves. Fortunately, the sleeves to the blouse I wore were short and the slacks I was wearing were comfortable. Maybe she was assuming because I was dressed similarly to him?

"No," Vaughn said readily. "She doesn't have anything invested in this and she's not financially tied to any of us." He spoke evenly, like he was actively trying to reassure someone that was interested in a business deal. "If this," he gestured between me and him, "doesn't work out, she's not stuck. The only people that will be in a bad position will be the three of us."

"That's good to know," Dad spoke up. "I realize that the four of you aren't really capable of going as far as getting married. But even if this thing that you're doing is to end, its best nothing more than feelings are harmed in the aftermath."

"Oscar," Mom barked at him, not at all in agreement with him.

"Now," he turned to her, giving her a shrug. "It is what it is, doll. Going in guns blazing is going to do one of two things," he began shrugging as he looked at me. "It's going to make this go up in flames faster than she's prepared for it to and she's gonna hold it against you. I don't know about you," he shrugged. "But I don't want my kid to hate me just because I put pressure on a questionable relationship to go the wrong way."

"Thanks, Dad," I smiled at him. There he was again, saving the day.

"Anytime, kid," he gave me a smile and moved between Mom and I to engulf me in a hug. He gave Vaughn a curious glance, "Your mother said there would be food." He moved forward with what he thought was important. "Don't tell me she tricked me into getting cleaned up just to try to intimidate your boyfriends."

"We have wings," Vaughn offered. "And burgers. I was hoping to narrow down a list of sauces to put on the menu. The whole point of this," he admitted as he spoke to my father. He directed him to a booth, close to the bar. "We've also got a few craft beers on tap, too. I was thinking we'd do a weekly beer tasting," he explained with a little level of excitement on his face. "Though I haven't really decided if that would be a thing or not. Real life became a distraction when I originally started planning things out for this place."

"Ah, I'm afraid I can't help you out with that," Dad said as he slid into the booth. "Recovered alcoholic. You've got Coke, right?"

"Of course," he said easily. "Do you have any preferences?"

I was a little surprised to see Vaughn talk to my parents like he was taking their order. He didn't write it down, but after he verified he walked to the bar to get the girl behind it to prepare two cups for them. I knew he had waitresses at the ready, they were in the back doing last minute paperwork so they could be paid for the night.

Which made it even more surprising that he brought both of them drinks. He looked at me, maybe feeling my attention on him. "You want something?"

"I didn't think you would be waiting on me," I admitted to him.

"Just because you're the girlfriend doesn't mean I'll be putting you to work after you've already worked a full day," he said to me, low in an attempt to keep it between us. "As I said before, this is a business that I don't want to tie you into. So relax." He nodded to the table, "Keep them entertained and the knives away from your mom."

"That one's all work?" Mom asked, the judging expression she hadn't heard what he said.

"Yeah, that's not to say that the other two aren't. Austin is focused on raising his son," I told her as I slid into the booth across from the both of them. I didn't mention Gavin, I didn't know what to say about him. I assumed when he got here he would be helping Vaughn out.

"Your mother mentioned there was a baby," dad hummed after sipping his drink. "Are you getting practice with that? Is that what I should assume?"

"It's not in the plan," I said, honestly. There was this gut instinct to lie to both my parents, to say that we were being careful. But we weren't. And it was at my insistence. "At least not right now."

Dad just nodded, accepting what I said without second guessing. Mom on the other hand just narrowed her eyes at me as she listened. "I don't have any problem with being a grandparent. But I don't want that to happen in a situation where you are outnumbered and out financed. I doubt there would be anything we could do to help you if you had a baby with one of your boys and then they decided to split."

I shook my head, "I get that this is unconventional but looking at it like it's doomed to failure and mentioning it at every opportunity might not be the way to go." I rubbed one temple and tried to keep my cool where my mother was concerned. "I would rather just see how it plays out without that negativity. You can understand that, right?"

Dad just looked at mom, like he was waiting for her response. Or maybe he was waiting for her to buckle and see reason. I could only hope that it wouldn't be the subject of conversation every time we spoke to one another. I didn't know how long I could handle it.

Mom's lips thinned and she looked away. "I know you can handle yourself," she admitted. "You've done so all this time. I just can't shake the need to protect my baby."

"Don't worry," Dad said to her, leaning close so he could press a kiss to her cheek. "She knows that."

The doors to the restaurant opened and I turned to see Kelli and Dave walk in. They were chatting with one another animatedly and only paused to take in the dining room. Kelli made loud, impressed noises and that got Vaughn's attention. He had been at the bar, talking with the pretty blonde that looked like she had been listening intently to him up until then.

Vaughn went to meet Gavin's parents with more enthusiasm than he did mine. But I guess the threats of bodily harm could do that. I watched as Kelli hugged him then Dave followed just after her. They were like doting parents to him, even after the last dinner we had with them.

He directed them to our table, "This is Nadia's parents. Pam, Oscar Evans, this is Gavin's mom and dad. Kelli and Dave Stockton."

Dave readily reached forward, across the table to shake dad's hand then mom's. Kelli only nodded politely while murmuring an uncomfortable, "It's nice to meet you."

Was this why Gavin wasn't here, yet? He wanted to avoid this? If I had known I would be stuck with the opportunity of my parents meeting his without him I might've been a little less on board with this.

I took Dave's hand, shaking it when he offered it to me. "I haven't seen your son since I left this morning for work. No idea where he is," I told him with a grimace.

"I called him before we came in," Kelli spoke up as she pulled her cell phone from her purse. "The baby was crying in the background so I'm assuming he didn't get the nap he needed."

"Gavin's put him into his exercise routine," Vaughn said with a shrug, like it explained everything. "I'm guessing Landon can't make it through a mile on the treadmill."

"Starting him a little young, isn't he?" Dave asked after a beat.

"Have to go farther than we did so you start 'em before they're even walking," Vaughn grinned a little. "Austin needs someone to carry the torch and take care of his ass when he finally goes lame."

"The trick to that," Dave said with a shrug, "Have multiple kids so there's bigger chances that more than one will get famous to take care of you."

"That's enough," Kelli huffed and sat down at the table beside my parents. She looked irritated, "I only ended up with three boys because I had hopes of having a girl. Instead I'm drowning in testosterone. The only saving grace I've got now is I don't have to wash anymore crusty socks."

"A bullet that I was more than happy to dodge," Mom chuckled a little bit.

"Is Nadia your only one?" Kelli asked, visibly relaxing.

"One and only, I had a rough pregnancy," Mom explained, something that I had heard before. "Damn near had a stroke while pregnant with her and after that he," she jerked a thumb towards dad, "decided that he didn't want to repeat the process."

Kelli nodded and Vaughn stepped in before the conversation could get directed towards us. "Here's some suggestion cards for you guys before things get started. We're going to focus on the wing sauces but you're welcome to try the burgers," he said to Dave. "Also, bar is open and I've got some craft stuff on tap. My staff is still working on getting their W-2's and all of that filled out. But I've got Sidney behind the bar if you want something special."

More guests began to filter in, people I didn't know or recognize. Vaughn played the attentive host, seating everyone and introducing people as he sat them close to others. How did he manage to do it after working the majority of the day? I couldn't just let him do all the work.

I got up and made myself useful. Getting drink orders for the closest tables. The girl at the bar, Sidney, was flirty but quick. I wondered if that's a job requirement when it comes to being a bartender. Gavin should fit right in.

Speaking of the devil, where the hell was he? I paused by the bathrooms, I pulled my phone out to see if there were any messages. There wasn't anything from Gavin or Austin. I had one waiting from Mara, one from mom letting me know that they were on their way. Fearing the worst, I called Gavin.

When he answered I didn't give him the opportunity to say anything. "Where the hell are you?" I asked, more than a little snappy. I was worried and I couldn't understand why either of them would choose to not show up. Sure, parents meeting parents was intimidating, but as far as I could see none of them seemed to be getting confrontational.

That was something, wasn't it?

I was immediately shushed by two sets of men. Had they put me on speaker phone? "Landon fell asleep on the way over and after the meltdown we had to deal with to get him here I'd like to get him to sleep a little longer than the twenty minutes it took us to get here," Gavin growled over the line.

"Go in, I've got this handled," I heard Austin, even though it was a hurried whisper. "You were supposed to help work the bar."

"It's busier than I expected it to be," I said, hoping to put a sense of urgency into both of them.

"Mom is already here," Gavin said with a whine. "I wish we could've done without inviting them." It was funny considering it had been his idea in the beginning. I knew, to him, that this was a step in making this as permanent as possible.

"Yeah and so are a lot of other people. You're leaving Vaughn juggling all of it," I pointed out, trying to get him to see past the fears he had about his mother. "I'm pretty sure she's distracted because the last time I looked she had a stack of suggestion cards that she was already filling out. We haven't even got food out."

Gavin made an irritated noise and I heard a car door open. "I'm on my way inside," he grumbled and the door closed, loud enough for me to hear. "Shit," he hissed into the phone and after a beat I could hear muffled crying. "Sorry, man."

"Maybe he can be another distraction for your mom," I suggested and Gavin immediately relayed that to Austin. It wasn't long after that they walked into the bar, Landon sitting on Austin's arm with his attention on the room full of people.

Almost like I predicted, Kelli was up to take the baby from him. Surprisingly, she brought him to my mother and the two of them fawned over him. While that was reason enough for warning bells to go off, I fought to ignore it.

There was more than enough to do to keep me from being stuck between the two of them. Mom might not have the need for a grandchild right now, I was willing to bet she wouldn't prevent Kelli from making comments about it. Especially if she took what dad said to heart.

I didn't get the opportunity to investigate it. Waitresses came out of the kitchen with trays of wings. Gavin got behind the bar and made the job of passing out drinks more seamless. I didn't intend to do this when I came to the bar, I was just supposed to be supportive and taste test food that Vaughn intended for them to sell.

This was supposed to just be a relaxing night for me. I couldn't say what it was, but I couldn't sit back and let Vaughn shoulder all of this on his own. Even after Gavin and Austin came in, I didn't take advantage and sit down. I kept working, wanting nothing more than this to be successful for the three of them.

Oh, how things have changed.

SCARLET LANTERN
Publishing

Made in United States
Orlando, FL
24 August 2022

21522858R00171